THE HOLIDAY COTTAGE

TIME WITH FAMILY CAN BE MURDER

MARIA FRANKLAND

First published by Autonomy Press 2024

First edition

Cover Design by David Grogan www.headdesign.co.uk

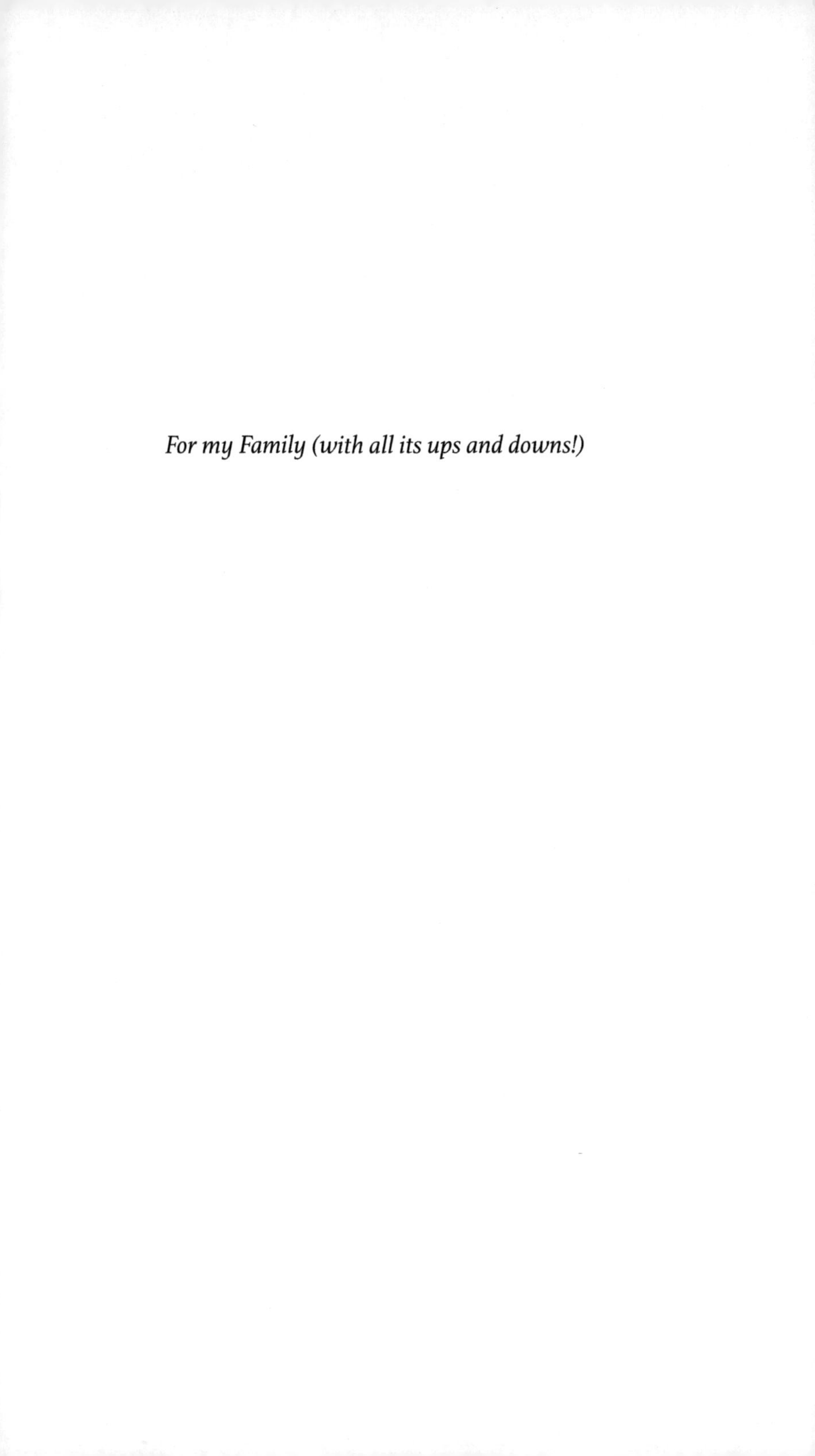

For my Family (with all its ups and downs!)

JOIN MY 'KEEP IN TOUCH' LIST

If you'd like to be kept in the loop about new books and special offers, join my 'keep in touch list' by visiting www.mariafrankland.co.uk

You will receive a free novella as a thank you for joining!

PROLOGUE

I TURN the iron over in my hands, its unscathed leaden surface offering little clue of the act it's just performed. Once a mere tool for pressing clothes, it now bears the guilt of a deadly purpose.

Murder.

Covered in layers of dust and grease from years of being used as a kitchen door prop, it has now evolved into something far more sinister.

Did I mean for it to kill? If I'm to be really honest - yes, I did. Can I deal with the inevitable repercussions? The enormity of what I've inflicted staining my conscience until the end of my days? No, I don't think I can. I bend to place the iron at my feet, as though trying to disassociate from it.

'What have you done?' The voice is heavy with accusation.

The room echoes with the sound of retching from one corner, the guttural noises cutting through the heavy silence. In another corner, soft sobs punctuate the air. The watching faces merge into one, united in shock, each expression unreadable. It's a fair question. What *have* I done? I meet their stares with a sense of numb resignation, unable to muster a response.

Several eyes flit between me and the lifeless figure slumped in a pool of blood between us. I open my mouth to speak, but the words catch in my throat, choking me with their weight. I close my eyes – willing the scene before me to disappear when I open them again.

But it's still there. As is the unspeakable horror that's emerging on each face as I continue to look around. One thing is certain – my fate is no longer in my own hands.

It's now in theirs.

BEFORE THE HOLIDAY

1

ERIN

'You're late back, aren't you?' I can't keep the suspicion from my voice as Nathaniel dumps his bag on the table. It's not that I'm necessarily bothered about him being late home – in fact, I much prefer it when he's out of the way. It's more that being late is so unusual for him. My husband is regimental to the point of being infuriating. *Everything* must run like clockwork and routine is key. He hates to admit it but it's a trait he's picked up from his father.

'Mum rang, that's all.' He strides to the fridge, his movements tense and hurried as he plucks a beer from it. 'I had to pull over to talk to her,' he says, his voice strained.

'For an *hour*?' I close the dishwasher door and watch as he snaps the top from his bottle. 'It must be serious if you're opening a beer this early. Is everything OK?'

'We're going on holiday.' He tugs a chair from beneath the table and brushes Alice's art paraphernalia to the side.

'Watch you don't mess anything up there. She's been working on that since she got back from school.' I dart forward to retrieve the mug of water she's been washing her brushes in before he knocks it all over her painting. 'What do you mean, *we're going on holiday*? Who?' My voice rises with each word.

'*All* of us.' He's avoiding my eye and his tone is flat, yet affirmative. Whatever it is that he's talking about here, he's not asking me. He seems to be *telling* me.

'All of *who*?' A sudden ill-ease steals over me as I begin to realise what this could mean.

'Everyone.' He slides his jacket off and drapes it over the chair next to him. 'The three of us, and Rylan, Kelli, Mum, Dad...' His voice trails off.

'And Martha?' My voice hardens as I spit her name out like a piece of stale chewing gum, while twirling the blind to shut out the fading day. I detest this time of year and the darkening nights. In less than two weeks, the clocks will turn back and I'll be stuck in this house every night within a marriage that's staler than two-week-out-of-date bread.

'Of course *Martha's* coming.' He unbuttons his shirt cuffs and slides them up his arms. 'She's my brother's wife. He's not exactly going to leave her at home, is he?' He looks down at the table as he fiddles with Alice's paint pots.

'Where?' I turn back to him. Not that I've got any intention of going on any sort of holiday with Nathaniel's family. However, I'm interested in what's being arranged, especially since no one has bothered to check whether I even want to go.

He pours beer into a glass. 'Mum's booked a cottage in The Dales for a week. It's half term next week so—'

'I don't care when it is. I'm not going.' I stare at him until he meets my eye again. 'And neither is Alice.'

'You've got to. Both of you.'

I laugh until I realise from his expression, again, so much like his father's, that he's deadly serious. 'Says who?' I pull out the chair opposite and sit facing him.

'It's why Mum was on the phone before.' His brow furrows as he loosens his tie. 'They read Grandad's will today.'

'And?' I clasp my hands together in front of me on the table.

'He's left specific instructions in a letter of wishes that came with it.'

'Specific instructions?' I echo. I liked Joe, Nathaniel's grandad but will be shocked if he's gone to his grave trying to force us all together. He knew full well how toxic things are and would have been the last person I'd have suspected of trying to control us all after his death.

'He wants us to mend our differences and unite as a family. His exact words, apparently.'

My mind races. Spending a week in the suffocating atmosphere that always pervades any family occasion with my in-laws? It's madness. There's no way.

'If you can't do it for *me* Erin, you can at least do it for him – he thought a lot of you.'

I shake my head. 'I don't mean to be insensitive, but your Grandad's not here anymore. It might have been his – I must say – *ridiculous* dying wish, but it's just never going to happen.' I laugh again – a hollow, sarcastic sound. '*Unite as a family.*'

'My parents are taking his wishes very seriously as it happens. Dad's even said that there won't be money from Grandad's estate until *after* the holiday.' Nathaniel picks at the label on his bottle, a sure sign he's nervous as he avoids my gaze again. He may not have expected me to be quite so opposed to the idea. 'Which is why we've *all* got to go, you and Alice too.'

'Got to go *where?*' Alice skids into the kitchen on her sliders, her auburn hair, which is exactly the same colour as mine, splaying out behind her.

'What have I told you about wearing those in the house?' I point at her feet.

'Sorr-eee.'

I roll my eyes. At only eleven she already has the attitude of a sullen teenager at times, though I can handle her far better than her father can. We've got the same kind of temperament – fiery and unpredictable, and he's often saying that he feels out of his depth with us.

'We're going on holiday next week,' Nathaniel tells her. 'With Grandma and Grandad.'

'*Grandad*?' She looks at me, as though trying to gauge my reaction. I've tried, I've *really* tried to hide the fact that I can't stand him from her, but she knows me far too well.

'Listen love. Could you just leave me and your dad to speak for a few minutes? I'll come and find you shortly.'

Pouting, she pivots on her sliders. 'But—'

'Maybe she'd like to hear about our holiday?' Nathaniel's voice is snappy as he twists in his chair to where I'm ushering our daughter back into the hallway.

I kick the door behind her and scoot back to the table. 'OK. Listen.' I pull up the chair beside Nathaniel. 'There is no way on this God-given earth that I am spending so much as a *day* in the close proximity of your family, never mind a *week*.' My voice rises. 'I'm not subjecting Alice to it, and I'm certainly not subjecting myself.'

'But – it's all arranged.'

'Well, you can go – but you can count us out.' I flick my finger at him. 'Besides, I'm working next week and I've booked Alice into dance school every morning while I'm not here – and she's looking forward to it.'

'I've already sorted all that.' He returns to picking at the label on his bottle. So far, he's scraped half of it away and has bits of sticky paper clogging up his fingernails. 'Which is the other reason I'm late home.'

'What do you mean – *you've already sorted it*?' I think I'll be opening a bottle of beer as well if he's about to say what I think he is. I don't care if it's only Monday.

'There was no problem cancelling the dance club – they've even agreed to roll her place forward.' He sounds almost apologetic, I'll give him that. 'And your manager was really understanding when I spoke to her too.' Clasping his hands behind his head, he leans back in his chair, showing the sweat patches that are beginning to emerge under his arms, another sign that his nerves are getting the better of him. 'She even said it was about time you used some of your holidays up.'

'You've spoken to my boss? You've arranged time off without even asking me first?' My voice rises again. 'I can't believe it! What did you say to her?'

'I-I told her I'd booked a surprise holiday for us.' His face floods with colour.

'Oh, it's a surprise alright. What is it, Nathaniel, am I suddenly no longer in charge of my own life *or* how I spend it?'

'Mum, stop shouting, will you?' Alice's voice echoes from the lounge. I can imagine the irritation on her face.

'Yeah,' Nathaniel says, raking his fingers through his receding hairline. 'You talk about *my* family's arguments, yet here you are, shouting your head off at *me* right in front of our daughter.'

'How dare you?' I hiss across the table as I throw my chair back across the tiles with a scrape. 'You have no right trying to tell me what to do.'

I stride to the fridge and tug out a beer. The prospect of being around my misogynist father-in-law for any amount of time is already sending me out in hives and as for Martha...

'I'll have another one of those.'

'Get your own,' I retort as I snap the lid from my bottle.

He stands from his chair and walks over to me. ' I know you and Martha don't get along but at least try to consider my mother in all this, will—'

'*Don't get along*? That's an understatement. She's the most spiteful, jealous, vindictive–'

'Alright, Erin.' He slams his palm against the fridge door. 'But like I said, if you won't do it for me, you have to do it for my mother. After all, she thinks more of you than she even thinks of *me*.'

'Give the emotional blackmail a rest, Nathaniel. First your

grandad, now your mum. I don't know what Gill was thinking of, booking a holiday like this without telling anyone beforehand. What's she playing at?'

'She told me it's what Dad asked her to do.'

'*Told* her to do, you mean.' This figures. As controlling as he is, Karl will have not only ordered Gill to book somewhere, but he will have then given her the task of breaking the news to us all and being forced to take our flack. While he sits back and does nothing – as usual.

'So you can't blame my mum, Erin. All she ever does is try to keep everyone happy.'

'Well as you can see, I'm a long way from happy. And I'm *still* not going. Nor can you force me to.'

A hush falls between us for a few moments as the music from whatever Alice's watching echoes from the lounge. Nathaniel's jaw has hardened and it's evident something new is whirring around in his head.

'Actually, Erin.' His voice is tight and clipped. 'I think we both know the *real* reason you don't want to go away with my family.'

'What would that be then?' *Here we go again.*

'It's Rylan, isn't it? You can't trust yourself to behave around my brother for a week, can you? That's why you're making excuses not to go.' He slaps his palm against his forehead. 'Of course – why am I always so blind?'

'How many times? That's all ancient bloody history – we were teenagers for goodness sake!'

'I've seen how you still look at him. And so has Martha. It's no wonder you and her don't get along.'

'You're siding with Martha now, are you? See? We've not even set off yet and we're arguing already.'

I can't believe he's going on about Rylan again. It's been months since Nathaniel used our former relationship as a bullet in his gun. If it can even be called a *relationship* – we weren't even old enough to vote or drink then. I'm on rocky ground here though – to a degree, Nathaniel's hit the nail on the head. I *do* feel uncomfortable around my brother-in-law but *not* for the reasons he's suspecting.

He pauses and his face softens. Something in my tone seems to have given him hope. '*We've not even set off yet.*' He repeats my words. 'It sounds like you could be seeing sense and changing your mind.'

'*Seeing sense!* If you want the truth, Nathaniel, I'm bloody furious at being cajoled into something you know full well I don't want to do.' I sink back into my chair, but yes, he's right. Resignation has begun to replace my fury. He's cancelled my work and Alice's dancing, he's told Gill we'll go, and now, even Alice's expecting a holiday. I don't see how I'm going to get out of it.

'I can't imagine your sister's any happier about it either.' Kelli's face swims into my mind, the only person who dislikes our sister-in-law even more than I do. Yet, as Nathaniel has repeatedly pointed out, mine and Kelli's allegiance over Martha only inflames the situation even more. And winds his dad up tighter than a cuckoo clock. Martha can't put a foot wrong in his eyes.

'No, you're right – she isn't.' Nathaniel folds his arms as he leans against the washing machine. 'But as you very well know, our father is not exactly someone we can easily argue with.'

'That's putting it mildly.'

'Look Erin.' He reaches for my arm. 'I'm sorry about what I said before. About Rylan, I mean.'

I tug my arm back and look away. 'It's not exactly the first time, is it?'

'Can't we just go along and try to make the best of it? If I promise that I'll take you somewhere hot and exotic next year? If you do this for me, I promise I'll make it up to you.'

I stare back at him as he smiles. I want to reply that I don't know if I even want to go to the end of the street with him at the moment, let alone somewhere *hot and exotic.*

But I keep quiet. For I know as well as he does that I'm backed into a corner with this lose-lose situation.

And I also know the extent of why I don't want to go.

2

KELLI

'I don't bloody believe this.' I hurl my phone onto the sofa. 'This is the last thing I need.'

'What's up?' Ben raises an eyebrow as the phone bounces up and lands in his lap.

'It's my bloody mother.'

'What's she done? From what I could gather, it sounds like you've got an all-expenses paid holiday to look forward to.'

'*Look forward to?*' My voice is nearly a screech. 'It can hardly be called a *holiday*. A cottage stuck in the middle of nowhere with my wretched family.' I pace up and down in front of the fireplace.

'Come on, sit down and calm down.' He catches me, mid-flight and tugs me down to sit next to him on the sofa. 'You'll give yourself one of your migraines if you get any more wound up.'

'I've spent my entire life being pressured and forced into things I don't want to do by my family, and this is yet *another* example.' I throw myself beside him.

'Ah, come on, Kelli – they're not that bad. You should have tried having *my* dad!' He smiles, though it's a smile that doesn't quite reach his eyes. He's right, to a point, but just because he spent his teens in a kid's home doesn't mean he's got carte blanche to pass his opinions on my family.

'With respect, Ben, you don't know the half of it.'

'Your family are like *The Waltons* compared to the one I started my life in.' He surveys me with his quiet brown eyes. There's a theory that we unconsciously choose partners who bear traits of our opposite-sex parent but in my case, this isn't true in the slightest. Despite our tumultuous childhoods, what Ben and I have found in each other is an oasis of calm. It's a refreshing place to be, free of drama and where we can both be ourselves. There are no expectations to conform to, and no hidden agendas.

I reach for his hand. 'I know it might sound heartless to say this, but at least you were able to get away from your family.' Ben's face darkens, so I quickly continue speaking before he shuts me down. This is the one topic that divides us.

'Yes, I know you had to go into care but at least you were away from all the trouble. Perhaps if you'd been immersed in it throughout your teenage years, you wouldn't be the lovely bloke you turned out to be.'

'Well thanks, but—' He flushes and his voice softens.

'My dad might appear like an OK sort of a bloke to you, but trust me – it's all for show. You don't know him like I do – and you've never heard how he speaks to my mother. Or the rest of us, for that matter.'

'I do listen when you tell me about it.' He squeezes my hand. 'Look, I know he's a bit of a bully but your Mum's really nice – and Erin – and your brothers are fine too.'

'Like I said, all you've ever seen is at the surface level,' I reply. 'You see what everyone wants you to see. Especially from my dad. He can't bear anyone thinking ill of him so he'll always show you his best side. Nathaniel can be the same as well.'

'So take me with you on holiday then.' He brushes a stray hair from my eyes.

'Honestly Ben – I couldn't put you through it. What we've got –

you and I,' – I point from him to me, – 'it's perfect as it is. We don't need to throw my dysfunctional family into the equation.'

'As far as I'm concerned, it's a no-brainer.' He pulls me nearer to him. 'You get some moral support – while I perhaps stumble on some material for my psychology thesis!' His voice has taken on an excited edge. 'Plus, maybe I don't want to be apart from you for an entire week. I might happen to miss you.' He smiles as he rests his fingers on my chin and tilts my face upwards to look at him.

Despite how upset I am, I can't help but smile back at him. And I have to admit that a week stuck in the dreary dales might be slightly more bearable with Ben at my side.

'I really don't see how I can get out of it if I'm honest.' My shoulders slump with resignation. 'They've probably purposefully booked it at half term, knowing I won't be teaching, and Dad – well, he's not someone *any* of us have ever been able to say no to. And if we were to try, Mum would just get it in the neck.'

'All the more reason for me to come along and support you then. *And* your Mum.'

'Mum *did* say I was welcome to invite you.' I nuzzle into the side of him. Ben makes me feel safe. 'You know how much she likes you.'

'I like her too. When is it anyway?'

'Next week.' I let a long sigh out. I guess if we're going to *really* make a go of things and eventually get married, Ben *does* need a proper taste of my family. Perhaps he needs to know *exactly* what he's getting himself into before it's too late, even if I am risking him literally running for our Yorkshire hills.

'That's settled then. Next week's a *reading week* anyway.' He shakes his fringe from his eyes as he draws air quotes around the words *reading week*. 'You show me a student who uses a reading week for actual reading.'

'I'm glad you're coming,' I begin. 'But I don't know how you'll handle it if my Dad starts on me in front of you.'

His face darkens. 'I'm afraid I'd have to tell him straight,' he begins. 'Diplomatically, obviously.' Ben must notice my worried expression. 'But do you know what – I reckon he'll be on his best behaviour in front of me – narcissists always are.'

'He won't be able to keep his charade up for an entire seven days.' I shake my head as I stare out at the darkness outside. This time, next week, I'll be incarcerated in what Mum has described as a gorgeous cottage in the heart of the dales. I could tell she was trying to feign some enthusiasm when we spoke before.

'The problem is as well, that I won't be able to cope with how he speaks to my mum. Honestly, Ben, I don't know how she puts up with it. I'd love to know what he's got over her, and why she stays with him.'

Ben rolls his head around as though trying to relieve some of the tension. I get to my feet to draw the curtains and shut the darkness out. If only it were so easy to close the darkness out in my family. 'It's not the first time you've said that,' he says. 'So maybe a holiday together might bring out this big, bad secret once and for all.'

'All I know is that he's controlled her with *something* for as long as I can remember. And she won't tell me what it is. She just plays dumb whenever I've tried to get her to open up.'

'Maybe she'll talk to *me*.' It's as though another light has gone on within him.

'She's not some pet psychology project.' I nudge him as I return to sit beside him. 'If my dad ever gets a hint that any of us are talking about him or *disrespecting* him as he puts it, he takes it out on Mum more than anyone. That's why we have to be careful.'

'Don't worry, I completely get it, and look, everything might be alright. Surely the two of us can go off on our own for walks and bike rides and that sort of thing? We're not going to be joined at the hip with your family for an entire week, are we?'

I force a smile as I shrug. All I can do is hope that I'm wrong about how things might turn out, and that Dad will be able to keep up a reasonable level of behaviour, for the sake of appearances if nothing else. There's certainly more chance of it if Ben's around. After all, to the outside world, Dad presents himself as a salt-of-the-earth family man who wouldn't hurt a fly.

But there'll be no outside world on this holiday.

3

GILL

'Have you sorted it?' I push the door to his office, trading the warmth of the hallway for the chill within. Karl doesn't bother to look up from his screen but at least he's not dismissing me with a swift wave of his hand, as he's often prone to doing.

'Yes – it's all done. I've found us a lovely cottage – it's a converted barn actually.'

I let the door fall closed behind me. The room is bathed in the soft glow of lamplight, casting long shadows across the rows of bookshelves lining the walls.

Karl continues to stare at his screen, which is infuriating. 'I'd better check if it's big enough for all of us before you go ahead and book it,' he replies, his tone clipped.

'You told me to get it booked, Karl – so I did.' I stand in front of his desk like a pupil before a head teacher. The familiar scent of old wood and leather mingled with the faint aroma of coffee from his desk is in danger of giving me a headache.

'I did no such thing. I distinctly recall saying, *let me see it before you book it.* You know how prone you are to getting these things wrong, Gill. Do you remember our trip to the Isle of Wight?' He raises an eyebrow over something that happened nearly two decades ago. Yes, I booked the wrong dates and ended up costing us a fortune, but he's never let me forget it, even if he masks it as a *joke* whenever he brings it up.

'It's fine – honestly. There's *plenty* of room for us all. And everything's there.'

'Well – I'll just have to take your word for it then, won't I?' He stacks his papers.

'All we need is our walking boots and bikes,' I continue, trying to steer the conversation away from his scepticism. 'Although there are a few there already.'

'Did you manage to speak to the kids?' Finally, Karl's watery grey-blue eyes, the same that our three children have inherited, look back at me from above his computer screen. His receding hair appears even thinner than usual in the dim light and he looks almost hopeful as he waits for my reply.

'Yes.' I tuck my hands into my pinny, ready to cross my fingers when I inevitably have to lie to him. 'I spoke to Nathaniel first, then Kelli.'

'What about Rylan?'

'He wasn't picking up so I spoke to Martha instead. She can't wait.' I attempt to load a brightness into my voice which I'm not feeling one bit. Since she was the only one of the three with a positive reaction, it's best to keep the focus of our conversation on her.

'It'll be good to spend some time with her. Well, with them all,' he adds quickly.

No, you meant what you said the first time. Though obviously, I wouldn't dare say this to him. Karl and Martha get on like a house on fire – two toxic people together. She'll no doubt be excited at the prospect of strengthening her allegiance with her father-in-law, as well as being able to do what she always does – to be thoroughly snarky and unpleasant to Erin and Kelli at every opportunity. Erin often rises to it but Kelli's learned to keep out of Martha's way.

'How come you're working so late anyway?' I sit in the seat at the side of his desk. He might be a retired CEO but he's still dressed in a shirt, trousers and shoes. The only thing missing from when he was still working is his tie.

'I'm just finishing off some accounts for the club. A treasurer's work is never done.' He glances at his screen and then back at me. 'Are Nathaniel and Kelli looking forward to getting away as well?'

'They seem to be. Oh, and I told Kelli she could invite Ben.' I keep my voice nonchalant. Karl's not going to like this as he'll have to keep a lid on himself all week. This is partly my rationale for inviting Ben in the first place.

I hold my breath as his jaw hardens. 'You should have checked with *me* before inviting outsiders on our family holiday.'

I'm glad Kelli can't hear what he's saying. 'They've been together for nearly two years,' I reply. 'He's hardly an outsider.'

'But my father hardly knew him.' The grooves Karl has worn into his forehead with all the frowning he does deepen as he shuts the lid on his computer. 'Which is what this holiday is *supposed* to be about. When Dad expressed his wish for us to reconnect, I'm certain that he wouldn't have been including some fly-by-night boyfriend of Kelli's in it all.'

'He's not some *fly-by-night boyfriend.*' Karl won't like me arguing back so I'd better tread carefully. 'They're even talking about getting engaged.'

'Since when?'

'After he graduates.'

'Ah yes. The psychology student.' He smirks as he pushes his glasses up his nose. 'I don't know what sort of job he thinks he's going to get with a degree like *that.*'

'Oh come on Karl – Ben's a nice lad. He and Kelli are perfect for each other.'

'I'm sure they are. However, I'd prefer it to be just family next week. Can I leave it with you to sort that out please?'

I swallow. To keep the peace, I usually try not to disagree with Karl but on this occasion, I'm going to have to, for Kelli's sake. 'I think,' I begin, 'that Joe would have wanted Kelli to be happy next week. And *we're* all in pairs, aren't we? You and I, Nathaniel and Erin, Rylan and Martha. Come on Karl, I can't exactly uninvite him now, can I? I'll look awful.'

The look on his face suggests that he thinks I can.

'Please Karl. He was at home when I spoke to Kelli, which will mean he'll already know about it.'

I could also add that there'll be no way on this earth that Kelli will come if Karl insists on us 'uninviting' Ben. From the tone of her voice when we spoke, she couldn't be any less enthusiastic about next week. Eventually, she said she'd come for me and me *only*, which felt like a miracle.

'I suppose he'll *have* to come then.' There's a resignation in his voice and my shoulders sag with relief. 'How did Nathaniel sound when you spoke to him?'

'Yeah – he's pleased.' It's back – my fake tone of voice to deliver my fake words.

'Was Erin there when you spoke to him?'

'No – he was on his way home from work. But he rang me back to say he'd spoken to Alice's holiday club and to Erin's boss.'

'And?'

'Erin's got the time off. They're all good to come.'

'Excellent.' Karl rubs his hands together. 'He's learning.'

'What do you mean?'

'At least that wife of his won't be able to come up with any of her usual excuses to avoid us. Not now that Nathaniel's taken the lead. Maybe he's got some of my backbone after all.'

'It'll be lovely to spend some proper time with Alice, won't it?' I need to change the subject before he starts digging into Nathaniel and Erin. I've heard it all so many times. 'She's growing up so fast, isn't she?'

I don't add that I've got it all planned out. My way of coping with this 'holiday' will be largely to bury myself in spending time with my granddaughter, my only grandchild. She will, no doubt, be the only person, aside from Martha, who'll have *any* excitement about going away. There'll be the inevitable confrontations, but other than that, my focus will be on Alice.

'Yeah, I guess she is.' He's *still avoiding my eye*. 'I only wish one of them would get on with having a boy. Nathaniel or Rylan, I mean.' He glances at the photo of our three children on the wall. I'd like to say it was taken in happier times but I don't think they've ever really existed. Nathaniel, with his floppy fringe and dopey grin, was in the first half of sixth form when it was taken. Rylan was about to start studying for his G.C.S.E.s and Kelli, swamped and tiny between her two sports-loving brothers, had only just moved up from primary school.

'The family name isn't going to get carried on at this rate,' Karl continues. 'Perhaps that's something I can broach with the boys next week.'

'Don't be daft,' I almost gasp, also bristling with how he still calls them *the boys*, especially since they're in their early and mid-thirties. 'We can't start telling them when they ought to be having babies! Besides, Martha's made it perfectly clear when it's come up in the past that motherhood isn't something she's considering.'

'Not at all? That's not what she's led *me* to believe.'

'Ever,' I say.

'So why hasn't she mentioned this to me? I know she's all for her career, but I thought she'd want them *eventually*. When her clock starts ticking, I mean.'

'Not all women want babies, Karl.' For a moment, I feel like laughing. With his knuckle-dragging beliefs, he'd have been better suited to the caveman era.

'She won't want to fall out of favour with you,' I say, almost under my breath.

'I'll speak to her,' he replies. 'I'll get her to see sense.'

'Karl – really – it's absolutely none of our business.' Besides, and I really daren't say this, one grandchild already having to witness the frequent drama and hostility perpetuated by this family is more than enough already.

Karl sighs as he rises from his chair. 'I suppose you could be right for once. I guess losing my father has made me concerned over losing our family name, that's all. By the sounds of it, Kelli's the most likely of our children to reproduce but if she's marrying the psychology student...' His voice fades as his gaze rests on the framed picture of his parents at the edge of his desk. It was amongst his father's things when we emptied his room.

'That's understandable. After so many years of him living here, his death's certainly left a void for us all.'

A wave of sadness crashes over me as I realise once again, how I've lost my greatest ally in Joe. He wouldn't hear Karl saying a bad word to me or about me. When he moved in full-time, it was as though the heavens had sent me a guardian angel. But now he's gone and I'm back at Karl's mercy.

In the immediate aftermath of his father's death, Karl seems to be meeker and milder than usual, but who knows how long it will last?

'Well, at least we're doing what he wanted to honour his memory,' Karl says.

'Yes – and like I say, everything's booked. This time next week, we'll be at our cottage. I just hope everyone gets along.' This is putting it mildly. I know, and Karl will be only too aware as well, of the potential this 'holiday' has to bring all the tension and any long-held secrets within our family right up to the surface.

'It's about time this family stopped all the petty feuding once and for all. My father was bang right in what he asked us to do. And now, as the new head of the family, woe betide *anyone* who causes any trouble next week.'

It's all I can do to keep a straight face. This would be the perfect time to mention that Karl's usually the person responsible for most of the feuding he's hellbent on overthrowing, but as always, I remain tight-lipped and change the subject.

'We'll have to get stocked up for the first day or two,' I tell him.

'The nearest town – and shop – is a good forty-minute drive from where we're staying.'

'And it's where exactly – this cottage you've found?'

'In the Yorkshire Dales.'

'Could we not have gone somewhere further afield?'

'We like The Dales, don't we? And so did your dad.' My voice is a little too bright. The cottage might be in the middle of nowhere but it isn't a million miles from someone I haven't been able to see for a while.

I just have to make sure I get the chance of a couple of hours to myself.

DAY ONE

4

ERIN

I LOOK AROUND AT ALICE, who's shaking her head as she stares at the cottage. 'Booor-ing,' she declares. The expression on her face probably mirrors the one on mine.

'I'm inclined to agree with her.' I nudge Nathaniel's hand as he pulls up the handbrake.

'For God's sake, both of you.' His head jerks towards me and then to Alice. 'Give it a chance – we've only just got here.'

'There's not exactly a lot for an eleven-year-old to do by the looks of it, is there?' I point at the building that's about to become our temporary prison. 'Not for an entire week.'

'I wish I could have just gone to dance school like I was supposed to,' she wails, evidently buoyed by my allegiance to her. 'All my friends are going.'

'And I wish I could have gone to work.' I feel like wailing too.

'Bloody hell, Erin. You're not even giving this holiday a go.' Nathaniel yanks the keys from the ignition and throws me a look I know only too well. 'We're here now so we'll make the best of it like everyone else. Right, Alice?'

She doesn't reply to him. Neither of us moves to follow Nathaniel from the car but we gaze instead at the imposing stone-built cottage amidst patchwork fields in front of us. There's no denying that it's beautiful around here, especially in the light of the fading day, but like Alice, it's the last place I want to be – the *very* last place. I roll down the window, allowing the cool breeze to wash over me, carrying with it the scent of wildflowers and the murmur of a nearby stream.

'Do we really have to stay here, Mum? For a whole *week?*'

'Like your Dad said, we're going to have to make the best of it.' Nathaniel beckons to me from the gate, mouthing the words, *come on*? Knowing him, he'll only be bothered about what everyone will think if they see him standing there like a lemon while we remain in the car. But to be fair, I'm beyond caring what anyone thinks.

'Come on.' I twist in my seat to give Alice my best attempt at a smile. 'I guess, we'd better show willing.'

'Hello,' Nathaniel calls as he ducks under a hanging basket and pushes the heavy-looking wooden door into a gloomy hallway. 'We're here.'

'And about time.' I can feel myself physically clench up as my father-in-law's voice echoes from one of the rooms. He always has this effect on me. It's only day one and he already sounds to be in a sour frame of mind. Alice rolls her eyes, clearly thinking the same as me.

'Helloooo.' Gill arrives before us in the dimly-lit hallway, her cheeks pink with what's probably excitement at our arrival. 'Come here, you.' She holds her arms out to Alice who steps towards her. She's getting to an age where she'll only accept hugs from me and her dad at bedtime. However, hugs from her grandma are another matter.

I shiver. I don't know whether it's just after the heat of our car, but it's decidedly chilly in here. I hope I've packed enough warm clothes for us. The floorboards creak beneath our weight, adding to the eerie atmosphere.

'Let me have a look at you.' Gill holds Alice at arm's length. 'It's only been a month since I saw you but I'm sure you've grown another inch.'

'I'm nearly as tall as you, Grandma.'

I laugh. By Gill's own admission, she's beginning to shrink and there really is only an inch or so between them. 'You should see our food bill.' I step towards my mother-in-law. 'It's good to see you.' I should probably say *thanks for inviting us* but that wouldn't be appropriate. I couldn't be any further from *thankful*.

As I hug her I get a whiff of her Daisy perfume and a dusting of the flour she's got all over her apron.

'Sorry.' She brushes my sleeve. 'I've been busy.'

'Something smells good.' Nathaniel sniffs. 'What are you making?'

'A hearty chicken casserole and Yorkshire Puddings.' Gill nods towards what must be the kitchen.

'And a pudding?' He looks at her hopefully. We never have puddings but his mum still likes to spoil them all.

'Apple crumble. At your dad's request. Anyway, don't I get a hug from you as well?' She smiles at her eldest son as he towers over her.

Karl appears behind her, his shadow looming over us all. 'Put him down for God's sake, Gill. He's a grown man.'

'If I want to hug my son, I—'

'What took you so long anyway?' Karl interrupts, frowning at Nathaniel as he steps back from his mother. 'Didn't you tell them we got the keys at three?' He moves his frown to Gill as though it's all *her* fault we're late.

'She did – but we couldn't have got here any earlier. I've been at work.'

Gill shoots me a grateful look. We've always had an unspoken allegiance and frequently speak up for each other.

'You were supposed to finish at *lunchtime*.' Nathaniel's voice is haughty. He changes when he's in front of his father – it's as though he's got something to prove. 'So we could beat the traffic.'

As Karl's gaze meets mine, I can feel the weight of his disapproval bearing down on me, sending a chill down my spine. His voice cuts through the air like a knife, sharp and biting, as he directs his attention towards Nathaniel and me. I can't help but tense up, my senses on high alert in his presence.

'Never mind all that, you're here now.' Gill beams at each of us in turn. 'And I expect you're ready for a cuppa after your drive.' She turns and steps around the side of her husband. He's staring at me as though waiting for an explanation of why I didn't finish work at lunchtime, like I was *supposed* to. He'll be waiting a long time for it.

I follow Gill from the hallway. 'I'm ready for something far stronger than a cuppa.'

Thankfully, we've got a case of wine still to bring in from the car. I don't think I could get through the coming week without it.

'It's just as well I've opened a bottle of Pinot then, isn't it?' She smiles back at me as she leads me through a breakfast bar area, into one of the largest kitchens I've ever seen.

I'd like to have a proper look at the beamed ceilings, the rustic units and the slate flooring but it's impossible to avoid the unwelcoming presence of my sister-in-law, Martha.

I cast a wary glance in her direction, taking in her rigid posture and the icy glare she directs towards me. The clink of her bracelets as she puts her glass down rings out with each movement she makes, a subtle reminder of the tension simmering beneath the surface. I can practically taste the bitterness in the air.

We nod at each other, neither of us seemingly able to muster the enthusiasm for a civil hello. She's found her place at the breakfast bar and was probably having a jolly nice time monopolising Gill's attention before we got here. I'll be the last person she wants to see. She married Rylan well before I married Nathaniel and has always seen me as some kind of rival for Gill's affections.

'It's chilly in here.' I rub at my arms.

'We've lit the fires,' Gill says. 'But I reckon the place is going to take some serious warming up.'

'Where's Rylan?' Nathaniel asks. It's not a question I'd be able to ask – Martha would shoot me down in flames. I try to keep my face straight as she shoots me a look. Perish the thought of me showing any interest in what her reply about his whereabouts might be.

'He's in the shower as far as I know.' Gill takes the lid off the crock pot and stirs the contents. 'I hope you're all hungry.'

'You always make too much.' I laugh.

'This one looks like she could do with fattening up.' Alice jumps as Karl comes up behind us and tousles her hair. 'You're starting to look like you've been stretched.' He laughs. 'What's up, don't your parents feed you? I'll have a glass of that as well.' He nods towards the bottle in front of Martha.

Alice leans into me, radiating discomfort. She's conscious enough about her height and changing shape without her grandad making barbed comments. I hope he's not going to be like this all week.

'So?' He glugs wine into a glass. He hasn't offered me one.

'So *what*?'

'*Are* you eating properly?' He takes a seat beside Martha at the breakfast bar as he continues to scrutinise Alice.

'Yes.' Her voice trembles as she replies. It always does when she's dealing with him. I'll have to keep an eye on the situation. Usually, we only have to cope with Karl in small doses – at the very most, overnight. Alice never knows whether her grandad's joking or being unkind to her. Personally, I can't believe we're even here. I should have put my foot down. I should have—

'Pour Erin and Nathaniel a glass, will you?' Gill points at the bottle Karl's placed back on the kitchen counter. Praise be to my mother-in-law.

'Come on, Alice – you can make yourself useful and help me unload the car.' Nathaniel nudges her back towards the door.

She trudges after him, dragging each trainered foot behind her as she goes. 'Please tell me there's wi-fi here, Dad.'

Nathaniel shushes her as the door bangs behind them.

'Is there anything I can help with, Gill?' I accept the wine from Karl with a forced smile and step towards the range with my heels clicking against the floor.

'Brownie points.' Martha mutters under her breath as she attempts to make her words sound like a cough. Karl looks to be stifling a smile. Gosh, we've barely been here for five minutes and already my hackles are rising with the two of them. I gulp the wine like my life depends on it.

'You look like you're ready for that.' Gill folds a tea towel into quarters and leans against the counter.

'You've had your hair done, haven't you?' I point at her neatly styled bob. 'It looks nice.'

'I'm glad someone noticed.' She rolls her eyes at Karl but he's too busy laughing at something else Martha's muttered. Probably about me. I'm not usually this paranoid but it's hard not to be around her.

'Is Kelli here yet? I didn't notice her car.' I'll feel better once she is. I can't exactly slag Karl off in front of her – he is, after all, her dad but we can unite against our common enemy – our dear sister-in-law, Martha.

'Ben's driving them over – they should be here soon.' Gill glances at the huge clock on the chimney breast.

'I thought this week was just about family?' Martha's bracelets rattle as she turns to Karl. 'How come Kelli's allowed to bring her boyfriend?'

'Let's not go there, shall we?' Karl shoots Gill a look. She turns away and busies herself at the sink.

'Why don't I set the table?' Placing my glass down, I stride towards the drawers at the far end of the kitchen and begin opening and closing them in search of the cutlery.

'Make yourself at home, why don't you?' Martha sniggers. It's my turn to give *her* a withering look. One that should convey how pathetic I think she's being. Especially since I *know* there can be a more reasonable side to her because Gill's told me she's perfectly capable of being civil, even *friendly*. Unfortunately, it's thinly disguised under layers of hatred and contempt – and all because Rylan was once my boyfriend.

'I want you *all* to make yourselves at home.' Gill frowns at Martha then points at one of the drawers. 'Thanks, love.' She comes up behind me and mutters into my ear. 'Just ignore her. She'll settle down if no one gives her any ammunition.'

'She'd better.' I mutter back as I grab a handful of cutlery, already fantasising about where I'd like to shove one of these forks.

'Why don't you give Erin a hand, Martha?'

'I can manage on my own.' I know Gill means well, but forcing Martha and me together is not a good move. Surely she must know that?

'I'm sure you can.' Karl twists in his seat as I pass him to head into the dining room. 'But Gill's right. Many hands make light work. Besides, it'd make a nice change to see the two of you getting along. That is, after all, what we're all here for.'

Making no attempt to hide the disdain from her expression, Martha slides from her stool. She'll never argue with Karl. Having said that, *none* of us would.

Not unless it was a matter of life and death.

5

ERIN

'I DON'T EVEN KNOW why you're bothering to set the table just yet. You know what Kelli's like.'

'What do you mean?' I squint at Martha as she stands in front of the window. The sun's just about to sink behind the hill but for the moment, it's blinding me.

'You know as well as I do that she won't bother getting here until the last *acceptable* minute.'

'I got the impression that she was already on her way. You heard what Gill said. *Ben's driving.*' I skirt around Martha and drag the heavy floral curtains together. It's a shame to shut the peachy sunset out but staring at it reminds me of the world that continues to exist beyond these four walls. I snap the light over the table on so we can see what we're doing.

'That doesn't mean they've set off yet though.' She sighs as she checks her watch. 'We'll probably end up eating at midnight at this rate.'

'Why would we?'

'There's no way Gill will dish up until *they* get here.'

'I know – it's called manners, Martha.'

We do what needs to be done without speaking any further for a minute, then she suddenly looks up as she's folding a napkin.

'So how have *you* been?'

I resist the urge to look around and see if anyone's standing behind us. Is she actually making conversation with me? If she is, I smell a giant rat. Martha *never* makes conversation with me, not unless she has a hidden agenda.

'Fine.' I'd better go along with it. 'Yourself?'

'Not too bad, thanks.'

We continue setting the table in silence. Martha lays the plates while I lay the cutlery. The table is the perfect size for nine of us, though what the atmosphere is going to be like at mealtimes is anyone's guess. I'll just have to ensure that I'm never sitting opposite or next to Rylan. If we were to catch one another's eye, or God forbid, have a conversation, who knows what trouble that might cause?

'We're away with *my* parents in a couple of weeks,' Martha says above the banging and clanking of Nathaniel and Alice coming in with the last lot of our stuff from the car. 'Apparently, they've got some news for us.'

'Right.' She really *is* making conversation with me. Maybe I should give her the benefit of the doubt. After all, we're going to be in close proximity for a *very* long time. 'I hope everything's OK with them.'

'Parents, eh?' Martha chuckles as she lays down the final plate. 'They bring nothing but drama. First Rylan's lot with this *let's all sort our differences* rubbish, and now with whatever mine are going to sling our way. You must be relieved you don't have any.' Without looking at me or waiting for a response, she heads to the door and back into the kitchen.

Bitch. I seethe under my breath, feeling a surge of anger and sadness welling up inside me. She knows full well that my mum's dead and that my father walked out when I was a baby. *You must be relieved you don't have any.* How can she say such a thing? I don't understand how some people can be so catty.

Crossing one slim leg over the other, Martha chats away with Karl as he tops their glasses up. I catch snippets of their conversation and mostly they're just trying to big themselves up. Karl's wittering on about how in demand he is, even though he's retired, and Martha's talking about some wealthy new client she's just bagged.

On the exterior, she is a really attractive woman and I can often see why Rylan sidelined me for her. With her glossy dark hair and elegant clothes, she exudes a confidence that I've never known even if, as my mum always used to say, *beauty is only skin deep.* Martha knows how to command attention and will, no doubt, want to spend this week being the centre of it. And God help anyone who gets in the way of that.

I catch sight of myself in the mirror as I head towards the wine glass I set down before. With smeared mascara and my hair half-in-half-out of its ponytail, I should probably up my game, just so I can regain some of my confidence while dealing with Martha this week. As I dab the streak of black from beneath my eye, she catches my eye through the mirror and smirks. It's far from a friendly expression.

It says *you'd better watch out.*

'How's my favourite sister-in-law?' Rylan nudges my arm as he passes me on his way to the fridge.

'Your *only* sister-in-law.' I laugh and hope I'm not looking too pleased to see him. 'Not too bad thanks.'

'Long time, no see.'

He glances in Martha's direction and I follow his gaze. As I would have had no trouble predicting, she's watching our exchange with a combination of interest and anger. 'Where are the others?'

Right on cue, Alice and Nathaniel appear in the doorway.

'Now then, Nate.' Rylan strides towards him and claps him on the back. Nathaniel nods back, clearly unable to reciprocate his brother's greeting. Plus, he hates being called Nate – I'm surprised when he doesn't pull Rylan up about it.

'Gosh, look at you.' Rylan mock-gasps as he turns to Alice. She giggles. 'You get more like your mum every time I see you.'

'What's that supposed to mean?' Martha steps down from her stool, looking daggers at her husband.

'It's the hair.' Rylan reaches out and tousles her hair in a similar way to how Karl did when we first arrived. Alice shrinks back. I don't blame her – I mean, what eleven-year-old wants her grandad and then her uncle messing her hair up? Unlike me, she takes a lot more care with hers and is always preening in front of the mirror.

'It's getting a bit long, isn't it?' Martha points at her and then at me. 'When are you both planning to get a proper haircut?'

Martha might be a hairdresser but I wouldn't go to her if she was the last hairdresser on the planet. She'd probably scalp me.

Alice's face twists into a horrified expression. 'I don't want mine cut, Mum,' she says.

'You don't have to—' I begin.

'You've got lovely hair,' Martha continues and for a moment, not only does Alice's face soften at the compliment but I soften too. Alice is at a funny age where she needs building up, not tearing down. 'But if you don't look after it now, it'll end up like your mum's.'

'There's *nothing* wrong with Erin's hair,' Gill says from where she's now sitting at the other side of the breakfast bar. 'Take no notice – they're only jealous.'

Martha snorts. 'What on earth of?'

'People pay good money to dye their hair the same colour as Erin and Alice's.'

'Not in my experience, they don't.'

I mutter something about needing to unpack, before grabbing my wine and striding away from her before I say something I regret. As I storm along the hallway to the stairs, my attention's caught by the inviting open fire crackling in the lounge. Closing the door after me, I inhale the welcome scent of burning coal and throw some more on. Though, even with this fire smouldering away, I'm *still* cold. The whole cottage must be like this. It doesn't have a good feel to it – in fact, with its low ceilings and dingy rooms, it's almost oppressive.

I look over the lounge, at the pile of board games beneath the table, games which Gill, no doubt, will be encouraging us all to play. My gaze falls on the leather recliner in front of the TV where Karl's left his glasses and newspaper. He's wasted no time in bagging the best seat in the house and if I know him correctly, woe betide anyone who dares to sit there throughout our stay.

I drop to my knees and delve into the glow of the fire with the poker, relishing this couple of minutes to myself as I try to get warm. 'Me time' is going to be in very short supply while we're here.

'Grandad says I can't have the wifi code until *after* dinner.' Alice flounces into the room and throws herself onto the sofa with tears in her eyes. 'He says I need to learn how to have a conversation.'

'I'm inclined to agree with him on that one.'

Alice's mouth forms itself into a deeper pout as she pulls her cardigan more tightly around herself. 'I might as well just stay in my bed all week.'

'Speaking of which, do we all know which bedrooms we're in? Has your dad put my stuff in ours yet?'

She pulls a face. 'Think so. Yours is next to mine. Someone's put labels on all the doors.'

'That'll be Grandad.'

'So you're both hiding in here, are you?' The door closes behind

Rylan who heads towards me with a bottle of wine. 'I thought you could probably use a top-up.'

'Thanks.' I hold my glass towards him.

'What's up with that brother of mine? He's got a face like a bag of spanners tonight.'

Alice giggles. At least *someone* can get a smile out of her.

'Ah, he'll be fine once he's got a couple of beers down him.'

'Didn't you bring *me* a drink, Uncle Rylan?'

'I don't think you're allowed wine.' He holds the bottle in the air. 'What do you say, Mum?'

'Definitely not.' I smile. 'Go and ask Grandma for some juice.'

We watch as she heads to the door. 'She's a lovely lass – a credit to you both.' Rylan smiles, though there's a sadness behind it. 'I just can't believe how fast she's growing up.'

Knowing Rylan as I do, he'd have loved being a father, but Martha's made no secret of the fact that she can't stand kids and never wants them. She used to *hate* being around Alice when she was toddling, and it was almost amusing watching as she tried to ignore her niece. It was difficult to try and get Alice to understand when she was younger that Martha was best left alone. According to Nathaniel, Rylan knew of Martha's child-free wishes fairly early on in their relationship but naively believed she'd come to change her mind over the years.

'So how's life treating you?' I probably shouldn't stay here in this room, talking to Rylan. Both his wife *and* my husband would be only too happy to jump to their own conclusions about a totally innocent conversation, simply because it happens to be *us* having it. But if I keep telling myself it's *their* problem for long enough, perhaps I'll eventually believe it.

'Can't grumble.' He takes the spot Alice has just vacated and sips at his wine. He and Nathaniel are very similar with their dark hair and blue eyes, though Rylan clearly works out more and is as cheery as my husband is dour. 'Though I can't deny that I'm more than a little concerned about what this week might bring.'

'I know what you mean.' I stare at the window. Darkness has completely fallen now and I should be cosy in front of this fire and the lamplight filtering from the corner of the room. But I'm far from it.

'It's always hard enough surviving Christmas – just for that one day,' he continues. 'I'm not entirely sure what my Grandad was thinking of bringing us all together like this. It must have been the concoction of painkillers that addled his brain.'

'I miss him, your grandad. I bet your mum does too.'

'You're not kidding.' He follows my gaze to the window, his eyes taking on a faraway look. 'She's lost her best ally against Dad.'

'I know.'

'One good thing about this week is that we'll be able to see how she's holding up against him now Grandad's not here to fight her corner.'

I jump as the lounge door bangs into the wall and am just about to tell Alice off for charging around when I realise it's Martha.

'Disturbing something, am I?' Her voice is sickly sweet and the look on her face says she'd like to rip my head off.

'Come and sit down, love.' Rylan pats the seat beside him. 'We were just on about Grandad.'

I mutter something about going to find Alice and make myself scarce as Rylan's attempt at humour with the words *I only have eyes for you, my sweet*, echo in my ears.

6

KELLI

'Oh God, as if we're the last ones to arrive.' The shapes of the three cars along the driveway loom against the darkness. 'My dad will have a field day when we walk in.'

'Just breathe, Kelli.' Ben reaches over the gearstick and rests his hand on my arm. 'We haven't even gone in there and you're already more wound up than a coiled spring.'

'The messages Mum's been sending me haven't helped. Three bloody times.' I stare at his chiselled profile as the light inside the car fades, the spikes of his hair almost reaching the roof. I wish it were just the two of us going away. I'd have looked forward to this week with every fibre of my being then.

'By the sound of them, your dad probably put her up to texting you.'

'I said we'd be here. Why can't that be enough for them?'

'Maybe she just wanted to know you were safe.' Ben reaches over the gearstick.

'I'm with *you*, aren't I?' As Ben's hand settles on my arm, a wave of calm washes over me. The tension in my shoulders eases, and I find myself leaning into his touch. With him beside me, being here feels less daunting, less threatening. It's not just his presence that reassures me; it's the way he looks out for me and anticipates my needs before I even voice them. In moments like these, I realise how fortunate I am to have him by my side.

'Someone's looking out of the window.' He points. 'Perhaps we'd better make a move.'

I let a long breath out and open the door. 'Let's do this.'

The air is thick with anticipation as we step out of the car, the tension palpable in the way my heart pounds against my chest. It's as if the very walls of the house are holding their breath, waiting to see how the evening will unfold.

'Gosh, just smell that fresh air.' Ben tilts his face to the sky and throws his shoulders back.

'You could hear a fly sneeze around here.' I follow his gaze, taken aback at how clear the sky is. Really, rather than going in there, having to play the dutiful daughter to my father and the friendly sister-in-law to Martha, I'd rather stay out here with Ben, breathing fresh air and staring at the stars. Plus, we've got plenty of beer in the boot.

'Are you coming in, or what?' Rylan rushes towards us from the door. 'There's a beer with your name on it, sis.'

'You must be a mind reader.' I lean into him for a hug.

'How are you doing, Ben?' He reaches around me to stretch his arm out to Ben.

'Not bad, thank you.' He returns Rylan's handshake. 'Happy to be invited to your family soiree.'

'You might not be saying that in an hour or two.' Rylan throws his head back with laughter, and in his presence, I relax a little more. He's great company, my brother. If we could be here minus Martha and Dad, and to a lesser degree, Nathaniel, it would be a good week. 'There's already been a few claws out in there.'

Ben opens the boot. 'Don't be telling her that,' he says. 'She's been worrying since you all got the phone call.'

'Let's just say – it's not the most *relaxing* environment. But I'm sure alcohol will see us through the worst of it.'

'Come on then.' I pass a bag to Rylan, hoist another over my shoulder, and then link arms with Ben. 'We'd better get in there and face the music.' But even as we walk, I'm aware that I'm dragging my feet after each other, heading for the door as slowly as humanly possible.

'Nice of you to join us.' Dad rises from where he's been sitting beside Martha as we enter the kitchen. Looking at his wine-stained lips and unsteady gait, he's already had more than a glass or two. 'Did you not think to let us know you'd be so late?'

'Sorry, Dad.' I mutter the two words which are an integral part of my vocabulary when I'm around my father. Even with Ben beside me, I'm a kid again, standing in front of my dad as he chastises me, while I wonder how far he'll go with his punishment. He might have aged and shrunk in stature but he's still as imposing as he ever was.

Ben must sense my discomfort as he nudges me towards my mother. 'Hi, Gill – sorry we're a bit late. Blimey, it smells good in here.'

'I'm just glad you've both made it safe and sound.' She smiles back. At least *she* looks genuinely pleased to see us, which is more than can be said for some people. 'I'll have five minutes with you both and then I'll get the Yorkshire puddings in.'

'So why *are* you so late?'

The sharp edge in Martha's voice slices through the air. It's not just her accusatory tone that makes me uncomfortable; it's the way she mirrors Dad's disapproving glare, the same one that used to make me shrink into myself as a child. I've spent years trying to distance myself from the memories, but every moment in my family's company tugs me back into the same old patterns, the same old fears.

'Cat got your tongue?'

I glare at her. Dad seems to have let it go, so what business does *she* have dragging it out? She's sporting a similar wine-stained mouth to him. Dinner is going to be very interesting with *both* of them so fuelled by alcohol.

'Auntie Kelli.' Alice races into the room and throws herself at me, saving me from Martha's scrutiny. 'I was beginning to think you weren't coming.'

'See?' Dad frowns at me. 'Your niece shouldn't be having to worry about *you.*'

'Oh my God. Is this so important?' Nathaniel plucks a beer from the fridge and slams the door. 'They're here now, aren't they?'

'Two more of those please, Nate.' I head towards him and slap him on the back.

'My name's not *Nate.*'

'Nice to see you too, brother dearest. Who's rattled your cage?'

'It's just – this bloody *family.*'

'Tell me about it.'

'Have you heard them over there?' Martha's voice rises as she points in our direction. 'Some holiday this will be if that's the attitude they're starting with.'

'Right – enough.' Karl's voice rises even higher than Martha's, sending a hush over everyone as he slaps his palm against the breakfast bar. I exchange glances with Ben. He's warned me that he won't be able to stay silent if my father is unable to behave himself this week.

But what we haven't discussed is what I once told him about Dad. I've wanted to bring it back up – if only to get Ben to promise not to mention *anything* – no matter what transpires this week. But I haven't, mainly for fear of bringing it back to the forefront of his mind. Yes, Ben might have had his share of toxicity with his own family and therefore be an empathetic listener, but I should never have told him *everything*. All families have secrets and often, it's easier, not to mention safer, for them to stay that way.

'What's going on?' Erin arrives at the kitchen door and nearly trips over the old cast iron which is being used as a doorstop. Her gaze finds me and we smile at each other. I want to rush over and hug her after not seeing her since the summer, but instead, I nod towards Dad. He's waiting for everyone's undivided attention and Mum's starting to look fractious. The last thing I want is for her to get it in the neck because he's angry with us. And that's usually what happens.

'Just spit it out then, Dad.' Rylan grins. He's probably the only one of us who could get away with saying that. Despite Nathaniel's lifelong attempts to win Dad's approval, to the extent of following him into the same profession, Rylan's always had the edge.

'Now that we're all here – finally.' Despite his obvious inebriation, he still manages to give me a funny look and I shrink slightly more into myself. 'I want you all to remember *why* we're here this week.' He pauses as though expecting someone to shout out the reason like we're at a quiz. But we all stay quiet.

'We're here not only to remember my father,' he continues, slurring his words. '*Your* grandfather.' He looks firstly at me and then at each of my brothers in turn. 'But also to honour his wish for some quality family time and togetherness. *Without* any falling out. Do you think you can all manage that?' He sweeps his gaze over everyone. It might be my imagination but I'm certain it lingers on me.

'Yes, Dad,' Nathaniel mutters and is followed by one or two other discernible grunts.

Without planning them, the words, *yes Dad* leave me too and I hate myself for them. It's no wonder I'm always such an easy target for him to bully – he'll be able to sense my mother in me. My brothers are always telling me how alike we are – in character as well as looks. But I don't want to be like her – at the mercy of my father's whims and moods. But nor do I want to stand up to him and risk her getting the brunt of it. It's happened before and I vowed at the time that I'd *never* put her in that position again. Or myself.

'Right then, let's all fill our glasses and we'll have a drink together before dinner.' He staggers back to his stool, flopping onto it like custard skin, and I console myself with the thought that at least he'll probably end up in bed early this evening.

7

KELLI

'They seem to be getting on well.' Mum nods towards where Ben's sitting across the breakfast bar from Dad, who judging from the way he's waving his arms around as he speaks, is delighted to be holding court in front of his newly-acquired captive audience.

'Hmmm.' I try to catch Ben's eye but he's firmly fixated on Dad. What I don't tell Mum is that he'll be hanging onto Dad's every word, but not for the reasons they think. Instead, Dad risks finding himself in one of Ben's psychology assignments about narcissism or misogyny. 'I'm just glad he said Ben could come.'

'Of course. He's practically family now.'

My gaze shifts to Martha, who, by the look on her face, seems put out by Ben's intrusion into her monopolising of my father's attention. It's always the same, when she's drinking, she gravitates to him and when she's sober she sucks up to Mum. Or at least, she tries to. What she doesn't seem to realise is that Mum can see right through her. 'At least Martha seems quiet, for now.'

'She wasn't earlier.' Mum nods towards Erin as she hangs coats in the hallway. 'She's already had a few not-so-sly digs at poor Erin. I know she can hold her own but she shouldn't have to put up with it.'

'Has Erin managed to keep a lid on things?'

'So far.' Mum sips her wine and I notice she's wearing a bit of make-up for a change. 'But we'll have to keep an eye on them. She's a loose cannon, that Martha, and never happier than when she's stirring up trouble.'

'You don't need to tell me. Alice doesn't look very happy either.' I jerk my head in her direction. She's perched next to her dad at the breakfast bar, and looks bored out of her skull. As I would have been at her age having to listen to the drunken ramblings of the grown-ups. Poor kid.

'She'll be fine once your dad gives her the wifi password.' Mum chuckles as she checks on one of the pans. 'Which is why we'd better get this dinner on the table ASAP and put her out of her misery. He said she can have it after dinner. The Yorkshire puddings are in now anyway.'

'I'll go and sit over with her for a few minutes. Plus, I'm interested in hearing what Dad's warbling on about to Ben.'

'After the amount of wine he and Martha have been putting away, I can't imagine it's anything meaningful. I'll just keep an eye on this lot in the oven.'

I pluck a couple more beers from the fridge, twist the caps off and hover beside Ben. Now he's perched on the high stool, we're at about the same height. I've never gotten used to seeing him interacting with my family. Somehow, he doesn't fit with them and really, I believe we're happiest as a team of two.

'Here, you sit down, Kel.' He slides from the stool as he accepts the beer I thrust at him.

'So you're one of those *gentlemen* types?' Dad laughs. 'Oh dear – I can see we're going to have to educate you.'

'Yes – he's a dying breed.' I look pointedly at my father but he doesn't take the bait. Which is probably just as well.

'Your dad was just telling me about his time as a town councillor.' Ben's voice is filled with enthusiasm which will please Dad no end, but the way his eyes are dancing with mischief affirms that he's merely enjoying having my father as a specimen beneath his microscope.

Dad's brief time in local government might be his favourite accolade but anyone would think he'd run for prime minister the way he goes on about it to whoever will listen.

'I'd have made an excellent prime minister actually,' Dad says. 'After all, one of my greatest talents is my ability to read and understand people – to really delve into their psyche. You'll know all about that, won't you, Ben?'

'It definitely sounds like we're on the same page, Karl.' I know Ben well enough to see that he's stifling a smirk.

'Yeah.' The buttons on Dad's striped shirt bulge as he puffs his chest out. 'If I'd been voted into parliament I could have made a real difference.'

Dear me. As my eyes meet with Rylan's, it's all we can do not to dissolve into laughter.

'So Ben – tell me more about *you*.' Dad leans back in his seat as if to scrutinise him more fully. 'We've barely spoken *properly* before, have we? Therefore, the jury's still out on whether you're suitable for my daughter.'

How embarrassing. I shuffle on the stool Ben gave up for me. Not only does Dad sound like a father from the 1900s, but he's also managed to make his words sound like a veiled threat.

'The Yorkshires are ready,' Mum calls from behind us and I heave a sigh of relief. At least some food might sober him up.

'Do you want a hand, Mum?' As the rest of them file from the kitchen, I linger behind.

'You could take the potatoes through.' Mum points towards the pan.

Balancing the steaming dish, I reach the door and pause at the sound of Nathaniel's voice hissing from a corner of the hallway. I know I shouldn't, but I'll listen in for a moment. After all, if I know as much as possible about what's going on between everyone, I'm in a better position to protect not only myself and Ben, but also Mum and Alice.

'What were you doing in the lounge with *him*?' He must be referring to Rylan. After all, other than Dad, he was the only other male present before Ben arrived.

'We were literally in there for a few minutes.' Erin's voice is defensive. 'Not even that.'

'You were smiling when you came out.'

'Sorr-ee. Should I have been crying? Would that have made you happy?'

'You don't have to be so sarcastic.'

'You don't have to accuse me of having an affair every five minutes.'

'What was he saying to you anyway?'

'Nothing much. He was just—'

'Don't mind me.' I breeze past them, hoping my interruption will put an end to Nathaniel's quizzing of poor Erin. He's as bad as Martha for the jealousy. Rylan and Erin can hardly be expected to ignore each other just to appease their respective partners. They went right through school together and were great mates until their stab at getting together put an end to that. I was devastated at the time – the end of their relationship felt like I was losing an older sister. So I was delighted, for all the wrong reasons, when Erin and Nathaniel got together some time later.

I head for the door where voices are echoing from behind it and push it open with my shoulder. The dining table, illuminated by the glow of chandeliers overhead, stands as the focal point of the room. Dad's already seated himself at the head of it with Martha one down from him and Rylan next to her. The table's lit up like a Christmas tree but the rest of the room's in gloom. And it's cold –

the whole cottage is cold. It looks like I'll be pinching some of Ben's thick jumpers.

'Another?' Dad waves the wine bottle he brought in from the breakfast bar in front of Martha's face.

'Don't mind if I do.'

'Don't you think you've had enough?' Rylan is clearly trying to keep his voice light and airy as I set the potatoes down on the table. I pull a face at him as if to say, *you're brave.*

'I'll be the judge of that,' she slurs.

'Where shall I sit?' Ben loiters around at the other end of the table.

'Wherever you like.' Mum comes in, laden with the casserole pot. 'Here, let me get past you – this is red-hot.'

'You should have let me carry that.' Ben says. 'Really, I want to help.'

'Like I've just told you – you're a guest.' Mum smiles as she slides her hands from the oven gloves.

'So he doesn't have to do anything all week?' Martha cackles. 'Is that what you're saying?'

I grimace as Ben pulls out the chair closest to Dad which is facing Martha. If he's sitting there, Dad's more likely to carry on the conversation about *whether Ben's good enough for me* from where he left off in the kitchen.

'Mum will be sitting there, won't you, Mum?'

But she's already heading back to the kitchen, presumably for the vegetables.

'He's fine where he is,' Dad says. 'Leave him alone.'

'Sit down here, Ben, with me.' I point towards the two ends of the table where we can face each other and be furthest away from Dad.

'I'm sitting there.' Alice scoots in and perches where I'm pointing at.

'I'll sit with you, love.' Erin comes in right after her.

'Don't you want to sit next to Dad?'

The expression on Erin's face suggests that she'd prefer to get as far away from Nathaniel as possible at the moment. After what I heard in the hallway, even if it was only a snippet, I don't blame her. 'Budge up one Alice,' she says.

'Why?'

I also don't blame Erin for choosing *not* to sit next to Rylan. Some things just aren't worth the hassle.

'I hope you two aren't fighting over who's *not* going to sit next to me.' Rylan looks from Erin to Alice and stabs a pretend dagger into his heart. 'I'm mortally wounded.'

The smile on Martha's face fades as Erin places her wine glass on the table and then slides into the seat beside Rylan. I end up between Nathaniel and Ben, who's left space for Mum beside Dad after all. The irritation radiating from Nathaniel is palpable as he looks across the table at Rylan. I can only hope we make it through this so-called holiday without my brothers coming to blows.

'Dig in.' Mum bustles back in and adds two bowls of vegetables to the food lined up down the centre of the table.

As Nathaniel reaches for the spoon in one of the casserole dishes, Dad's voice makes me jump.

'The dishes will start at the top of the table, if you don't mind, and will then be passed round clockwise.' He circles his finger around us all.

What a pillock my father is. It's a good job Mum's cooked plenty since under his instruction, she'll be served last. Surprisingly, she doesn't challenge him. I guess she's learned to choose her battles.

8

GILL

'I HAVEN'T HEARD you all so quiet since we arrived.' I cast my gaze over my family, happy to see them all tucking into their dinner with gusto. 'Is everything OK?'

'Delicious, thanks,' replies Rylan with a wink.

'The chicken's a bit dry,' Karl says. 'But I guess that's the price we pay having to wait for latecomers.'

I glance down the table towards Kelli who luckily isn't rising to his bait. Bitter experience has taught her well.

As we continue eating, the silence grows heavy with something I can't put my finger on. Nor do I really want to. All I know is that I don't like this quiet between us – it makes me nervous. As I glance around the room, I take in the elegant furnishings and the walls which are adorned with scenes from around The Dales. I can't help but imagine the other families who'll have eaten around this table and the differences between them and us.

'So what does everyone fancy doing this week?' Evidently, it's up to me to elicit some kind of conversation. There seems to be an atmosphere not only between Nathaniel and Erin, but also between Rylan and Martha. I should have maybe put some music on to lighten the mood but if I jump up and do it now, it'll look too obvious. Besides, Karl would no doubt complain if I were to leave the dinner table to mess around with the radio.

'Ben.' I direct my question to him, knowing he's the most likely to give me a considered answer. 'What do you think?'

'I, erm.' I've clearly put him on the spot when he's just taken a mouthful of chicken. All eyes are on him as he chews and swallows. 'I'm easy really. I just hope the weather holds up for whatever we end up doing.'

'It'll be a long week if it doesn't,' Nathaniel says. 'Has anyone thought about that? About what we'll do if it rains all week?'

'Forever the optimist. That's what weather forecasts are for, brother dearest.' Rylan grins. 'Besides, you'll have packed your waterproofs, won't you?'

'Rain tomorrow, then sunny and cold, according to my weather app, for the rest of the week. So in other words, awful and then perfect.' If only the same could be said about our unfolding holiday.

Everyone laughs. Probably because I used to religiously watch the forecast on the TV until the kids clubbed together for my iPhone. I swear by my weather app now and revolve my plans around it.

'We're not spending the entire time *together*, are we?' Nathaniel stabs at a potato. 'There is such a thing as personal space.'

'Ben and I might go off and do our own thing a bit,' Kelli says. 'If no one else minds.'

'Did you not hear a word I said in the kitchen before?' Karl drops his fork onto his plate with a clatter. 'This week is about being a happy family *together*.'

'But—' begins Nathaniel.

'And woe betide *anyone* who decides to spoil things.' Karl glares at him. 'And while we're on the subject of being happy – Alice, for goodness sake, put a smile on it.'

Her head jerks up from where she's been staring into her dinner. 'On what?'

'On your face, what else?' Karl shakes his head. 'I saw cheerier faces at Dad's funeral.'

Alice flushes. I make a mental note to take her off after dinner and spend some time with her. The rest of them can sort the clearing up.

'Smile, I said!' Karl's still on at the poor love.

'Let her have her dinner in peace, Karl.' I rest my hand on his arm. 'Besides, she's probably missing her GG as much as the rest of us.'

Alice's face falls some more at the mention of GG, the term she adopted as a toddler for her great-grandad. There can be no denying what a huge Joe-spaced hole he's left behind. For all of us.

'It's not just Alice being a misery here – it's *everyone*?' Karl tugs his arm away from me. 'In fact, the only person making any attempt at conversation is *you,* Gill. What's up with you all?' His gaze lands on Martha.

'Well, it's not as if I can talk to either of my sisters-in-law, is it?' She drops her gaze from Karl back to her plate as she pushes vegetables around on it. 'It's obvious neither of them can stand the sight of me.' She looks up and firstly at Erin, then at Kelli. 'Can you Erin – Kelli?'

'Leave it out, will you, love?' Rylan nudges her, grimacing as he exchanges glances with Kelli. 'I'm with Dad on this. Let's just all get on with each other this week – who knows, we might even enjoy ourselves.'

Alice snorts.

Karl points at the door. 'I think you can leave this table until you learn some manners, young lady.'

'No! Karl. You're being—'

As Alice jumps up from her chair and shoots to the door, Erin also pushes her chair back with a scrape, drowning out any pleas I was trying to make. 'Alice come back here and sit down. And Karl, just for the record, if my daughter needs chastising, either I or her father will be the ones to do it, thank you.'

But it's too late. Alice's angry footsteps are already on the stairs.

'Yeah, and a grand job you both do of it too.' Martha's voice drips with sarcasm.

'Do you know what?' Erin lifts hers and Alice's plates from the table. 'This is a lovely meal, Gill, and I'm sorry to have to do this, but I'm going to eat with my daughter in the other room. Neither she, nor I have to put up with this.'

'Sit back down, Erin,' Nathaniel snaps. 'Now.'

Thankfully, she completely ignores him. I'd hate to see anyone follow in *my* footsteps. However, I can't imagine Nathaniel ever having anything like the leverage over Erin that Karl's always had over me.

Kelli pushes her chair back as if she's going to follow Erin as well but I shake my head at her before she stands from it. Her trying to peace-make will only inflame things, especially with her father.

'Birds of a feather...' Martha begins and I shake my head at her as well.

'I honestly don't know what's up with everyone,' Rylan says. 'Maybe we should just have a mass argument and get it over and done with. Everyone can tell everyone else what they *really* think and feel about them, we can clear the air and then get on with the rest of the week.'

'Yeah, right.' It's Nathaniel's turn to snort.

'The Yorkshire puddings aren't up to your usual standard, dear.' Karl holds one at the end of his fork. 'What happened?'

I'm on the verge of blaming my unfamiliarity with the strange oven as I'd normally do, however, some very different words trip out of me. 'Well you know what you can do in future, don't you, Karl?' He's been sitting there drinking while I've been slaving away in that kitchen and yet he's daring to complain.

As Karl opens his mouth to reply, Ben pipes up. 'So, have we all brought our own bikes then? I looked online and there are some excellent routes around here. I enjoy a bit of off-roading,'

'That's the plan,' Rylan replies. 'We'll be needing to work off all this delicious grub anyway. Take no notice of Dad – Mum, the food is delicious. Anyway,' he looks back at Ben. 'What sort of bike have you got?'

I relax as the conversation is dominated by bikes for a few minutes until all falls silent after Rylan mentions the coast-to-coast bike challenge he and Erin did when they were in sixth form.

'Bloody marvellous,' Martha declares. 'From what I can gather, we're going to be spending this entire week taking a trip down Rylan and Erin's memory lane. I might as well pack my stuff and go home now.'

'Let's just change the subject.' I elevate my voice and force a smile. 'What are we going to do this evening? There are plenty of games in the lounge to enjoy ourselves with.'

No one speaks. Not even Ben.

9

GILL

It's a blessed relief to escape from the table – away from the undercurrents and bubbling tensions between everyone. From their body language, things seem to have deteriorated between Nathaniel and Erin and I suspect this week could bring it all to a head.

'Can I come in, love?' I poke my head around Alice's door and she looks up from her book. If I know my husband correctly, she'll be lucky to get that wifi password tonight after his sending of her from the table. Unless someone sneaks it to her, of course...

'As long as it's *only* you.' She appears to be trying to look behind me as if she's expecting her grandad to have followed me up. As if I'd have let him into her room, the state he's in. He and Martha are welcome to each other's company this evening. Rylan looks equally fed up about how drunk his wife is as the rest of us are.

Alice's face is tear-stained and I feel dreadful about it. She's supposed to be on holiday and yet she's spending her first night alone, in her room, in tears. As I cross the carpet, my eyes fall on her two bags still on the window seat. Clearly, she's as enthusiastic about unpacking them as everyone else seems to be. Even I haven't unpacked my things yet and that's normally the first thing I like to do on holiday. After having a cup of tea.

I sit beside my granddaughter and draw her towards me. She puts her book down and allows herself to be close which is a positive start.

'Why don't Grandad or Martha like me?' Alice's voice trembles with uncertainty as she searches my eyes for answers.

'They do like you, sweetheart.' I reassure her, squeezing her shoulder gently. 'But sometimes adults can be a real pain in the neck, can't they?' I nearly add, *when they've been drinking too much wine* but that wouldn't be true. They hardly need wine to be pains in the neck.

'I should have been at the dance club this week.' There's a shake in her voice as she nestles deeper into my shoulder. 'And even Mum didn't want to come here.'

I suspected this would be the case which is why I rang Nathaniel to make the arrangements instead of Erin. Nor did I try to persuade him otherwise when he promised to contact Erin's place of work before broaching the subject of the holiday with her. Usually, I wouldn't hear of such a thing. But Karl had told me in no uncertain terms that everyone *had* to be here. Then, he'd given me a look that served to warn me of the consequences if I didn't make it happen. Not that I needed that – I wanted everyone here as much as he did. Whether we can *keep* them all here is another matter, although I'm sure the possibility of funds from Joe's estate might hold some sway.

'Is everything OK with your Mum? And Dad?' I shouldn't be asking Alice to divulge problems my son and daughter-in-law might be having, but short of asking one of them what's going on *outright*, how else am I supposed to get to the bottom of things? If I'm going to help them, I need to know.

'Not really. They just keep sending me to my room while they shout at each other.' She stares down at her hands.

The poor lamb. She's only just started secondary school and doesn't need this stress to be going home to every day.

'How long has it all been going on, love?'

Alice pales to the roots of her lovely red hair. 'You won't tell them I said anything, will you?'

'Of course I won't. But if I know what's happening, perhaps I can help.' Rising from the bed, I creep across the thick carpet and peer across the landing – just in case. But Erin's loading the dishwasher with Kelli so we're safe to keep talking up here. I close the door after me with a click and turn back to face Alice.

She shuffles up to make space for me.

'Right, sweetheart. Tell me what's been going on.'

She's still hesitant.

'You know you can trust your grandma, don't you?' I sit back beside her and once again, I drape my arm around her skinny shoulders.

'They've been shouting a real lot since last week.' She looks up at me. 'But it was even before then as well.'

The last week would coincide with their knowledge about this holiday. I knew there would be a certain amount of reluctance to come here but I never imagined it could cause actual rows for anyone. There must be more to the shouting than merely this holiday and I already have my suspicions about what it could be. 'Do you know what's causing the problem, love?'

She shakes her head. 'No, but I daren't take any of my friends around anymore. It would be so embarrassing.'

'I know and I'll do my best to help with it all, I promise.'

'But you won't say I told you?'

'Of course not.' I nudge her as I stare at her earnest face. Come what may, I'm going to do everything in my power to make this week away a happier one than it's started out for my only grandchild. No matter what rubbish is rotting away within the so-called adults, I'm not having Alice affected, so will do whatever it takes to protect her from it all.

Ultimately, however, the only person's behaviour I can control is my own. Anything could happen among the rest of them.

'Look, love, we're here now and I promise we'll make the best of it. You and me can spend some proper time together, can't we? I've been looking forward to that.'

She fiddles with the corner of her pillow, evidently unconvinced and still downcast. 'But Grandad said we've all got to stay together.'

'He doesn't mean for every moment of every day. But never mind Grandad – for now, we just need to turn that frown upside down. I know, we could do nails and face masks – what do you think?'

She brightens slightly then her face falls again, the dusting of freckles on her nose wrinkling as she frowns. 'But I haven't brought anything with me.'

'One of the others might have. Or we'll find a shop.'

'There isn't anything for miles, Mum said.'

'We're not that far from the nearest shops. We can have a drive out tomorrow if you like.'

'OK.' She sniffs.

'Now how's about I go and get hold of that wifi password for you?'

Judging by the sudden light in her eyes, that was the right thing to say.

'Just don't tell your grandad.' I squeeze her hand as I rise from the bed.

'I'm a bit hungry, Grandma.' She pats her slender midriff. 'I couldn't finish my dinner before.'

'That's easily sorted.' I wink at her. 'How about crisps and chocolate cake?'

Her face breaks into a smile. 'Yessss.'

'You read a bit more of your book. Give me ten minutes or so to do a bit of creeping around.'

Her smile broadens which makes me so happy. A smile, after all, is top of the list of a Grandma's job description.

I stand on the landing for a few moments to discern how the land lies and where everyone is before returning downstairs. I expect I'll be doing this a lot more this week. Karl's, Ben's and Martha's voices echo from the dining room, where they're evidently putting the world to rights about something or other. I can only hope it doesn't result in an argument breaking out if Ben dares to disagree with something Karl might say. In any debate there are only ever two opinions – Karl's opinion and the wrong opinion. No one can ever disagree with him without a fallout ensuing. I can also hear Kelli, Rylan and Erin's chatter as they rattle around in the kitchen. This just leaves Nathaniel unaccounted for. Wherever he is, he'll no doubt have a glass of something in his hand – he hasn't been without a drink since he arrived earlier.

Which gives me just a moment to myself before I do what I need to do for Alice.

I slide my phone from my apron pocket, along with a number on a dog-eared scrap of paper. I haven't dared to store it in my phone for fear of Karl demanding a look at it to carry out one of his 'checks,' as he calls them.

> We've arrived. It's going to be difficult to get out but I'll find a way.

No sooner have I typed the message when a row of dots appears. At least I don't have to wait for the reply. I'll be able to turn my phone off and tuck it away.

> That's good. I'll look forward to seeing you soon then. Keep me posted.

As I delete the messages and drop the phone back into my pocket, I feel a sense of rebellion. Karl might think he's got me exactly where he wants me and similarly, the kids might also believe that I'm totally under their father's control, but they'd all be wrong. Yes, I've got to toe the line to a certain extent – only because of the consequences if I don't. But nobody knows this other side of my life. Not yet, anyway.

Through the bathroom door which has been left ajar, I catch sight of my reflection in the mirrored tiles. Deep down, I'm still Gill. Worry lines and dark eye circles might be concealing the girl I once was. I might also be hiding beneath a pinny and the conservative jumpers and skirts Karl prefers me to wear but I'm most definitely still in here. And there's nothing whatsoever he can do to change this.

Yet, as I stand a little longer, savouring these unexpected moments of free time and the promise of further freedom, the foreboding that's been lying heavy in my belly intensifies. Try as I might, I'm unable to shake it.

DAY TWO

10

ERIN

As I awaken with a start, the soft glow of dawn is filtering through the curtains, casting long shadows across the room. For a moment, I wonder where the hell I am. Then the realisation hits me like a cricket bat to the head. It's day two of the week from hell. One night survived and six more to get through. Nathaniel's been in a foul mood since we got here, Alice's mood is even worse and right now, amidst the last of the autumn birdsong that's drifting through the open window and the drum of the rain, Karl is loudly berating poor Gill about something she's forgotten to bring.

'I wasn't the only person in charge of packing,' she protests, making no effort to keep her voice down from the other side of the landing. I check my watch – it's later than I thought. I don't usually drink as much wine as I did last night but needs must.

'And I'm not your bloody mother,' she adds. At least she still has it in her to defend herself against him. Whatever their history as a couple, and whatever the reason that she feels compelled to stay with him, I'm glad he hasn't completely squashed her spirit. Judging by how drunk he was last night, he's probably more likely to back down than normal. Who wants to row when they've got a stonking hangover?

I stretch out in the bed, grateful that Nathaniel's already up. The low rumble in my belly reminds me that I hardly ate anything last night, what with Karl sending Alice from the table like he did. There was no reasoning with her after that and I was thankful that Gill was able to get through to her.

'Help yourself to porridge.' Gill points at the huge pan simmering on the stove as I exchange the gloom and chill of the hallway for the slightly warmer kitchen. I've felt chilled through ever since we arrived here. As I head to the stove, a happy memory of my grandmother, who always used to make porridge in a pan like this, emerges in my mind. She'd sprinkle it with sugar and tell me to eat from the edges so I didn't burn my mouth. My grandma is one of my happiest childhood memories, a relationship which has luckily been emulated between Alice and Gill. I'm so pleased they're close, especially with my mum no longer being around.

'I hope you're not planning to wait on us all week, Gill.' I grab a bowl from the stack she's left beside the pan. 'This is your holiday too. In fact, I think we should take it in turns.' I glance towards the fire. I bet she laid and lit that as well.

'What do you mean – take *what* in turns?' Alice says as she shovels her porridge down. The poor love's probably starving after last night as well. I tried coaxing her to finish her dinner but she was too upset.

'Well there's six days still left here, isn't there?'

Not that I'm counting them down or anything.

'So six evening meals left to cook. How about we take one night each? We could even compete to see who cooks the best meal?' Something lifts within me – at least I'm doing *something* to take the edge off the ghastliness of being here. Which is more than can be said for any of the others.

Martha gives me one of her infamous withering looks as she

glances up from her phone where she's sitting at the breakfast bar. 'I detest cooking,' she says. 'Rylan does it all in our house.'

'You're not that bad at it!' He reaches for her and squeezes her shoulder. Evidently, they've resolved their issues from last night. 'What about that three-course meal you once cooked me?'

'I was trying to impress you then.' She peers at him from beneath her fringe.

'As if you ever had to try.' He grins back at her.

Watching their interaction provokes a wave of anger in me. I shouldn't let myself even go there – it can only ever be counter-productive. The fact that Rylan and Martha got together almost the moment after I left for university is something I've never really forgiven him for. So to hear them talking about their early days together never fails to illicit a reaction within me, as she very well knows. As I finish ladling porridge into my bowl, I can sense her eyes boring into me. I won't give her the satisfaction of even looking back at her.

'So,' I continue, swallowing my fury as best I can and striding towards the breakfast bar with my bowl. 'I'll cook tonight, shall I? With Alice.'

'No, Mum – no!'

Ignoring my daughter, I perch on the stool as far away from Martha and Rylan as possible. 'Tomorrow night we'll have Nathaniel cooking, then Rylan the night after, followed by Karl, Martha and lastly Kelli.'

'What about me?' Ben points at himself. Despite the obvious hostilities, he seems relaxed around us all. Dressed in joggers and a hoodie he's sprawled on the rug in front of the fire with a book.

'You're a guest,' Gill calls from the kitchen at the same time as me and we both laugh. Martha pulls a face.

'I'm game.' Karl pours himself a coffee. I'm quite surprised he's willing to get involved. But then he spoils himself. 'It's got to be better than last night's casserole, hasn't it?'

Gill's smile fades as she comes up beside me with her breakfast. 'Ignore him,' I hiss. 'It was lovely.' She squeezes my arm.

'Here, Gill. I've saved you a place.' Now that Martha's sobered up, she'll be on a full-on charm offensive with our mother-in-law. 'We haven't spent that much time together since we got here, have we?'

She looks daggers at me as if to say, *butt out*. I've even had *I was here first* from her in the past which isn't strictly true. She might have married into the family before I did, but I first met Gill, Karl, Nathaniel and Kelli when I was only sixteen, which was long before she muscled in.

'Do you mind?' Gill's voice is full of apology as she glances at me. I shake my head so she heads around to the other side of the breakfast bar. I can hardly tell her that actually, I *do* mind. Martha getting one over on me is never a good thing.

Kelli saunters in with her hair on end, rubbing her eyes.

'Afternoon,' Ben calls out.

'Why didn't you wake me?' She pulls a face as she slips into the seat Gill was about to take beside me. 'It's so quiet around here – that's probably why I've slept so late.'

'Quiet – with our lot?' Gill laughs.

'The quiet's actually eerie.' Kelli lowers her voice, seemingly just to talk to me. 'There's almost an air of impending doom about the place, don't you think?'

'Well I heard noises all night,' Alice says. 'It sounded like there was someone out there.'

'It was only the bogeyman.' Karl laughs as Nathaniel pulls a face at him. I feel like asking Karl if he's ever going to act like Alice's grandad. He should be spoiling her, protecting her, making her laugh and feel special. To say she's his only grandchild, I can't believe the way he treats her at times. However, from what I can gather, he'd have been completely different if she'd been a boy who was going to carry his precious family name on.

'What are we doing today then?' I'll change the subject before he upsets her again.

'It's a bit wet for any cycling.' Gill looks towards the window. 'But there's a better forecast tomorrow.'

Alice looks as gloomy as the weather. 'We can't just stay in *here* all day. I'll go mad.'

'We can have a drive out somewhere,' I tell her. 'Just you and I.'

'We'll come with you.' Kelli nudges him. 'Won't we, Ben?'

'Have you forgotten what I said last night already?' Karl's voice booms from the top end of the breakfast bar. 'We're spending this week together as a family, therefore we'll start as we mean to go on. We'll *all* go for a *walk* after breakfast.'

Everyone falls silent, obviously not daring to argue back. Everyone, that is, apart from me. I stare at the driving rain against the window pane. 'What if some of us don't want to go for a walk?'

'We've got waterproofs here – they're all in the shed.' He gestures to the window. 'So we can get wrapped up and go for a walk, OK?' He gives me one of his looks and from the opposite side of the breakfast bar, I can feel Nathaniel's eyes on me too. He's still not speaking to me and I'll be damned if I'm the one to instigate any peacemaking between us.

'Good.' Karl takes my silence as my submission. 'I'll hear no more about it then.'

I bite my lip. How Gill's put up with the man for all these years, I have no idea. Karl used to terrify me when I was a teenager but now he just irritates me beyond measure. Kelli shoots me a sympathetic look which conveys *there's no point arguing with him.* I'm biding my time though. I'm *not* Kelli, and Karl hasn't got whatever hold over me that he's got over her. It's the first time I've considered this, but I'm relieved I had the father I did – the one who walked out on me when I was small. It's preferable to the father Kelli, Rylan and Nathaniel have been lumbered with all these years – a father who is only satisfied when he's exerting his tyrannical influence over everyone.

For now, I twirl porridge around my mouth and resign myself to a level of supposed obedience – at least on the surface.

Hopefully, the fact that we're getting out of here soon and unleashing some pent-up energy might also release some of the tension that's been building inside these four walls since we arrived.

It already feels like we've been here for several days.

11

ERIN

ALICE and I step into the shed and the dim light filters through cracks in the walls, casting eerie shadows that seem to dance across the floor. It takes a moment for my eyes to adjust.

'Right – Grandma said to look in the bag in the corner. Ah – there we are.'

'I'm not wearing *those*.' Alice remarks as I thrust a pair of waterproof trousers at her. 'And can we hurry up and get out of here?' She nods in the direction of the door. 'It's even creepier in here than it is in the house.'

'They'll keep you dry,' I insist, my tone tinged with frustration. 'Other than rabbits and squirrels, who's going to see you anyway?'

'*I'll* see me.' She pouts. 'Oooh, what's in those?' She lifts a lid from what looks like a pot but a closer inspection shows what she's *really* unearthed.

'Put it back,' I shriek. 'Now!'

She jumps in response to my elevated voice and snaps the lid back on it. 'Why, what is it? – Grandma...' She glances at Gill who's just appeared in the doorway. 'Do *you* know what's in these jars?'

'It's – it's just some stuff for plants – it's poisonous.' If I tell her what's really in them, she'll be running off into the hills. She's already hearing noises at night. 'Go inside and get ready while I get your grandma some waterproofs.' I nudge her and she rises to her feet.

Gill steps back so Alice can leave and then comes into the shed.

'What *have* you found?'

'You'll never believe it.' I peer into one of the urns to double-check the contents and then snap the lid back on.

'What?'

'Human ashes,' I reply, tilting the urn so I can read the inscription. 'Two lots, by the looks of it.'

'Just left here in the shed?' She bends down beside me and picks up the other one. 'Let me see.'

I reach into my pocket for my phone and shine its light on the plaque. '*Joyce Callaghan 11.2.55 to 23.3.23*,' I read from it.

'Blimey,' Gill says, squinting at the plaque on the urn she's holding. 'This one has the same date of death. *Bruce Callaghan 25.5.54 to 23.3.23*.'

'They died together.' I shiver. Rain drums against the roof, its relentless patter echoing our unease. 'Do you reckon they died *here*?' I glance through the open door of the shed through the rain at the gloom of the cottage.

'They must have been the owners.'

'How did you find out about this place?'

'Through a friend of a friend,' she replies, jumping slightly as the shed door bangs in the wind.

'Did you find out any more than that?'

'Just that their son,' – she gestures at the urns, – 'inherited the cottage, but because it's been on the market for a while, and wasn't selling, he decided to let it as a holiday cottage. We're the first people to stay here, according to the agent.'

'And he's left the ashes of his parents *here* in this shed?' I stare at the urns, feeling colder than I have since we arrived. I've felt an uncomfortable vibe the whole time we've been here. Maybe now I know why.

'Well, everyone handles things in different ways,' Gill says.

'I wonder what the story is about them dying on the same day.' It's my turn to jump as the shed door bangs again. 'Perhaps they were in an accident together.'

'Come on – let's go and get ready.' She tugs at my arm.

'We'll have to google their names,' I reply as my cold fingers fasten the bolt back up. I'm willing these next few days to pass even quicker now I've been 'introduced' to the former owners of the place. It's cold and dark enough here as it is.

'Some things are best just left alone, Erin.' Gill leads the way back to the cottage door. 'I think I'd rather not know any more details about who they were or how they died.'

'It looks nice on you, that does,' Gill remarks as I tug my hat over my ears. 'Green has always been your colour.'

'Well, it was one of my favourite birthday presents from you.'

I glance across the room at Martha to gauge her reaction. She won't be happy with our mother-in-law complimenting me instead of her.

'Have you still got the matching gloves?' Gill continues.

'No, I lost one when we did that walk-up Pen-Y-Gent. That day when the weather was nearly as awful as today. Don't you—?'

'It's *my* birthday next month, remember?' Martha's head jerks up from where she's tying her boots by the back door. 'Do you fancy going somewhere nice for lunch, Gill?'

'Oh, erm, well, yes – I suppose so.'

Kelli and I exchange glances as we have done several times since we got here. Our unspoken words convey that if we're waiting for Martha to include us in this cosy lunch invitation, we'll be waiting an extremely long time.

'I've seen you both, you know.' As Gill heads towards Alice, Martha rises to her feet and twists her hair into a bun at the back of her head.

'Seen us – what?'

'All your little looks at each other – I'm not stupid.'

'You're talking complete rubbish.' I stride toward the door where everyone's waiting outside.

'You should hear what Kelli says about you *behind your back*,' Martha mutters as she barges past me. 'And what Gill says.'

I try to keep my expression as nonchalant as I can. I would never give Martha the satisfaction of thinking she's got to me. I can't imagine Kelli or Gill saying *anything* against me, but then they do talk about Martha behind *her* back, so who knows?

I splash through the puddles to catch up with Nathaniel. Not that I really want to, but for the sake of keeping the peace, I need to try and appease him if I can. We fall into step alongside each other and trudge a few paces behind his parents.

Tightening the cord on my kagool hood, I blink the rain from my eyes. 'Nice day for it, don't you think?' I nudge him with a smile and watch for his reaction.

'Don't act like nothing's going on, Erin.' I can tell from the line of his jaw that he's just as upset as he was last night. Before he got stuck into the box of beer we brought. I glance around to see where Alice is. She's seen and heard more than enough of her dad and me exchanging cross words lately. I'm pleased to see her engrossed in conversation with her Auntie Kelli and Ben.

'But there isn't. I've no idea what you're going on about.'

'Rylan. I've seen the way you look at each other.'

'Look.' I move closer to him and try to link my arm with his, but he shakes his away. 'You're reading something that isn't there,

Nathaniel. Maybe it was fourteen years or so ago, but it's dead and buried now.'

'How come you were cosying up in the lounge last night then? Martha told me she walked in on you.'

'She walked in on *nothing* and we weren't *cosying up*. I was already in there, then Alice came in, then Rylan. It was – oh come on, let's not do this. The week's trying enough, don't you think, without the two of us being at each other's throats about a load of nonsense.'

He won't even look at me. 'I just can't get it out of my head.'

'Well try, please. You've already spoiled the first night with your foul mood. Oh God, your dad's at it again as well.' I roll my eyes to the sky.

Karl's striding some way out in front and Gill's almost running to keep up with him, the shriek of her voice suggesting she's also trying to appease him. What she could have done to upset her husband is anyone's guess but by the jerking of his limbs and his indiscernible raised voice, I can tell that, once again, *something's* set him off.

'Are you OK?' I reach for Nathaniel's hand. No matter what atmosphere might be rumbling between us at the moment, I know how much it upsets him to witness his dad going at his mum like this.

'I just wish he'd leave her alone.' His voice is soft but he still yanks his hand away.

If it was any other situation, I'm certain Nathaniel would intervene. But where his father's concerned, it's as if he steps back in time in his powerlessness whenever he's around him. Things aren't brilliant between the two of us right now, our main problem being his insecurity, but I still feel sorry for him despite everything else.

However, I'm annoyed at the underhand way he forced me and Alice into this holiday, largely because it echoed how Karl might have gone about things. I try not to draw comparisons between them as although Nathaniel is rough around the edges, he's a long way from being anywhere near the bullying and controlling league of his father.

'Do you think she'll ever leave him?'

'To be honest…' Finally, he looks at me as he brushes raindrops from the end of his nose. 'I don't think she could. There's the practical side of things, of course.'

'Then there's this supposed deep, dark secret,' I say.

He shakes his head. 'Sometimes I think all that's invented – as another one of his control mechanisms. I mean, look at her.' He nods towards his mother, swamped by the large yellow raincoat and waterproof trousers we found in the shed. She's completely dwarfed beside the bulk of his father. 'What deep, dark secret is *she* going to have?'

'Mum – Dad, look, there's a cave.' I love it when my daughter forgets herself for a few moments and regresses from her near-adolescent state to showing the awe and wonder of a child again. She comes up in between us and links arms. For a moment, I yearn for the days when she was a toddler and would swing between us from our arms as we walked in the park. Back then, I had less qualms over everything. Not like I have now.

'This could be a good place for a tea stop,' Kelli calls from the back of the line.

Gill says something to Karl who slides the rucksack from his back. Clearly, they agree for a change.

As we head towards the mouth of the cave, I can see there's enough room for us all to get out of the rain, but it'll certainly be cramped in there. Not to mention interesting.

Karl, as I could have put money on, serves his own tea first. Not for the first time, I find myself ruminating on the loss of his father, Joe, and imagining it had been the other way around. Joe was an absolute gentleman, so much so that it's hard to explain where Karl's chauvinism and lack of chivalry originate from.

'Cheers.' Gill raises her plastic cup into the air.

'Cheers.' I take a grateful swallow and enjoy the warmth travelling from my cold lips down to my stomach. Tea always tastes better from a flask, especially on a day like this.

'How's my favourite niece?' Rylan plonks his bag on the stone floor and perches on the ledge in the corner beside Alice. 'I see you've saved me the best spot, sitting beside you.'

She giggles and if it wasn't so dark in here, I'd probably be able to see her blushing too. She's always liked Rylan making a fuss of her. I glance across the gloom and meet Nathaniel's narrowed eyes, as he watches. He's no doubt got something else to berate me with later now. It wouldn't be the first time he'd made a song and dance about our daughter preferring to be around Rylan to being around *him*.

'Here, let me warm you up.' Rylan takes his scarf off and drapes it over her shoulders. Then, in the tight space behind them, he manoeuvres his arm behind her and rubs at the top of her arm. 'You OK?' he asks.

She pulls a face. 'I guess so.'

'This holiday can't be much fun for you – you should have been allowed to bring one of your friends.'

Alice doesn't reply but her face says it all. *As if I'd invite one of my friends to a place like this.*

'How about we find a film to stream later? Something really funny? I'll even provide the popcorn.'

'You've got popcorn?' Her eyes widen.

'Sure have.'

Nathaniel's jaw hardens and I can tell he wants to say something. If I know him correctly, he'll be racking his brains to come up with a better offer so that Alice will want to look forward to spending time with *him* instead of her uncle. But communicating with our daughter has never been his strong point. It's as if he wonders what to say to her, and this is even more pronounced as she's getting older. Therefore, he's often been distant to the point of being aloof. I think he'd have been different if I'd had a son like he wanted.

If, on this holiday, Alice is gravitating more towards Rylan and Ben, Nathaniel's only got himself to blame.

12

KELLI

Ben takes my gloved hand in his as we allow ourselves to fall away from the rest of the group. We've all broken off into pairs, and Alice is walking with her mum.

I steal a glance ahead, half-expecting my dad to whirl around any moment, his booming voice commanding us to catch up. He looks like he's arguing with Mum over something. As always.

But since we've stopped for a drink and set off again, I've gone really cold and lacking in energy in the autumnal rain. It doesn't help that I was tossing and turning all last night.

'Your mum sticks up for herself more than you gave her credit for.'

I peer at Ben's face behind the side of his hood and can see that he's watching them too. To give Mum her dues, she does appear to be sticking it back at him.

'She's definitely got better at defending herself since I left home,' I reply, pulling my hood tighter. 'It's as if she was protecting me by not arguing back as much when I was there.'

'Why, what would have happened?'

'Well, whenever they argued, I always jumped in, I couldn't help myself. I tried to keep out of it but when someone's bellowing at your mother and smashing things against the walls...' My voice trails off.

As we continue to trudge through the muddy woods, memories I've long tried to suppress claw their way to the surface. The tension between my parents resurrects ghosts of past arguments, dragging me back to a time I'd rather forget.

'I was thinking,' Ben says, 'when we were having dinner last night that if your dad is as unpleasant as he is with all of us here watching them, I dread to think what he could be like when he and your mum are alone.'

'You haven't seen it when he lords it over her with money and that sort of thing.'

'Really?'

'Yeah – I can see it in her eyes that she feels absolutely worthless when he starts up about that.'

Our synchronised steps create a rhythm as we continue to walk; the rustle of our waterproof sleeves and the swish of our legs brushing against each other, adding a comforting background melody to our conversation. The damp earth beneath us yields with each footfall, releasing an earthy aroma that mingles with the scent of rain-soaked leaves.

'Hasn't your mum ever worked?'

'Nope.' I look ahead at her as she starts to ascend some steps into a clearing. There's a slight brightening of the cloud up there. With a bit of luck, it might stop raining soon.

'Well, I'm obviously no expert on families, am I?' Ben's laughter rings out, but it lacks its usual warmth as it echoes in the damp, misty air. 'However, I'd have said that the woman staying home was the exception rather than the norm these days.'

'Dad said she never needed to work. But that was *his* decision, rather than hers.'

'So she wanted to have a job?'

'Oh yes. Especially by the time we were all at nursery or had started school. She nursed my Grandma at the end, so I can't imagine how much she'd have wanted and needed to get out of those four walls after she'd died.

'Your Grandma?'

'Yeah, I can only remember her vaguely. I was quite young when she died.' An image of her with Grandad enters my mind. The framed photo has had pride of place on the bay windowsill for as long as I can remember. As a child, I often used to stare at the face of this smiling woman who would always be a stranger to me and would feel envious of Nathaniel who could remember her well.

'Was she Joe's wife?'

'Yeah, and all I can recall was her being ill in bed. I don't remember ever seeing her get out of it. But I'm glad you met my grandad – I just wish Dad was more like him.'

'Did your Grandma live with you too?'

'For a time.' I can't believe we've got onto a subject that's been at the root of so many of the arguments between my parents over the years.

'What's up? You've gone quiet.' Ben lets go of my hand and throws his arm around my shoulders. Cold droplets of rain cling to our clothes, adding to the damp chill that permeates the woods. I lean into him, hoping to get warmer but that's not possible with someone also wearing a soggy kagool.

'I was just thinking. From what I've been told since, Mum was on her own with my grandma when she died, and to be honest, I don't think Dad's ever forgiven Mum for it.'

Ben shakes his head. 'It's not as if you can plan these things, is it? Oh, I'll die at six o'clock because that's convenient for everyone else.'

'Nathaniel remembers even more of the rows going on and Mum being in tears all the time.'

'Has she ever spoken to you about it?'

I stare at my mother's back, feeling slightly guilty for discussing her like this when she's so close by. She wouldn't be happy. 'I've tried asking her about my grandma dying a few times, as there's clearly a story there but, even after all these years, she clams up for some reason. She still seems quite affected by whatever it is.'

'They must have been close – if she was looking after her.'

'I guess so.'

'Other than that, your mum's spent her whole life keeping house and looking after you guys?'

'Pretty much. She'd have loved to paint but Dad always poured scorn on that, saying it was a complete waste of time.'

'It's never too late.'

'Try telling *him* that. He doesn't seem to want her to do *anything* on her own.'

'He's an interesting guy, your father. I don't think I've ever met *anyone* with such a lack of redeeming features.' With being such different heights, we're struggling to wade through this sludgy mud while arm in arm so he lets me go, squeezing my hand as he does. 'I'm sorry, Kelli. He's your dad – I shouldn't have said that.'

'It's OK. Like I've said before, you don't know the half of it.' Regret floods me as soon as the words escape my lips. If Ben doesn't remember what I told him about Dad a few months ago, with what I've just said, I risk reigniting his memory. And with that, I also risk him slipping up and saying something to Dad.

'So tell me then. From what you've told me already, there seems to be far more keeping your mum tied to your dad than just his grip on the wallet strings. Maybe we can get to the bottom of it this week.'

'To be honest, I've never been a hundred per cent sure of the facts,' I reply, staring at my lovely mum's back. I can see why Erin and Martha fight over her but there's just no need. There's enough of her to go around. 'I just hear the snarky comments from my dad at times but I've never been able to make head nor tail of them.'

'It sounds like you should have another go at talking to her.'

'I have. Rylan and Nathaniel have too.' I nod towards my brothers, walking in front of us. 'She just changes the subject and says the past is in the past. But you can tell by how she says it that there's more than she's letting on. I know my mum and there's always a look in her eyes that I can't put my finger on.'

'What about your dad? Have you ever tried talking to him?'

'You're joking, aren't you?' I laugh. 'Can you imagine trying to engage *him* in a meaningful discussion?' I shake my head. 'The only time he properly lets himself go is when he's drinking but, even then, it's all about *him*.'

'Maybe he'd talk to me.' Ben gestures to himself.

'He'd be more likely to chuck you out when you say something to *offend* him.' I let go of Ben's hand and draw air quotes around the word 'offend' with my gloved fingers. There is, after all, no rhyme or reason to the things my father takes offence to.

'If he did, would you come out to the car and keep me warm?'

'Of course.' I give him a playful push as I survey everyone in front. Rylan and Martha seem to be enjoying each other's company which is a surprise after their hostility towards each other last night. Nathaniel seems quiet – Erin and Alice are doing all the talking there and thankfully, up at the front of the line, Dad's striding forward with his hands plunged into his pockets. He looks to be giving his vocal chords a rest for a change and seems quiet for the time being. Mum's probably making the most of it.

'Anyway, I promised you that I'd be on my best behaviour, didn't I? I'm only here, well, mainly for you, *and* as an observer.'

I laugh again. 'I dread to imagine your *notes*.'

'Some of these family dynamics are so interesting to watch that they'll probably end up in my thesis.'

'What's your thesis going to be about then? Have you decided?'

'Families who divorce each other.'

'If only.'

I could quite cheerfully divorce my father. Nathaniel too, at times – he can be so much like Dad that I don't know how Erin puts up with him. And then there's Martha, although I don't really see her as family. I wouldn't trust her as far as I could throw her.

'Well we're only on day two and I still see ructions ahead.'

'Yeah,' Ben replies as he dodges another muddy puddle. 'There's certainly quite an atmosphere between you all.'

'All our 'past stuff' is why my Grandad seems to have forced us all here. This must be his version of banging our heads together.'

'Rylan seems like a decent sort though.' Ben nods to where he's striding along, holding a golfing umbrella over himself and Martha. 'I haven't quite sussed your other brother out yet.'

'I don't think *anyone* ever could.' I shake my head, then I chuckle. 'I knew you'd be in your element this week with this lovely opportunity to psychoanalyse everyone. Go on, spill it – I reckon that's the real reason you came.'

He swings his arm around me again. 'I came for you – you know I did. But to be honest, it *is* nice to be around a family – and to be almost part of it. Even if I'm the only one here who's not a Hawthorne.'

'You could always marry me and take my name if you want to belong to this dysfunction *forever*.' I playfully slap the top of his arm as we continue.

'Oooh, is that a proposal?' He turns and winks at me, his eyebrows sodden with rain and water dripping from his chin.

'Not yet. Besides I'm a traditional girl. You've got to ask me.'

'Does that mean I've got to ask your dad for your hand in marriage first?'

'Don't you dare. He doesn't need his ego inflating any more than it already is.'

Although as I stare at the back of my father's head, I know there are many worse attributes he could display before his inflated ego.

13

KELLI

'Gill... over here.' Erin's pointing at something on her computer screen. Her hair is damp and frizzy from the rain and she has patches on her jeans where the wet has seeped through her waterproof trousers.

As Martha tries to lean over to look at it, Erin turns the screen towards her and shuffles from the breakfast bar, over to one of the easy chairs near the fire.

'What's so secret?' Martha screws her face up. She's as impeccable as always, having changed into leggings and a long, cosy-looking jumper since we got back. Not a hair or an eyelash out of place. Not like me with my panda eyes and hair clinging to my neck like seaweed.

'It's nothing. Just something I wanted to show Gill,' Erin replies.

'Have it your own way.' Martha slides from her stool and towards the door. 'Hey watch it,' she snaps at Alice who almost collides with her as they meet in the doorway.

Mum begins reading over Erin's shoulder. 'I thought we'd agreed to leave this alone.'

'Did we?'

'What are you going on about?' I move closer to them. As soon as I see the photo of the end of this lane with a police cordon across it, I know what it's about. Erin's already told me about the urns they've found in the shed.

'We'd better keep this from Alice.' I frown at Erin.

'I'll go over there and distract her while you read it.' She rises from the chair and passes me the laptop. 'Close it down when you're done.'

Tragedy of a couple who couldn't live without each other

Further to the deaths of 68-year-old Joyce Callaghan and her husband, 69-year-old Bruce Callaghan which were reported last week, their post-mortem examinations have now identified their causes of death.

Police made the grim discovery at Poppy Cottage, near Ingle Tarn in the northern area of the Yorkshire Dales of the couple in front of the fireplace of the kitchen area in the eighteenth-century listed building. They were responding to telephone calls from the couple's concerned son who had been unable to gain access to the house.

Mrs Callaghan, who had been diagnosed with an inoperable tumour, was found lying on the rug. The post-mortem showed evidence of suffocation, consistent with having a cushion held over her face.

Her husband's death had resulted from taking a cocktail of prescription drugs, including his wife's strong pain relief and sleeping tablets—.

'What's this you're reading?' Dad swoops down and sweeps the laptop from my hands.

I jerk my head at Erin, hoping she'll take the hint to get Alice out of the way.

She does. 'Come on,' I hear her begin as she grabs Alice's arm before my attention returns to my father.

'I was reading that,' I tell him, but he's now too engrossed in it himself to answer. 'Well, I never.' He glances around. 'We're in exactly the same place as where it happened.'

I shiver. Trust him to make light of it. The look on Mum's face is like nothing I've seen before. Disgust mixed with fear as he snaps the laptop closed.

'Playing God,' he asserts as he slides the laptop onto the kitchen counter. 'Well you know what I think of that, don't—'

'Their remains are in the shed,' I say.

'They're what?' Martha looks almost amused.

'Their ashes. They're in urns. Erin and Mum found them earlier which is why they were googling it.'

'Ugh.' Her hand flies to her mouth. 'Maybe those noises Alice was hearing—'

'Not a word to her, do you hear me?' Rylan looks up from where he's pouring a drink. 'You'll scare the poor lass half to death if she hears about any of this.'

'What would you care?' Martha frowns.

Nathaniel's watching them too, through narrowed eyes.

I give Martha a withering look before crossing the kitchen to join my brother. But as I look back to where I was just sitting, a cold feeling snakes its way up my spine and I feel even more uncomfortable within this house than ever before.

'What's that black thing propping the door open?' Alice bends to pick it up. She raises it to eye level and turns it over in her hands. 'It weighs a ton,' she remarks. 'It looks like the iron from Monopoly, doesn't it?'

'We'll have a game of that soon, shall we?' Rylan calls out. 'I'll whoop all your arses.'

'Is that a gauntlet I hear being thrown down?' Ben laughs. It's good to see how easily he's getting on with Rylan. It's a shame the same thing can't be said about my other brother whose raised voice is drifting from the lounge. It's obvious what his problem is though, to be honest, I can't believe he's still harbouring a grudge over the relationship between Rylan and Erin. It was a lifetime ago. He needs to get over himself.

'He's definitely a chip off the old block,' Ben whispers to me and jerks his head in the direction of the lounge. 'Maybe you should make sure Erin's alright. Or do you want me to go?'

I pull a face at Ben and nod towards Alice as if to say *watch what you're saying in front of her*. Thankfully she's still too busy inspecting the iron to be taking any notice of us.

'My history teacher would love to see this,' she says before jumping as Dad suddenly arrives in front of us. 'W-what are you doing?' she stammers.

I have to admit that I jump as well. He came out of nowhere.

'Yeah, go into the lounge.' I nudge Ben. 'I'll be along in a minute.'

'You sure?'

'*That's* not a toy you know.' Dad looks from Alice to me as Ben moves away but hovers in the doorway. 'Do you think it's a responsible and adult thing to do?' Dad jabs his finger in my direction.

'What?'

'To let an eleven-year-old mess about with such a heavy object.'

'I'm fine – I was only thinking that I might draw it.'

'Grandma would probably draw it with you.' I look over to where Mum's been cornered by Martha. She's been doing everything she can to monopolise her since we got back from our walk, seemingly to keep her from getting too 'cosy' with Erin. 'It's nice that you've both got the same talent for art.'

Dad snorts. 'It wouldn't be nice if she dropped it on her foot though, would it?' He reaches for the iron, however, I beat him there. Like a kettlebell, I swing it from Alice's hands and hold it behind my back.

'Like Alice just said, she's absolutely fine.' I square up to my father, though as he steps closer to me, I'm already regretting it. My new-found bravado ebbs away as quickly as it appeared as I see the glint of anger in his eyes. I'm just like Mum in that respect. She's always trying to stand up to him – until he retaliates.

'Don't *ever* think you're too old, Kelli.' The look in his eyes has intensified. But I won't be the first person to look away, no matter how much I'm quaking inside. I'm in my twenties now – I refuse to let him bully me.

'For what exactly?' I hope he can't hear the tremble in my voice – not when I want to convey strength. 'A repeat performance – is that what you mean?'

Alice looks at me, curiously. However, the combination of her watching, and what I've just said seems to do the trick.

'You'll keep,' Dad mutters as he storms off, rescuing me from a wave of fear not unlike the one the eight-year-old me remembers feeling. However, as he leaves the room I realise I'm shaking.

Ben assembles the Monopoly board on the dining room table as the rain continues to hammer outside.

'One of us can't play,' Alice moans. 'It says eight people on the box.'

'We'll be a team.' Rylan reaches and draws her towards where he's taken the same chair as last night. 'Come and sit next to me.'

'Actually, I'm her father – she can sit with me,' Nathaniel says from the other side of the table, while pointing at the chair beside him.

'Leave the poor girl alone.' Mum slides a tray of tea in front of me while frowning at Nathaniel. 'She's fine with her uncle. Now who wants some cake?'

'Meeee.' Alice smiles at the chocolate cake.

It's obvious from her face that she's happier being partnered for Monopoly with her uncle rather than her father. And I don't blame her, with the miserable mood Nathaniel's been in since we all got here. I should probably try to have a word with him but I would, no doubt, get my head bitten off for interfering.

'I'll be the banker.' Dad sits at the end of the table again. I'd have placed a bet on him grabbing that role. 'And then I'll check everyone's money to make sure that no one's taken more money than they're entitled to. Someone pass me some cake please.'

'Some things never change,' Rylan says and even Nathaniel stifles a smile.

We spend a surprisingly amenable hour-and-a-half playing Monopoly, with plenty of laughter and banter, but as people start to win and most importantly, when people start to lose, I'm reminded why this sort of game is no good for this family.

'Don't be flipping the board, Nate.' Rylan chuckles as Nathaniel lands on his Mayfair square. 'He used to do that, you know.' He nudges Alice. 'Whenever your dad was losing, he'd just throw the board from the table, scattering pieces and money everywhere. Then he'd storm off.'

Alice laughs back. 'Dad doesn't like losing one bit. He even gets mad if he gets the questions wrong when we're watching a quiz show.'

'He can be a right mardy arse, can't he?'

'Watch your language in front of my daughter, Rylan.'

'Oh, get over yourself.' I nudge my brother. 'She's heard it all before. Especially in *this* family.'

The room falls silent as Erin takes her turn, landing on *go to jail.*

Martha laughs. 'Never mind, Erin.'

Rylan nods at a card in front of Erin.

'Oh yes.' She smiles back at him.

'Why are you helping *her*?' Martha points at Erin and then jabs the same manicured finger into Rylan's arm.

'Didn't anyone ever tell you it's rude to point?' Erin snaps back. 'He was only reminding me that I can use my *get out of jail free* card.'

'Having someone helping you is cheating,' she persists.

'Well, I'm hardly going to win, am I?' Erin points at her handful of twenties and fives and her turned-over rail stations. 'So get over yourself.'

'Geez.' I shake my head. 'It's only a game.'

'Right, it's time for you and me to wipe the floor with them all.' Rylan puts his arm around Alice. 'How many hotels shall we have on Bond Street?'

She giggles. Then I jump as Nathaniel throws his chair back with a scrape. 'I've had enough,' he announces. 'I'm off to get a beer.'

'At least he's not flipping the board over,' I laugh. He glares at me before storming from the room. Everyone else laughs too. Apart from Dad, of course.

'A beer sounds like an excellent idea.' Ben throws the dice. 'To be honest, I'm going to concede too. There's not a lot of damage I can do with the three pink ones and the electrical works.'

'You can sell them all to me,' Karl says. 'Come on Rylan – we'll play this out – you and me. No way am I going to let you beat me. Over my dead body.'

'I concede too.' I spread my cards in front of Dad. 'Fill your boots.'

I follow Ben into the kitchen.

'Where's Nathaniel gone? I'll have one of those too.' I nod at the bottle in his hand.

He reaches back into the fridge. 'He'll be licking his wounds somewhere after everyone laughed at him.'

'Have you heard them in there?' The raised voices of Erin and Martha echo from the dining room.

Ben passes me the bottle opener. 'We seem to have got out of there at exactly the right time.'

'I've had enough, Auntie Kelli.' Alice runs into the kitchen with her hands over her ears. 'They're all arguing. I just want to go home.'

'Come here, sweetheart.'

As she runs to me and I wrap my arms around her, the crash

from the other side of the wall says that someone in there *has* flipped the board over.

Here we go.

14

GILL

'YOU CAN HARDLY BELIEVE this is a family of mainly adults, can you?' I say to Ben as he helps me pick up the last of the houses from the dining room carpet. 'Flipping the board is usually Nathaniel's trick.'

'Was Martha losing that badly?'

'I think she was feeling a bit put out when Rylan offered to loan Erin some money. *Monopoly money,*' I add quickly, like that really makes any difference.

'Is Alice OK?' He asks, his eyes meeting mine. To say he's grown up without his own family, he's more well-adjusted than my lot put together. With some of the things that have gone on in our house over the years, *no* family might be preferable to the dysfunction and chaos that surrounds ours.

'She's fine – just a bit fed up. I'm going to take her out of here shortly.' Thankfully, the reminder of my face masks and nail polishing promise seemed to do the trick before and nearly even made her smile.

'There.' Ben secures the lid on the box. 'It should live to see another battle.'

'Thanks,' I smile at him. 'You're a goodun. And I know things might be a little interesting here, but I'm so glad you were able to come.'

'I wouldn't have missed it for the world.' He smiles as he rises to his feet and turns towards the door.

It's a curious comment and as I watch him leave, I wonder what he meant by it.

Rising to my feet, I also head to the door, checking into the hallway before pulling out my phone and closing the door behind me.

I can be with you within an hour but I'll have my granddaughter with me. We'll need to say I know you from you once doing some work on the house.

I don't want you taking any risks. What if she goes back and says something to the others?

She won't. I'll speak to her. She knows what her grandad's like.

Is there no way you can come on your own?

Unfortunately not. I've promised her I'd take her out for a bit.

OK. Though it's going to be awkward.

But it's worth it to see you!

I smile at his last text and then delete the conversation from my phone – just as Karl walks in. He's looking more and more like his dad these days – from the bald spot on the top of his head to the clothes he's begun to favour. I wouldn't be surprised if the checked shirt he's wearing didn't come from Joe's shirts I bagged up for charity after the funeral.

'What are you smiling at?'

'Nothing much – if you must know, I was remembering Nathaniel and the Monopoly when he was younger.'

He eyes me suspiciously. 'I heard Alice telling her mum that you're going out.'

'Just to get a few bits from the shops at Settle.'

'I'll come with you,' he announces. 'I wouldn't mind a drive out.'

'Why? You wouldn't normally traipse to the shops with me.' I can't believe this. However, I need to keep my face straight and my voice level or he'll get suspicious. More importantly, I need to talk him out of it.

'My plan was to go with Alice actually – just the two of us, if you don't mind.' I give him what I hope is my most beseeching look. 'She's a bit upset after all that carry on before.'

'So I'm not welcome, is that what you're saying?' His face hardens.

'Of course not – it's just that I'd like some girly time with Alice – you must have noticed that she's a bit out of sorts at the moment.'

'*Girly time.* You're hardly a girl anymore, Gill.' He smirks and I wrestle with a huge urge to do or say something that might wipe it clean off his face. He seems to be able to pluck the most hurtful throwaway comments out of thin air to hurl at me. He never fails.

'Actually Karl, I believe that however *old* I might be, there will always be something of the girl inside me.' I stare at him as though daring him to mock me even further. 'And nothing you can say or do will change that.'

'Whatever.' He continues to chuckle as he strides to the door. I don't know what's worse, him mocking me like this or the other sort of treatment he's prone to giving me. 'I'll leave you to enjoy your *girly* time then. Have fun.' He raises the back of his hand in a wave as he leaves the room.

I let a long breath out as I feel for the phone in my pocket. That was very close. I'd better get out of here before he changes his mind.

~

'Why doesn't Dad like Uncle Rylan?' Alice tugs her seatbelt across herself.

'Has he said something to you?'

Not that he needs to have done. Nathaniel makes his feelings perfectly obvious when he's around Rylan. One of these days, I'll string that son of mine up. He's carried this petty jealousy towards his brother for years and he's got no right trying to inflict it on Alice.

'Dad said it's *him* I should be spending time with while we're on holiday, not my *uncle*. But I *like* Uncle Rylan.'

'I know you do.' I take a deep breath. I'm pretty sure Erin's already told Alice the truth so I should be on safe ground reiterating things. 'You already know about Uncle Rylan being your Mum's boyfriend for a little while when they were teenagers, don't you? I think it's *that* that still upsets your dad.'

'Yeah, Mum's told me. But she said it was *years* before I was even born. And Uncle Rylan's with Martha now so I don't get it.'

'*Auntie* Martha,' I say in a firm voice. 'You know how upset she gets when you don't say Auntie.'

Alice pulls a face as we turn from the drive from the cottage onto the pretty country road. It's a shame it's so wet today. Every tree and every field emanates a hue of gold or orange – it would be lovely in the sunshine.

'Anyway, I'm sorry you've been having such a rotten time.' I reach over the gearstick and touch her arm. 'Hopefully, we can make up for it. So, after I've called in on someone I need to see, we'll drive on to Settle – there's a couple of wonderful shops I need to show you. And I've got my credit card.' I glance at her while pulling my most excited face.

'Who are we going to see?' There's a tinge of disappointment in her tone.

'Just the man who built our conservatory. I want him to do our porch next and I said I'd call in with the measurements while we're over this way.' I keep my voice as nonchalant as I can. I've never been a good liar but with something like this, I must do my best.

'Oh – OK.'

~

'But this is someone's house.' Alice frowns as we pull up onto the kerb at the stone-built terraced cottage five minutes away from where we're staying.

'This is where he lives.' I look up to see Jason peering around the curtain and have to work hard to contain my joy at seeing his face for the first time in months. With Karl keeping such a tight rein on me, it's usually impossible to get away for any length of time. But here I am, and even if I can just see him for half an hour, it's worth it. Then hopefully I'll be able to get back here later in the week.

I turn back to Alice. 'You mustn't mention that we've been here to *anyone*. We're just going to have a quick cup of tea, I'll have a chat with Jason and then we'll get ourselves to Settle.'

'Why can't I say anything?' Her voice rises.

'I want the porch to be a surprise for Grandad's birthday. And if you tell *anyone*, they might spoil the surprise. Is that OK?'

She nods and I heave a silent sigh of relief. Alice will have forgotten we called in here by the time I've distracted her with a little shopping afterwards. Luckily, she's still too young to jump to any other conclusions from what I've told her. I'm well aware that if she were a couple of years older, it would probably be a very different story. But for now, she trusts me and takes what I say at face value.

'We're not staying here for long, are we Grandma?' She pats at her pocket, evidently ensuring that she has her phone on her. 'Why do you have to have a cup of tea if you're just giving him some measurements?'

'Because it's polite – and he does a good job.' I tug the keys from the ignition. 'Don't worry, love – I'm sure he'll let you have the code for his wifi while I have a chat with him.'

As we get out of the car, Jason throws his door open, looking a bit too enthusiastic to be merely someone about to discuss a porch. I glance at Alice who seems non-plussed about the whole thing. Then just in case Karl's followed me here, I glance up and down the lane. After all, he's done it before.

And if he could see me now, with Jason, my life wouldn't be worth living.

15

GILL

'How come you've been gone so long?' Karl's in exactly the same place he was in last night, sitting beside Martha with a bottle of wine between them. I can't decide whether this is a good thing or not. The room's filled with the scent of coal and cooking dinner. With neither the fire to lay or the dinner to prepare, it looks like I can relax for a change.

'We got busy in the shops, didn't we, love?' I smile at my granddaughter as I flick the overhead light on. 'There, that's better – it was a bit gloomy in here.'

Alice nods. She's brightened up hugely to what she was like when we set off.

'Go and show your mum what we bought. Where is she?' I look around the room.

Martha shrugs as if to say *who cares?* 'Do you want a glass, Gill?' She points at the bottle. 'Come and sit down for a bit.'

'If you don't mind, I'd rather have a cup of tea. Does anyone else want one?'

'No thanks.' Kelli and Ben chorus from where they're huddled in front of the fire. They've both got started on the beer too. I check my watch – it's just after six.

'Back in a minute.' Karl swipes for the car keys from where I dropped them on the kitchen counter. I know exactly what he's planning to do. I take a deep breath as I head for the kettle, telling myself not to allow his behaviour to erode my mood. I've had a lovely few hours away from here, being able to see Jason, albeit briefly, and also spending some quality time with my granddaughter.

'This looks good.' I glance into the oven.

'It's a pasta bake,' Rylan says. 'My favourite. I'd forgotten what a whizz Erin is in the kitchen.'

Martha slams her glass onto the breakfast bar. 'What's that supposed to mean?'

'Yeah.' Nathaniel looks up from whatever he's reading in the corner behind Kelli and Ben, scowling. 'What *is* that supposed to mean?'

'That she's a good cook, that's all.' He throws his hands into the air.

Martha spins around on her stool to face him. 'Are you purposefully trying to wind me up or what?'

'Of course not love – I was only joking.'

'Well, you're about as funny as a toothache.' Nathaniel slams his book on the arm of his chair. 'So leave it out – right?' He rises from his seat and storms out of the room, presumably to find Erin. He'd better not be planning to give her any grief. Especially not when Alice has also gone to find her. I'm not having anybody upset her this evening.

Kelli and I exchange glances. She's probably thinking the same as me – is Rylan, who acts like butter wouldn't melt in his mouth, deliberately trying to cause trouble?

'It's seven miles from here to Settle.' Karl slams the keys on the counter in front of me. 'And seven miles back.'

'So?' I wrap my fingers around the warmth of my mug as though trying to comfort and protect myself.

'So would you like to tell me why you've clocked up over seventeen miles in total? Where else have you been?' He rolls his sleeves up as though preparing for a fight.

'*Nowhere*! Perhaps it's from when we were trying to find somewhere to park.'

'For three miles. Don't give me that rubbish!'

Kelli jumps up from where she's playing chess with Ben. 'Leave it out, Dad. You really shouldn't be checking up on her like—'

'Mind your own bloody business.' He puts the flat of his palm up to her as she approaches us. 'This is a private conversation.'

'But you're having it in front of us all.'

'It might have been the diversion,' I say, praying Kelli will heed his warning. 'Roadworks. We were diverted for a little of the way.' I can only pray he doesn't jump in the car to investigate my story of *roadworks*.

Without saying anything else, he retakes his seat beside Martha, keeping his eyes on me the whole time.

As if I'm even trying to explain myself like this. Normally I'm angry when he checks the mileage, but this time, because I *have* been somewhere I supposedly shouldn't, I'm ten times more defensive than I normally would be. If he were to find out that I've been anywhere *near* Jason, all hell would break loose.

But thankfully, Karl has no idea where Jason moved to. Or that it was Jason who told me about the availability of this cottage in the first place.

'I'm sick of them arguing all the time.' Alice, who hasn't even taken her shoes and coat off yet, darts past us all in a flood of tears. She runs to the back door. 'I've had enough.' Then she slams it behind her.

'Oh, for goodness sake, now what?' I start after her but Karl jumps down from his stool and comes after me. He catches my arm just as I get to the door and tugs me back. 'Just leave her be for a few minutes. She doesn't need *you* pandering to her all the time.'

'I'll go after her then.' Rylan drops from his stool.

'It's got nothing to do with you.' Martha stretches forward and reaches for his arm in the same way Karl just grabbed mine, but he shakes it free.

'She's my niece. It's got everything to do with me.'

'She's just seeking attention.' Martha grabs the bottle of wine by its neck. 'That's why she's stormed off. She's not going to go far, is she?'

'Go after her, Rylan,' Kelli says. 'It's nearly dark out there and you know she's scared of the dark.'

'She certainly wouldn't have gone out there if she knew what you'd found in the shed this morning.' Martha glugs more wine into her glass and purses her lips.

'Ugh, don't remind me.' Kelli pulls a face.

Erin and Nathaniel's raised voices echo from upstairs. I wonder if they even realised how much they've upset their daughter.

'It's a big fuss over nothing if you ask me.'

I stare at Martha, wondering how I could ever have tried giving her the benefit of the doubt over the years. While she's beautiful on the outside, she is one venomous individual within. And she's really upped the ante this week.

I want to say, *well no one did ask you, Martha.* But instead, I say, 'It's the second time in as many days someone's made her cry.' *Without* looking at my husband as I say it.

'That's night two done and dusted.' I press the button on the dishwasher and turn to Kelli who yawns and stretches.

'And we've all survived so far,' she says, still in mid-yawn. 'No one's killed anyone else yet.'

'Give it time.' I drain what's left in my wine glass and force out a laugh.

'It's nice it just being me and you, isn't it, Mum.' Kelli clinks her glass against my empty one and looks around the semi-darkened room. 'Peaceful for once.'

I have to agree. And it *is* a pleasant cottage, despite its deeply sad history – Jason's recommendation when I mentioned what I was looking for was spot on. It's even more pleasant now everyone's gone up to bed, most of them in various states of inebriation. At least with just me and Kelli left, there are no barbed comments to contend with. No loaded atmospheres or jealous looks. Best of all, before she went to bed, there was a smile back on Alice's face again. After Rylan coaxed her back inside, Erin, Kelli and I managed to cheer her up with an hour spent doing nails, beauty and hair. Martha was invited to join in, but unsurprisingly, chose not to. Instead, she's had a face as long as the time we've been stuck here so far – which feels like forever. I was relieved when she announced she was going to bed.

I don't know who jumps the most, Kelli or me, at the sudden overhead bang and the throwing open of a door.

'Who's bloody done *this*?' It sounds like Erin.

Kelli and I look at each other before rushing to the door to see what all the shrieking is about.

'What's the matter? Who's done *what?*'

Erin's on her way down the stairs, her dressing gown flowing out behind her and her red hair looking wilder than usual as she clutches a pint glass to her chest.

'What the hell's up with you?' Nathaniel shouts from behind her as he ties his own dressing gown.

'Look at this! Just look at this!' She holds the glass in front of me and Kelli as we all get to the bottom of the stairs.

'It's just a glass of water,' I say, totally puzzled. Maybe it has something to do with all this 'spiking' stuff I've heard about in the news. But then, we'd be talking about *drugs*. Surely it isn't anything along those lines? None of my children have ever had anything to do with drugs.

'No, Mum – look closer.' Kelli points into the glass.

'Is that ice or...' My voice trails off as I flick the switch for the overhead light. A closer inspection shows that this innocent-looking pint of water is actually filled to the brim with shards of broken glass. 'Oh my God.' My hand flutters to my mouth. 'If you'd drunk that, you'd have—'

'I dread to think what damage it could have done to you.' Kelli stares at it.

'Exactly,' Erin says, her face as white as a sheet. 'So who'd fill the glass on my bedside table with pieces of broken glass, that's what I want to know.'

We all fall silent. I look from Erin to Nathaniel. I know they've been arguing but he wouldn't do something like this. He can be a lot of things but this sort of behaviour wouldn't even enter his head.

'Oh my God, have you heard that?' Kelli points up the stairs.

In our silence, the moans and shrieks of people having sex echo from above. By process of elimination, it can only be Rylan and Martha.

'I can't stand here listening to that.' I turn on my heel back towards the kitchen. I feel slightly sick.

Finally, everyone's in bed and the house is in silence, apart from a couple of creaks and knocks which are hopefully just the boiler, coupled with the fact that we're staying in a very old cottage – and nothing to do with what once happened here and what, or who, is in the shed.

When we're at home, I'm familiar with every sound the house makes, so to hear these new ones which I can't quite put my finger on is somewhat disconcerting.

The recent commotion has left me feeling on edge and not at all sleepy. There's only one thing I can do – pour myself another glass of wine. Kelli joked when she first arrived about how alcohol will get us all through this week. At the time, I thought she was being melodramatic, but now, I know exactly where she's coming from. It's just one thing after another with them all.

My head jerks in the direction of a sudden noise on the stairs. *What now?* It's impossible to have five minutes of peace here – even though it's approaching midnight.

'Grandma.' Alice's hair is on end as she shivers in her nightie in the kitchen doorway. 'There's someone outside – I've just heard them.'

'Come here.' I grab a coat someone's left on one of the breakfast bar stools and drape it around her shoulders. 'You're freezing.'

'I couldn't sleep anyway but then I heard someone in the garden.' She points towards the hallway.

'It's a creaky old house, that's all.' I draw her into me. 'Let's get you in front of the fire and I'll make some hot chocolate.'

'I really did hear something out there. My room's on the other side, isn't it? Can't we wake Uncle Rylan or Ben up to have a look?'

It's interesting how she's requesting one of the others to be woken, and not her own father. And she hardly even knows Ben. Have things really got so bad for them all at home?

'OK, *I'll* have a look then.' I draw my cardigan more closely around myself as I glance at the back door. 'If it'll put your mind at rest.'

'No, Grandma. I don't want you to go out there on your own.' Her eyes widen in fear. 'Please wake one of the others up.'

'Just wait in here, sweetheart. I promise I'll be fine.'

'Please Grandma, I'm scared.'

'I tell you what, I'll take this with me.' I grab the iron propping the door open and head to the door.

Despite her terrified protestations, I open it with a creak. 'I'll just be a moment. You go and get warm.'

DAY THREE

16

ERIN

'WHAT I'D LIKE TO KNOW.' I slam my cereal bowl at the head of the table. 'Is who put pieces of broken glass in the drink of water on my bedside table?' My gaze rests on Martha. 'Who'd do such a thing to me?'

'It was probably there from the *last* people who stayed here,' Karl says. 'They must have forgotten to move it.'

'We're the first people to stay here since...' Gill's voice trails off.

'Well Erin must have left it there *herself*,' Karl continues, his hair still wet from the shower. He's the only one out of us who's fully dressed this morning. 'She'd had a few to drink on the first night, hadn't you, Erin? You probably can't remember things properly.'

'Of course I can,' I snap. 'I took a clean glass up on the first night.'

'Are you absolutely certain?' Gill asks.

'I got the glass out of the kitchen cupboard and filled it with water from the bathroom. Someone else has filled it with glass.'

Alice, still wearing her fleecy pyjamas, looks like she might cry. Perhaps I should have sent her from the room before having this confrontation but it's too late now.

'I'll ask you all again, shall I?' I lower myself to my chair. 'Who put bits of broken glass in my drink?'

'Well, *we* were otherwise engaged last night.' Martha giggles and winks at Rylan as she tightens her gaudy pink dressing gown around her waist. He blushes and their little exchange only serves to make me even angrier.

'Perhaps I should just call the police and let *them* speak to you all?' Clearly, no one's taking this seriously. Even Kelli and Gill haven't jumped to my defence like they normally would. They're probably hoping the situation will just go away.

'Don't be ridiculous,' Karl says. 'What are the police going to do?'

'If I'd swallowed that glass...' I begin, my throat feeling sore at the prospect. 'Imagine the damage that could have been done.'

Still, no one says anything. Really, I know there's only one person here who is capable of such a thing, but looking at her smug face, she's never going to admit to anything. Who else here would want to hurt me like that? 'I'm sure the police would be very interested. They'd probably class what's happened as attempted—'

'Now you really *are* being ridiculous,' Karl cuts in. 'And in the hope of a civilised breakfast, I'd like to change the subject if you don't mind.'

'So whoever has tried to do this to me just gets away with it?' I gasp. 'I'm not letting this go. Would *you* Karl? If someone had put broken glass in *your* drink?' I look at Nathaniel. 'And *you're* supposed to be my husband,' I snap. 'How can you just sit there without defending me?'

'I'm with Dad on this,' he says. 'The cleaners have probably swept something up and forgotten to move it. You did have a few drinks on our first night here – you might not have remembered seeing it.'

'Gill, can you see that a complaint is made to the letting company?' Karl looks from me to her. 'Evidently, the cleaners of this place need to be held to account for their actions.'

'But—'

'No one *here* has put glass in anyone else's drink.' His voice booms around the room. 'So let that be the end of the matter.'

I open my mouth to go on but really don't know what else I can say. My only option is to go to the police – but what further trouble could that cause? Perhaps Nathaniel's right. It doesn't seem likely but perhaps I *did* miss something on the bedside table on the first night. I've certainly had lots on my mind since we got here. Well, *before* we got here, really.

'So, from what I'm gathering,' Karl's now directing his words at Martha. 'Might I be able to expect some grandson news in the not-too-distant future?'

'Dad!' Kelli gasps.

What a complete arsehole. I can hardly believe he's just said such a thing. Maybe it's to completely deflect the attention away from the glass situation. Or maybe he is just an absolute arsehole.

He briefly averts his attention to Kelli and then back to Martha. 'It's a simple question. It's definitely about time the two of you got on with it. As losing my father has demonstrated, it's not as if Gill and I are getting any younger.'

The direction this breakfast table conversation has gone in has pushed the topic of the glass in the water into the shadows. However, I'd love to hear Martha admit directly to Karl that she has no intention of having babies – ever. But I bet she stays quiet. She'd fall out of favour with him so fast her head would spin if he knew there was no chance of her having a baby. Her disdain for Alice since the day she was born is one of the many things which have demonstrated how she doesn't have a maternal bone in her body.

'And you as well.' I nearly choke on my cereal as I realise his eyes are now on me. 'If you were to have another child, perhaps Alice wouldn't be quite so, how shall I put it—'

'Don't put it any way at all.' Gill snaps, thankfully coming to my rescue. 'Whatever children our kids and their partners decide to have has got nothing to do with us.'

Nathaniel meets my eye and I quickly look away. I know he'd love a son, but I'm well aware that a large part of his yearning would be to court favour in his father's eyes and to get one over on Rylan. Despite how difficult Karl is, it's clear that both brothers still seek his approval and validation. But I decided long ago that a second baby definitely won't be happening. I can't think of anything worse.

'Is there anything so wrong with wanting to continue our family name?' He says. 'Since we're here in my dad's memory, it doesn't seem unreasonable to—'

'Just leave it, Dad, will you?' It's Nathaniel's turn to snap. The fact that I didn't acknowledge him looking at me before seems to have worsened his mood. But I'm getting to the point where I'm beyond caring.

'Alice thought she heard someone snooping around last night.' Gill shields her eyes as she looks towards me. The sun is beating from the window onto the back of my head.

'You're joking – Alice, why on earth didn't you wake me?' I stare at her. She's *never* not woken me before if she's been scared in the night.

'I could hear that Grandma was still up,' she replies. 'So we had a look together.'

'And there was nothing there,' Gill adds.

'You went outside? You should have woken someone.'

Gill nods. 'It was fine.'

It's on the tip of my tongue to mention how I wouldn't have ventured outside, especially near that shed containing the urns after dark. But a, I'd sound daft, and b, Alice can't know about them.

'Erin, close those curtains, will you?' Martha squints too. 'That sun's far too bright.'

'Give over,' Gill replies. 'It's nice to have some sunshine in here after all that rain yesterday.'

'I couldn't agree more.'

'It'll all be in Alice's imagination anyway.' Martha spreads marmalade onto her toast.

'What will?'

'These so-called noises. Just like the broken glass is in her mother's.'

I give her a look which I hope conveys what I'm thinking about her. I'm certain it was her with the glass but there's no way of proving it.

'I really *did* hear someone out here, Mum. And I'm sure I saw a shadow when I looked out of the window.'

'Yeah, right.'

'To be honest,' Gill continues. 'If it was just the noises Alice heard I'd let it go. But – she's saying that she actually saw someone out there.' She pours herself a cup of tea. 'Therefore, I was thinking of making a report to the police – just so they're aware of it if anyone comes back tonight. Maybe they could have patrols around here, or something. Especially if it's going to help Alice to feel safer.'

'The Police.' Karl shakes his head. 'No chance. How would that make me look? Like I can't protect my family, that's what. Like I said, you should have woken me.'

'After everything you'd had to drink, Dad?' Rylan laughs. 'We'd have had more success raising a corpse.'

'At least we can go for that bike ride today.' Gill forces a smile and I can see she's trying to soften the conversation and break the negative mood. 'Once breakfast is over with, shall we get ourselves ready to go?'

There are a few mutterings of agreement. I have to admit that a bike ride sounds better than a walk. At least I can be more on my own with my thoughts and not really have to talk to anyone. Nothing could be worse than when I was trudging along yesterday with Nathaniel – while I eventually managed to lift his mood a bit, talking to him was like pulling teeth. It's like we've run out of things to say to each other.

'My puncture still needs fixing,' Alice says.

'You'd better get out there then, hadn't you?' Nathaniel replies. 'When you've eaten that.'

'Won't you help me, Dad?'

'I've shown you a million times how to fix a puncture.'

She looks back at him, crestfallen. Really, she's got about as much of an idea as I have about fixing one.

'I'll help you, don't worry.' Rylan gets to his feet. 'I'll just nip up for a shower then I'm at your service.'

Alice stuffs the last of her toast into her mouth and springs to her feet. 'I'll go and get dressed.'

'Didn't you hear what Nathaniel just said?' Martha twists in her seat as they head to the door. 'Let her bloody fix it herself.'

They both pause for a moment but then continue.

'Oi, I was talking to—'

'Just give it a rest, will you?' Dropping what's left of my toast onto the plate, I glare at her. Then I rise from my chair and head after them.

'Go inside while I have a quick word with Uncle Rylan,' I tell Alice as Rylan lowers her tyre into a bowl of water.

'Do I have to?' She pulls a face.

'Just for a few minutes. Don't worry, you'll see lots of him when we get out on the bikes today.'

Rylan laughs. 'It's the best part of the holiday, isn't it, Alice? Being able to catch up with each other.'

Her face brightens as she gets back to her feet. 'Don't be long, Mum.'

I watch as she heads back to the door. She's probably so reluctant to go back in there for fear of whatever Martha or her grandad might say. But there are others around to keep an eye on things.

'What's your quick word then? Bingo!' Rylan lifts the tyre from the water, dries it and chalks it.

'I know you can't do anything about your dad,' I begin. 'But can you *please* have a word with your wife?'

'What do you mean?' Rylan lifts his eyes to meet mine. He's got such different eyes to his brother – they look the same but his are filled with warmth and friendliness.

'It's all the sly digs she keeps having at Alice,' I reply. 'She's eleven years old for goodness sake, it won't do her self-esteem any good.'

'You know what Martha's like.' Rylan sticks a patch on the tyre.

'I do – but that's not good enough. Whatever her problem still is with me, I can't have her taking things out on Alice.'

'I've reassured her until I'm blue in the face.' He doesn't look at me but keeps his gaze fixed on the tyre.

'She bloody well needs to get over it, Rylan.'

'She doesn't mean any harm to Alice, you know. It's just that, well, sarcasm is her middle name.'

'Well if you don't speak to her – believe me, I will and I won't hold back. Look she's there, watching us now.' I glance to the upstairs window as I sense the daggers showering down at me. 'You do know that you've married someone who's *exactly* like your father, don't you?'

'What's that supposed to mean?'

'An absolute narcissist.'

'Leave the psycho-analysis to Ben.' He frowns. 'I don't need it.'

'But it's true. I don't know how you put up with it.'

'Whatever you think of her, Erin – she's still my wife. And let's be fair here. She never stood a chance of you actually *liking* her after I chose her over you back in the day.'

'That's not the reason. I've tried to get along with her. I've really tried. She—'

'Maybe you should deal with your own husband first.' Rylan gestures towards the door and then grins as he returns his attention to Alice's bike.

'Oh, for goodness sake.' I turn on my heel, feeling Nathaniel's angry eyes boring into me well before I see them. 'What's the matter with *your* face?'

'I want a word with you,' he replies, jerking his thumb towards the shed. 'In private.'

'Not in there. Come over here.' I head over to the coal bunker and wait behind it until he joins me. This isn't going to be pretty. 'Go on then, Nathaniel. Spit it out.' Really, I know what's coming.

'What is it with you and him?' He rounds on me.

'It's *you* with the jealousy problem. You need to get a grip.'

'I've had years of this.' He throws his arms in the air. 'You probably only got with me in the first place to wheedle your way back in with him.'

'Yeah right.' I would laugh if the situation wasn't so tedious. 'That would be a little drastic though, wouldn't it? How many times do I have to tell you – Rylan and I are ancient bloody history.'

'So why's he always hanging around you? And Alice?'

'He's not.' My voice rises. 'So just leave it, will you?'

'Whispering in corners again?' Karl's voice booms from the doorway. 'This is supposed to be a *family* holiday.'

'Well done, Nathaniel,' I snap. 'You've gone and got *him* involved.'

I storm past him and head back to the house. 'Your son's a pillock,' I hiss as I barge past Karl. 'I wonder where he gets it from.'

Despite my bravado, I'm in tears as I reach the bottom of the stairs.

'Oh gosh – dare I ask what the matter is?' Kelli rushes down the steps towards me. 'My lovely brother, I take it?'

I nod, while brushing angry tears from my eyes. 'I shouldn't let him upset me.' I pull a tissue from my pocket. 'But I'm honestly wondering how I'm going to survive another five days of this.'

'Four days, ten hours to be precise.' She glances at her watch. 'And fifty minutes. Not that I'm counting.'

I smile through my tears.

'You and Alice stick with me and Ben.' She puts her arm around me.

'Thanks. We will.' I lean into her. 'Without you and Gill here...'

'Anyway, like I've said to you before, I'm forced to be part of this wretched family – I was *born* into it. At least you had a choice!'

'I suppose so.' And I resist the temptation to say, *I still have.*

'OK. I've plotted a route for us,' Karl announces as we gather around our bikes. 'We've got a stop planned at a cafe for some lunch and I'll lead the way to get there.'

'As if we'd have expected anything else,' Kelli mutters and Gill shoots her a look as if to say *leave it.*

'Right, off we go then,' he calls from the front. 'Make sure you all keep up.'

'Hang on,' I call from the back as everyone starts setting off. 'My tyres are as flat as pancakes.' I step off my bike to inspect them. 'I've got punctures in *both* of them.'

Ben squeezes his brakes and both he and and Kelli look back at me as I squeeze both tyres. Ben lowers his bike to the ground and walks back towards me.

He crouches beside the wheels of the bike to inspect them. 'They're not punctures.' He runs his fingers over each tyre. 'Look, they've been slashed.'

17

ERIN

I DON'T KNOW who's in the worst mood, Karl or Nathaniel, as we're finally ready to set off after our previous false start.

'Take no notice of Karl,' Gill hangs back with me. 'He's just annoyed that we'll miss the lunch reservation I made.'

'It was hardly my fault,' I tell her as I wobble out of the drive onto the lane. 'It's the fault of whoever decided to slash my tyres.' I stare at Martha out in front, her dark hair billowing from beneath her helmet. I could cheerfully go and push her off that bike. Preferably when a lorry is coming.

'I know it's not your fault.' Gill's unsteady on her bike too. 'But being reasonable is hardly on Karl's list of attributes, is it?'

He has attributes? This is what I want to say, however, because I'm talking to my mother-in-law about her husband, I clamp my lips tightly together and keep my eyes on the road ahead.

'We're just lucky,' she continues, jerking her head back in the direction of the cottage, 'that there was a few bikes in the garage.'

'Yeah, but no doubt Martha will be disappointed.' I won't hold back where *she's* concerned. 'Did she know about the spare bikes?'

'Now, now Erin.' Gill's starting to get out of breath. 'I know more than most how difficult Martha can be, but cutting someone's bike tyres isn't her style.'

'She'll have wanted to leave me out of the *family* bike ride.' If I wasn't clutching my handlebars for dear life, I'd be drawing air quotes around the word *family*.

I change up a gear to attempt this first hill, but am so out of practice on a bike that I discover I've actually changed down a gear. If I'm not careful, I'll be losing my chain and incurring more of Karl's wrath.

I haven't ridden a bike for years and neither has Alice. There's too much traffic around at home, so I prefer to drop her off in the car. 'Nathaniel,' I try to project my voice to him. He's way out in front with Rylan, almost looking as though they're racing each other. And Alice seems to be doing everything she can to keep up with them. Where speed and height are concerned, my daughter has no fear. Anything to do with noises, that have the potential to be ghosts or murderers though, and it's a different story.

'What now?' He glances back. At least he's replied to me – he was completely ignoring me before we set off.

'Make sure you keep an eye on Alice,' I shout. He might have the hump with me but surely we can still communicate about her?

I remain at the back of our group, and there can be no doubt that I'm the slowest out of the lot of us, but after twenty minutes or so, I'm beginning to enjoy being out on the bike. Away from the others, I can abandon myself to the liberating sense of freedom I used to love about my bike when I was younger. I recall my teenage years when Mum was still alive and the long hot summer when Rylan and I first got together. We'd cycle between each other's houses or Mum would pack us up some sandwiches so we could go off on our bikes for the day. He was my first love and we had so much fun together – laughing, always laughing.

My attention drifts to my husband, hunched miserably over his handlebars, having given up on keeping pace with Rylan. Judging from the slouch of his shoulders, I bet he's not enjoying a second of being out in the fresh air like this. Which is part of the problem. He never enjoys anything anymore.

We pause for a water break and to get our bearings. Karl and Gill bicker about where we are and where we're supposed to be.

'This helmet's hurting,' Alice complains. 'It's giving me a headache and it's nipping my chin.'

'Have a look at it for her, Nathaniel, will you?' I say. 'It probably needs loosening.'

Surprisingly, he lowers his bike to the ground to do as I ask.

We set off again, me leading this time – for as long as it lasts. Apparently, it's a straight but hilly road to the cafe we were previously booked in at. Gill's rung ahead and while we've no longer got our table, they're rustling up some sandwiches for us to eat outside. So all's well that ends well.

'Nathaniel – watch what she's doing, will you! Alice, get over to the side!' Kelli's voice shrieks from behind me, followed by a screech of tyres and then a scream. I pull my brakes on so fast that I almost shoot over the handlebars then twist around to see what's happened.

At first, I think I'm imagining what I'm seeing.

My daughter's lying in the road. Only a moment ago, I could hear her laughter behind me, yet now she's as still as a rock.

'Oh my God! No!' I throw the bike to the ground and hurtle back to her.

As I get there, Kelli crouches beside her and feels around on her wrists.

'Oh my God. Oh my God.' She looks at me with terror in her eyes. 'I can't find her pulse. Erin, I really can't.'

I think mine's probably stopped as well.

'You must be able to,' Nathaniel drops to his knees and begins searching too. 'Alice!' he cries. 'Alice – can you hear me?'

The driver of the car rushes at us. 'I was overtaking you all,' he gasps. 'I allowed plenty of room but she swung out right in front of me. I couldn't brake in time.'

'I told her to get herself over,' Kelli cries as Ben flies to her side, then to me, she says. 'She was next to Nathaniel but he didn't seem to realise how far out into the road she was. It all happened so fast.'

'Somebody, just do *something*,' cries Gill who's not far behind Ben. 'Please!'

I drop into a crouch. 'This is all *your* fault,' I screech as I elbow Nathaniel out of the way. 'Let me get to her. Alice. Oh my God. Alice!'

'She's breathing,' Ben shouts. 'Look, she's trying to open her eyes.'

'Thank God. Oh, thank God.'

'Where's her bloody helmet? Why the hell wasn't she wearing her helmet?'

'Everyone try to calm down.' Karl lays his bike onto the kerb and heads over too.

'Give her some room,' I yell. The last thing she'll want is to open her eyes and see *him* at her side.

'I'm just so sorry.' The driver plucks his phone from his shirt pocket. 'Like I said, she just spun out in front of me. I'll call for an ambulance.'

Martha points at the rucksack Nathaniel discarded at the side of the road.

'Her helmet's in there?' I ask.

She nods.

Alice opens her eyes, a soft moan echoing from her.

'Where does it hurt, love?' I daren't touch her. I don't want to make anything worse than it might already be.

'Thank goodness she's alright, that's all I can say.' Gill leans over to touch the side of Alice's face. 'Grandma's here, sweetheart,' she says. 'You're going to be just fine.'

'We don't know that for sure. Nobody is to move her,' I shout as Karl steps closer. 'Stand back.'

'Erin's right for once,' Karl says. 'Alice could have spinal injuries for all we know.'

Everything's in slow motion as I hold my daughter's hand, the voice of the driver spinning around me as Kelli relays our details for him to give to the emergency services.

'You wouldn't think she'd been knocked off her bike by a car,' I remark as tears cascade down my face. 'There's barely a scratch on her, really.'

'Her bike took most of the impact.' Ben points at where it lies twisted at the other side of the road. A couple of cars coming the other way have stopped to have a look at what's going on.

'Never mind her bike. Look at *her.*' She's closed her eyes again. 'Alice – Alice can you still hear me?'

She continues to moan. At least she's moaning. We can't let her fall asleep.

'Where does it hurt the most, love?' I need to keep her talking.

She tries to point but only manages to raise her hand a couple of inches off the road.

'From what I saw, it was her head she hit as she landed,' Ben says.

'She could have a serious head injury because of *you.*' I screech at Nathaniel. 'How could you have let her ride without her helmet?'

'I'm not her only parent,' he yells back. 'You could have been keeping an eye on her too. But you're too distracted with—'

'Shut up, for goodness sake,' Gill yells. 'The last thing this poor mite needs to hear are her parents going at one another when she's lying in the road like this.'

'There's an ambulance on its way,' the driver says. 'I'm just so sorry.'

'It really wasn't your fault.' Kelli reaches out and touches his arm. 'I saw everything that happened. There wasn't anything you could have done.'

'Well, I know who I blame.' I can't even look at my husband. 'If anything happens to her because of *you*...' My voice trails off as Gill gives me one of her looks before turning her attention to the driver. 'How long did they say they'd be?'

'They're prioritising her,' he replies. 'But they're coming from Settle.'

'It's only seven miles,' Gill says. 'And they'll have the sirens on, won't they?'

'Should we put something under her head?' Rylan asks. 'She can't be very comfortable laid there, on the concrete.'

'Don't touch her! Don't bloody move her!' I flail my arm out to prevent him from coming any closer. 'Everyone stand away now.'

'Mu-um.' Alice says as I cloak her in a blanket the driver hands to me. 'My head really hurts.' Relief washes over me at the sound of her voice. If she's speaking, at least that means she's less likely to have any permanent damage.

'I know, sweetheart.' I say. 'And we're going to get it looked at very soon.'

'How long's it going to bloody be?' Nathaniel throws his hands in the air. If he thinks he's coming to the hospital with us, he can think again.

This is all his fault.

18

KELLI

'THEY'VE BEEN in there for ages. I hope to God she's OK.' Mum's pacing the waiting room, just as she's been doing for the last hour.

'Shall I get us some more tea?' Ben asks.

'Not for me thanks. I feel like I've been swimming in the stuff. Mum?'

She shakes her head as she burrows her hands into the pockets of the trousers she usually wears when long-distance walking. 'This is one of the few situations where tea feels as though it wouldn't be very helpful.'

'As if things weren't bad enough *before* between Nathaniel and Erin,' I say as Ben sets off in the direction of the drinks machine.

'What was he thinking of, letting Alice ride without her helmet on?' She points to her own head and under normal circumstances, I would chuckle at the state of her hair after the wearing of her own helmet. But until we get word that Alice is alright, there's nothing we could possibly laugh at.

'He wasn't even watching her, Mum. I know things aren't right in his marriage but he's acting like he just doesn't even care about his own daughter. You heard him when she asked for help with her puncture. What the hell's up with him?'

'We're going to have to intervene.' Mum wrings her hands as she sits beside me. 'Alice being so unhappy was worrying enough, but now her safety's been compromised too.'

'I bet Dad will have a field day berating them both after this.'

'That doesn't matter right now. All that matters is that she's OK. And your dad won't feel any differently.' Mum cups her hand over mine.

'Mum.' I nod to where Erin's poking her head through the double doors of the treatment room. We both leap to our feet.

'It's OK. She's going to be OK,' she tells us as she steps out, wiping tears from her eyes. She looks knackered.

'Oh, thank God.' Tears flow down Mum's cheeks again as she throws her arms around Erin.

After a moment, she steps away from Mum. 'She's got a concussion,' Erin continues, 'and they're going to keep her in overnight for observation but otherwise, she's fine. *Made of tough stuff*, they said.'

'Have they checked her over thoroughly?'

'Yes – that's why we've been so long. She had to go for a scan but it's shown she's going to be completely alright. Anyway, she's asking to see you.'

'Who? Me?' Mum asks, pointing at herself.

'Of course. Who else would she want when she's lying in a hospital bed, other than her Grandma?'

Her dad, I think to myself but I don't say this out loud as Mum disappears into Alice's room. I've no idea why Nathaniel isn't here. When I get hold of him, he's going to get a piece of my mind.

'We're going to need some overnight things,' Erin says. 'Obviously, I'm going to stay here with her tonight.'

'I'll get hold of Nathaniel, shall I?' At least it'll give me an excuse to let him know that she's alright. 'They should have got the bikes back to the cottage by now.'

'Thanks – but I really don't think I could face him today,' Erin replies. 'I need to calm down and get my head around things. Could you and Ben get a taxi back to the cottage and then drive back here with our things? I know it's a lot to ask but—'

'Of course we can.' Ben arrives back with a plastic cup filled with a liquid that's masquerading as tea in his hand. 'How's she doing?'

'She's concussed,' I reply. 'But she's going to be fine.'

'She's been very lucky,' Erin adds. 'The doctor said it could have been much worse. But she'll be as right as rain after a good night's rest.'

'And then we can make a huge fuss of her,' I say, though perhaps Erin won't even come back to the cottage after this. Maybe she'll just want to take her home and I wouldn't blame her.

'We'll get going now then,' Ben says, grimacing as he takes a gulp of the machine-brewed tea. 'We'll bring you both some goodies back as well. It'll be a long night for you in this place.'

'Shall I ask Nathaniel to get your overnight stuff together?' I ask.

'I'd rather *you* sorted it,' she replies. 'We both just need a change of clothes, also pyjamas, toothbrushes and our phones and chargers. If you forget Alice's phone, she'll be sending you back for it.'

'She must be feeling better then.' Ben laughs.

'You certainly haven't been exaggerating when you've talked about your family.' As we leave the lift, Ben takes my hand. 'But hopefully, things will calm down after this.'

'You'd think so, wouldn't you? If this isn't a wake-up call for my dear brother, I don't know what will be.'

'Have you ever had any counselling Kel?' He squeezes my hand as we pass by the chapel.

'Erm, no. Why? Should I have?' His out-of-the-blue question pulls me up short. It's not the first time someone's asked me this.

'Yes – I really think you should.'

'Why?'

'Let's get out of here,' he replies. 'Then I'll tell you.'

We fight our way through the packed reception area towards the revolving doors. It's a relief to swap the cool, antiseptic-infused air for the October sunshine.

'I hate hospitals.' I shudder, recalling my own foray into one when I was interrogated for what felt like hours by social workers at the age of eight. And even though it was obvious that I was covering things up because I was scared, I still got sent home with no further questions being asked at the time. Therefore Dad was allowed to continue ruling not just over me, but over all of us.

'It's just that you're such a people pleaser,' Ben begins as we walk along the path where the leaves have started to fall. 'To be honest, you're not dissimilar to your mum.'

'That should be a compliment, but it doesn't really feel like one.' I sigh as I wait for him to continue.

'It's more of an observation.' He looks at me and I'm not sure I like being subject to his scrutiny in this way. Not in these circumstances, anyway. 'There's something inside you that seems to accept the way people like your father, your brother and your sister-in-law treat you.'

'You mean Nathaniel and Martha?'

'Who else? They speak to you as though you're rubbish most of the time. And you accept it.' He drives his hands into his pockets as we walk along. 'It's almost like you believe that's all you're worth. It shouldn't be like this – it drives me mad.'

'Nathaniel's been the same since childhood. He's like it with everyone.'

'That doesn't mean it's OK,' Ben replies. 'I've been watching your brother quite closely, as it happens.'

'Oh yes?'

'He seems to be seeking some kind of power but because he doesn't get it, he falls into victim mode.'

'Yeah, you've probably got a point.'

'But either way, he's incredibly manipulative with you and your mother.' He slings his arm around my shoulders as though we're having a casual conversation about what to have for dinner instead of denouncing one of my brothers.

'You mentioned Martha as well.' I might as well let him get it all off his chest.

'Well, she's an out-and-out narcissist. It's little wonder she and your dad get on so well. They feed each other's enormous egos. But if they ever fell out, it wouldn't be pretty.'

'None of this is helping me work out how to deal with them though, is it?'

'You need to stop being sucked in by *any* of them. Just stick with me, your mum, Erin, Rylan and Alice as far as family's concerned. Nathaniel isn't quite as lost a cause as your dad and Martha. Is he any different when it's just you and him? Any nicer?'

I think for a moment, trying to bring an example to mind. But I can't. 'Not really,' I eventually reply. 'However, it's difficult not to be sucked in when it's people you're actually related to. It's not like I can just walk away.'

'You could, if you really wanted to.'

'I've got Mum to consider so I just want to change things. *Them*, if possible.'

'You'll never change a narcissist, Kelli,' he says as we approach the entrance to the hospital car park. 'But you can change your response to them. They feed off another person's misery.'

'My dad's certainly inflicted plenty of that over the years. Anyway,' I playfully push Ben's arm, 'this is all getting very deep for a sunny Monday afternoon.' I raise my gaze into the sky as I dump myself onto the perimeter wall of the hospital, wishing I was sitting with Ben in a nice beer garden instead of returning to face that miserable lot. 'For now,' I continue, 'we should just be glad that Alice is alright and we should concentrate on getting in and back out of the cottage with the minimum of interaction with that lot.'

'Alice is going to be fine, you heard what Erin said.' Ben drops his phone into the pocket of his jeans. 'Anyway, I've ordered an Uber – it'll be here in five minutes.'

'Thanks and thanks for caring – you know – about *me*, I mean.'

'I'm not expecting you to be able to deal with them differently overnight.' He sits beside me. 'But you can't keep allowing them to have the impact they're having on your life forever. They'll grind you into the floor.'

'But as I said, they're my family.' I'm only too aware of my glum-sounding voice.

'That doesn't mean you owe them anything.'

'You've seen and heard what my Mum puts up with. And that's only the tip of the iceberg. I have to be around for her more, especially now Grandad's gone. She needs me to protect her.'

'From your dad?'

I nod.

'Your mum can fight her own corner. I've seen and heard her. And look, she's a mature woman. If she really wanted to, she could leave him.'

'She couldn't – she really couldn't. There's the money side of things for a start and—'

'She could always come and stay with us.'

'Our house would be the first place he'd come looking. Besides, she wouldn't agree to it in the first place.'

'You don't know unless you talk to her.'

'It's not just about the money Ben – there's other stuff – things even I don't know the full details about.'

'Perhaps I could try to talk to your mum – I know how worried you get about her and honestly love, you can't continue through your life like—'

'Ohh look. Saved by the taxi. Can we change the subject now? Particularly in front of the driver. I know it's all pretty horrendous but let's just focus on Alice, shall we? We can talk about everything else later.'

'When?'

'Just *later*. It's all making my head hurt.'

19

KELLI

'How's she doing?' Rylan springs from the chair the moment we open the door. 'The hospital wouldn't give me any details over the phone.'

'It's a concussion,' I reply. 'And she's going to be absolutely fine.'

'Thank goodness for that. Have you heard this, Nate?' Rylan leans against the breakfast bar and looks at our brother. 'You can slow down on that whiskey now, can't you? Alice is OK.'

'That stuff's not going to help matters.' I stride towards him and reach for the bottle but I'm too late. He tugs it towards him like a baby hanging onto their milk.

'Mind your own bloody business,' he slurs as he turns away from me.

Great – he's pissed already. Perhaps it's just as well Erin's not coming back tonight.

'Did you not hear what I just said, Nate? Your daughter's OK.'

'But everyone's blaming *me* for what happened, aren't they?' He still won't look at me.

'Do you want to know what I think—' I begin.

'No.' Dad smirks as he cuts his sandwich in half. 'But just like your mother would, I'm sure you're going to tell us.'

I glance at my father and then back to my brother. 'I think you should sober yourself up, Nathaniel, and get your arse over to that hospital.'

'Is she not being let back out today?' Martha arches a perfectly plucked eyebrow as she pours a coffee from the jug. I'm quite surprised to see she hasn't hit the alcohol as well.

'They're keeping her in for observation,' Ben says. 'Erin's asked us to take an overnight bag back for them.'

Nathaniel slumps even further over the breakfast bar. 'Great.'

'Is she allowed visitors?' Rylan drops his cup into the sink. 'I might come back with you.'

'It's Nathaniel who should be going, not you.' Martha's face hardens. 'Besides, you heard what Kelli said – she's going to be OK.'

'I can't go.' Nathaniel stares into his glass. 'I need to give Erin time to calm down. Like she said, it was all my fault.'

'To be honest.' I sit beside him. 'I do think you need to let her calm down. But you also need to put this bottle away, sober yourself up and get your thinking cap on about how you're going to make things better.'

'Hear, hear,' says Rylan and I shoot him a look of gratitude.

'There speaks the voice of experience.' Dad laughs as he drops his knife into the sink. 'How many times have you been married and had children, Kelli?'

I open my mouth to retort but then recall my conversation with Ben. I'm not going to allow my father to draw me in anymore. What was it he said, *I can't change him but I can change the way I respond to him.* Judging by Dad's expectant face, he's itching for me to argue back, to give him some 'feed' which will, in turn, give him an excuse to let rip at me. Particularly with Mum not being here at the moment – his usual emotional punchbag.

I head for the stairs. I *will* go for some counselling as soon as I'm able to. It's time to end Dad's days of being able to pull my strings. And in doing so, maybe I can help Mum too.

'Just drop me off here, will you.' Mum gestures to the left. 'I'll walk the rest of the way.'

'Why?' Rylan asks. 'It's easily a twenty-minute walk from here to the cottage.'

'Here?' As instructed, Ben brings the car to a stop at the side of the road.

'I just want some fresh air,' Mum replies. 'After being stuck at that hospital, I could do with clearing my head.'

'I'll come with you.' I unclip my seatbelt.

'No, honestly, love. I could just do with a bit of a walk on my own, if you don't mind.'

'Are you sure that's wise?' Rylan leans between the two front seats. 'It's starting to get dark.'

'I'll be back well before it gets anywhere near fully dark.' She laughs as she slides her gloves from her pocket. 'Honestly, you lot. The last time I looked in the mirror, I was a fully grown, late-fifty-ish woman. I'll be fine.'

'Have you got your phone with you?'

'Of course.' Mum pats her pocket.

'And you know the way back?'

'Yes. Now do you have any more questions or can I get out?' She turns in her seat to look at Ben.

He smiles. 'It's only because they love you, Gill.'

She pats his hand. 'I know. Anyway, thanks for everything you've done today. I'll see you soon.'

I watch as she walks away from the car, and I'm momentarily overwhelmed with love for the woman who exudes such strength, yet also so much vulnerability. I don't know what I'd do without her.

'Come on,' Rylan says, as he pats my hand. 'You heard what she said. She doesn't need us lot watching her as she walks along the road.'

We pass her as she's zipping her jacket up and she waves after us. I'm rattled about her walking on her own in the dusk, no matter how much she said she wanted to. After all, I've spent my whole life worrying about her.

~

'Whose turn is it to cook tonight?' Trust this to be Dad's first question the moment we walk in.

I point at Nathaniel who's slumped in the armchair in the corner next to the fire. At least someone's bothered to light it.

'I guess it's a takeaway then.' Rylan laughs.

'We'll be lucky,' I say. 'Most places only deliver within a five-mile radius. One of us will have to collect one.'

'That's him out then.' Rylan nods in Nathaniel's direction. 'Though I don't fancy eating takeaway, to be honest. Not after all that chocolate I ate from the hospital machine.' He pats his stomach and I laugh. There isn't an ounce of fat on him. 'Come on, Martha. We'll whip something up together, shall we?'

'Where's your mum?' She peers at us from beneath her fringe.

'If you're expecting Mum to cook, you know what you can do,' I reply. 'She's been at that hospital for hours. So get off your fat, lazy arse and pull your weight for a change.' The words are out before I can stop them. For a moment, Martha looks as shocked as I am at my outburst.

'My arse…' She slides from her stool at the breakfast bar and sashays towards me, still dressed in the leggings and hoodie she wore to cycle in. 'Can hardly be described as *fat*. Unlike—'

'It can certainly be described as lazy though, can't it?'

I smile at Ben as Martha opens her mouth to retort but Dad beats her to it.

'Where *is* your mum?' He closes the lid on his laptop. He's the only one who's changed out of what he wore to cycle in and is now back in his usual checked shirt and chinos.

'She's gone for a walk to clear her head.'

'*Clear her head?* Why?' He tips his head as he awaits my reply.

'She's been stuck in that hospital all afternoon. I don't envy Erin and Alice having to *sleep* there.' I shudder as I come further into the kitchen. 'Is there any coffee left in that pot?'

'Dinner's nearly ready.' Rylan looks up from the pan of stir fry he's cobbled together. 'What are we going to do about Mum?'

'I'm starving,' Martha announces. She's back in her favourite spot at the breakfast bar with yet another wine bottle. For someone so slim and attractive at the surface level, she can sure pack the wine away. I'll have to casually ask Rylan if she's like this at home, with the drink *and* the willingness to be waited on. She hasn't lifted a finger with the dinner but then it's Rylan's fault for letting her get away with it. Ben and I always take turns to cook.

'I can cover it over for a bit. Can you try Mum's phone again?'

I reach over to where I've left my phone charging and hit the redial button. *This is Gill. Leave a message.* I smile at her happy voice but my smile quickly fades at the realisation of how long it's been since we dropped her off. 'Her phone's still off.' I look around at the others.

'It's nearly half past eight.' Martha glances at the clock, her ponytail swinging with the motion. 'And my stomach feels like my throat's been cut.'

I glance at her milky-white throat, adorned with an expensive-looking necklace, probably bought by my brother, and can't help my thoughts from wandering.

'We're not eating without Mum,' I tell her. 'It's pitch black out there and she said she'd only be twenty minutes.'

'How long ago was that?' Rylan mops his brow with the tea towel. For the first time since we've arrived, we seem to have got it heated up in here.

'Over three hours ago now.' Ben frowns. 'I haven't had a drink yet so I think we should have a drive around.'

'Good idea,' Dad says, looking over the top of his glasses. 'I'd appreciate that.'

Just as my astonishment at him being polite threatens to dislocate my jaw, he spoils himself.

'Just don't be all night about it,' he adds. 'And make sure you find her. I'll keep checking the *find my phone* facility I set up in her phone, but it's no good if hers isn't switched on.'

'Gosh, he's all heart, your dad, isn't he?' Ben pulls the door behind us, shaking his head. 'He doesn't appear to be remotely concerned for your mother's welfare – he seems more bothered that he's lost control of her whereabouts. And Martha just wants her dinner.'

'I reckon Mum's found herself a pub.' I gaze into the sky which is as clear as it was when we first arrived. 'She'll have decided to have a bit of *me* time. I hope so anyway.' I pull my cardigan more tightly around myself. 'The temperature's really dropped, hasn't it?'

'Did you notice any pubs around here?' The lights on our Golf flash as Ben points the key at it.

'Not the way we've been coming and going.' I slide into the passenger seat. 'But that doesn't mean there aren't any further afield.'

'True. Well if we find her in one, maybe I could be persuaded to have half an hour longer with her.' I smile at him. It's good to be out of that oppressive cottage and to be on my own with Ben. I also feel like I'm doing something useful to find Mum instead of just sitting around, speculating and worrying about her.

As we head up, down and around the winding country roads, there isn't a pub in sight. The only sign of civilisation in the five-mile radius we cover is a small row of dark terraced cottages.

'None of them even look occupied.' Ben cranes his neck as he pulls up at the side of the road. 'They're probably holiday lets like ours.'

'But it's half term – that's why Mum picked this week – for mine and Alice's sake. You'd think the cottages would be all booked out – it's quite pretty around here.'

'Who wants to stay in the middle of nowhere with only cows and sheep for company?'

'Beats my family.' We both laugh.

'Look – that one's got a light on.' I point at the cottage in the centre of the row.

'There are no cars around it though, are there? The owner might just leave a light on a timer to deter burglars.'

'I doubt a burglar would bother coming all this way. Should we knock on the door, just in case?'

I stare at it for a moment before sighing. 'I don't think there's any point. It's not as if we dropped her off anywhere *near* here. This is the complete opposite direction to the cottage.'

'I think we should try – just in case. I'll go.'

His seatbelt swings back with a clunk. The whoosh of cold air hits me as he opens the door, leaving me in the darkness. I watch as he knocks on the door before cupping his hands against the window with the light on. He even tries the door handle before returning to me, shaking his head.

'OK, let's just go back for now, shall we?' He shuts the door again. 'We've been driving around for well over half an hour. She might even have gone back to the cottage by now.'

'Surely someone would have rung to let us know.' Then I realise – my phone's still plugged in on charge. Hopefully, Mum's getting warm by the fire and someone will have made her a cup of tea.

'If there's no sign of her when we get back, then maybe we need to report her missing, Kel. The police will check these houses, and any more we might not have found, I would have thought.'

My stomach twists at the thought of making a call to the police.

I can only cling to the hope that she's already back at the cottage, waiting for us.

We race from the car to the cottage door. 'Is she back?' I gasp as we burst in. Spent plates are stacked on the breakfast bar. If they've eaten, that *must* mean she's returned. After all, Rylan said they'd wait.

But she hasn't.

'What are we going to do?' I sink into the chair and shiver. The fire's gone out and if we don't find Mum soon, I don't know what I'm going to do. 'Pass me my phone, Ben. I'll try her again.'

'I just did.' Rylan shakes his head. 'It's still going straight to her voicemail.'

'I'm going to call the police.' I open my phone screen. 'It's been four hours and it's pretty cold out there. She could be lying in a ditch for all we know.'

'As if you drove off and left her to walk back alone,' Dad says through gritted teeth. 'If anything's happened to her, Kelli, I'll be holding you *personally* responsible.' The look on his face sends a tremor through me. Ben was right earlier – I really *do* need to go for counselling. I can't let him do this to me anymore.

'What about *him*?' I point at Rylan. 'He was in the car with us as well.' It's always been the same old tale. I get it in the neck instead of my brothers.

'Perhaps, instead of point-scoring against your brother,' Martha says, her voice syrupy sweet on the surface but with an icy edge. 'You should be making that call to the police.'

'I'll be in the other room,' I say. If I have to spend another moment in that woman's company, I won't be responsible for my actions.

I call 101 and wait. 'Yes, I need to report a missing person,' I begin.

'What's happening?' Rylan pokes his head around the door.

'It's alright. You can come in. I've finished talking to them.'

Ben follows him into the room and sits beside me. 'I've put a plate of food in the microwave for you. You haven't eaten all day.'

'I couldn't eat a thing. Not until my mother's back here safe and sound.'

'What did they say?'

'They've taken a description and said they'll keep an eye out for her.'

His eyes widen. 'And that's it?'

'They're going to circulate her details on the local news and they said someone will be round here to see us – probably tonight if they get time, but if not, it'll be in the morning.'

'*In the morning.*' Rylan rakes his fingers through his fringe. 'But she could freeze to death out there all night.'

'That's what I said. I asked if they could get the police helicopter up – they'd definitely be able to find her with that.'

'True. With the infrared whatsit.' Rylan lets out a long breath, walks to the window, and tugs one of the curtains to the side. 'It's impossible to see a thing out there. She must have taken a wrong turning and got lost… then if her phone's died or lost signal…'

'Which is all best case scenario.' I blink back tears. I can't give in to them yet – that would be like giving up hope that Mum's somewhere keeping warm with a glass of something in her hand. 'I just need to know she's OK. I'm giving it an hour from now and then I'm ringing the police back.'

'Someone should let Erin know,' Rylan says. 'What if she sees something on the news? I'll call her now. Mum could have even gone back *there* for all we know.'

Erin's frantic voice echoes around the lounge as she processes what Rylan's telling her. 'As if today could have got any worse,' she says, her worried voice echoing from the speaker of his phone. 'What are we going to do?'

'There's nothing we *can* do other than just wait for her to come back,' I reply. 'Ben and I have already had a drive around, looking for her.'

'I just can't believe this.' Her voice is filled with tears.

'I didn't want to tell you,' Rylan says, 'but then we decided that you needed to know – just in case she gets in touch with you. Also, they're circulating her description on the news shortly.'

'You were right to let me know,' she replies. 'I can't imagine finding out that way.'

'Who's he on the phone to?' Martha pokes her head around the door.

'Shhh.' I raise my finger to my lips and frown at her.

'I'm just sorry to pile more stress on you,' Rylan says. 'You've already had a pig of a day.'

'Is that Erin?' Martha's eyes flash with anger.

'Shall I get a taxi back over?' Erin says over the loudspeaker. 'Alice is fast asleep – I know I should stay with her but the nurses—'

'No, you stay put until she's discharged,' I reply. 'There's nothing you can do here. We're just waiting for the police.'

'*The police?* Oh honestly, this is a nightmare. What are *they* doing to find her?'

'Not a right lot to be honest. But hopefully, that will change once they turn up here and we put a rocket up them.'

I glance at Nathaniel, now stretched out on the sofa, oblivious to everything going on around him. Our mother's been missing for hours and he's so drunk he doesn't even know what day of the week it is. It's just as well Erin isn't here. If she were to see the state of him, I don't know what she'd do.

20

GILL

I TAKE a deep breath as I stare at the cottage which is lit up like a Christmas tree. From the outside, it looks almost cosy and welcoming yet I know only too well what lies at the other side of the door.

As my gaze flits to the police car parked next to Ben and Kelli's Golf, the enormity of what I've done starts to hit me. Poor Kelli will be out of her mind with worry – all so I could spend some time with Jason. I can't believe I've done this to her.

In the moment, the decision felt like the right one. To put *me* first for a change. Only when Jason's hallway clock struck eleven, did it dawn on me just how selfish I was being.

When I first set off walking after Ben dropped me off earlier, I had no intention whatsoever of ending up at Jason's. But as I got to the junction which would take me either back to the cottage or towards his house, a wave of indignation crashed over me and I couldn't stop myself.

My lot have had me at their beck and call, day-in-day-out for as long as I can remember – so why shouldn't *Jason* get some proper time with me? We cooked, we talked, and things just felt so natural and easy – not like they do at home. Most importantly, he's helped me to accept that things can't go on as they are any longer.

As the evening wore on and I felt more and more comfortable in front of his fire, the prospect of returning to Karl became less and less appealing. If it wasn't for my kids, particularly Kelli, I dare say I might not have come back here at all.

I know I could have and *should* have let someone know I was safe, but that would have risked the message being traced back to Jason's house and I'm not ready for the fallout that would inevitably cause. Instead, as soon as I knew where I was going, I turned my phone off so Karl wouldn't be able to use the *find my phone* function he's set up.

'I should come in with you really.'

I looked at Jason in the darkness of the car when he pulled up around the corner, firstly realising just how much I've missed out on by keeping him on the fringes of my life, but secondly, realising how important it is to handle this situation delicately.

I shook my head. 'There'd be mayhem if you did that.'

'You can't blame me for worrying about what will happen when *you* go back in,' he said. 'If I'm there—'

'Look, I *am* going to address things, really I am…' My voice trailed off and he must have picked up on my hesitancy by the look he was giving me.

'But I need to do it in my own time and in my own way,' I added.

'OK – then promise me you'll keep in touch. I'm at the end of a phone. And I'm only ten minutes away if you need me.'

I stand in the doorway, observing the tear-stained face of my daughter and the dark circles under the eyes of my son as they sit facing two police officers across the dining room table. I don't think I could feel any more terrible than I do at this moment.

'I'm here,' I say. 'I'm really sorry.'

'Oh my God. Mum!' Kelli flies across the room, hugging me so tight I can hardly breathe. 'Where the hell have you been?'

'I got lost,' I fib as I step into the room. 'And my phone had run out of charge. I ended up at some houses, and I was cold, and...'

'What houses? Is that where you've been all evening?'

'We told you she'd be safe, didn't we?' The female police officer's face relaxes into a smile. 'We will need to ask you a couple of questions though, Mrs Hawthorne. Your family have been very worried about you.'

'Where the hell have you been?' Karl appears in the doorway, looking more angry than relieved – just as Jason predicted.

'At someone's house. I was lost and upset and she let me stay.' Tears leak from my eyes. I never planned to cry but knowing my kids have been so worried that they've called the police makes me feel guiltier than I have in a long time.

'*She*?' Trust Karl to pick up on that. It's all he cares about – whether I've been around a he or a she. After all, in his eyes, I *belong* to him.

'I didn't want to come back at all, if the truth be known.' I swipe my coat sleeve across my cheek but I can't stem the flow of tears I've suppressed for far too long. 'I've had enough of it all.' I stare at Karl, silently daring him to have a go at me in front of these officers.

'Come here, Mum, come and sit yourself down.' Rylan stands from his chair, hooks his hand into the crook of my arm and leads me to the table as though I'm a hundred years old. 'Martha,' he says to his wife who's appeared behind Dad. 'Go and make Mum a cup of tea, will you?'

I sink to the chair, the tears falling faster than ever. I don't think I've ever felt this exhausted. 'I can't go on like we have been,' I sob. 'This family. It's...' My voice fades. I'm crying so hard I can't even get my words out.

'I've had enough,' I eventually repeat. I don't know what else to say. 'I've really had enough.'

Yes, I'm crying with the constant aggro that exists within my family, particularly in my marriage and the secrets we harbour, but I'm also crying with guilt, for what I've put Kelli and Rylan through tonight. And I'm crying for the situation with Jason. And I'm crying with fear over what's coming.

It's the first time I've ever done anything like it and I can only hope they'll all be able to understand my reasons when I feel up to explaining them.

'Would you prefer us to call back and talk to you later?' The policewoman's voice is kindly as I rub at my head. 'Or would you like to speak to us now? We can go somewhere private if you like?' She looks around at everyone as though trying to gauge their reaction to this suggestion. Karl won't like this one bit.

'Can you all leave us for a few minutes.' I accept a box of tissues from Kelli and pluck one from the top.

'I'll stay with her if you don't mind,' Karl says as he steps further into the room.

'Is that OK with you?' asks the policewoman.

'I'd prefer it if *everyone* left us,' I reply. 'Thank you,' I say as Martha slides a cup of tea beside me.

'Fine then.' Karl strides after Kelli and Martha as they file from the room. Rylan, the final one to leave, turns back to me and winks. 'It'll be alright, Mum,' he says as I pop some headache tablets into my mouth.

As I sit facing the two police officers, I'm reminded of the enormous threat Karl's wielded over me for years. *Just remember what might happen if you ever try to leave.* I'm shocked he hasn't reminded me of it since I came back tonight.

'OK, my name's Sergeant Lara Greene and this is my colleague PC Tom Burnham. Are we alright to call you Gill?'

I nod and blow my nose. 'I'm just sorry your time's been wasted like this. And I'm sorry to have worried everyone.' I need to set their minds at rest and get rid of them as quickly as possible. There are other things which need to be dealt with.

'You're back, that's the main thing.' She studies me for a moment. 'I do have to ask whether everything's OK, Gill. We need to make sure you're safe.'

I nod. 'Of course I am. We've just been having a few problems – like every family does.'

'Go on.'

'I guess today, everything's got on top of me more than it usually would. My granddaughter got knocked off her bike by a car earlier, you know.'

'Yes, we've heard about that – it does sound like it's been a very stressful day all round.' Her tone's sympathetic and I find myself relaxing a little as I sip my tea. After all, no one's accusing me of anything.

'Aren't holidays supposed to be relaxing?' The constable smiles and Sergeant Greene gives him a look as if to say, *leave the talking to me.*

'I understand that you've been away from your family since around half past five this evening.' She glances at her watch. 'That's quite a long time for them to be worrying about you.'

'I know.' I drop my head into my hands which serves also to ease my headache. 'I just needed some space.'

'You mentioned going into someone's house before? Whose house would that be?'

Oh gosh. What if they want to check out what I tell them? My thoughts tumble over each other for a moment. *What shall I say?* I could tell them the truth, and for them, that would probably be the end of it, but for all I know, someone could be listening outside the door. I certainly wouldn't put it past Karl.

No one can find out about Jason by overhearing me telling the police. No, I've got to bide my time for another day or two.

Certainly, until Erin's back here and Alice has settled down again. Until then, I can't breathe a word.

21

GILL

'I'm going up Mum.' Kelli rises from her chair and squeezes my shoulder. 'I'm done in.'

'OK, love. Hopefully, I won't be far behind you.'

'Before I go, can I ask you – did it go alright when you talked to the police before?' She shakes her hair, the same dark colour her dad's used to be, behind her shoulders and stretches her arms towards the ceiling.

'Yes, they just wanted to know where I'd been, which as I told you, was at that woman's house. Mainly, they wanted to check that I'm OK.'

'And are you?' Kelli leans onto the back of the chair she's just vacated and looks at me with the love and concern in her eyes which is one of the things that's held me in this dreadful marriage of mine for so many years.

'Yes.' I yawn and stretch too. 'I've calmed down a bit now. You know what it's like when everything gets too much.'

'You know you can always talk to me, don't you?' Her voice is soft.

'I do.' I rub at my head. 'And I will, I promise. Has everyone else gone to bed, it seems very quiet?' I look towards the door. I've barely moved from the dining room since I returned, feeling happier in the dimly lit space surrounded by paintings of the dales. Karl tried interrogating me after the police had gone, but I just kept reiterating what I'd already said, that I'd been walking, trying to clear my head and that I ended up bumping into some woman. End of.

Eventually and miraculously, he left me alone in favour of getting another drink and returning to the others. But I'm pretty sure I won't have heard the end of it. Not by a long chalk.

'Rylan's turned in,' she replies. 'Ben's just got in the shower and I think Martha and Dad are watching something in the other room.'

'Are they in there?' I jerk my head in the direction of the lounge.

She nods. 'Thick as thieves, aren't they?'

'Dad should be spending his time with *you*.' I sigh, resisting the urge to add how heartless it is that he treats his daughter-in-law better than his own daughter.

'They're welcome to each other.' Kelli rolls her eyes and I'm proud that she doesn't allow the situation to get to her. She's never been as anxious to gain Karl's approval as her brothers always have been. They grew up vying with each other for his attention. 'Anyway, enough of all that – who was this woman whose house you were at?'

'I thought you were going to bed.' I smile.

'I am – but I just want to know.'

I should have known that Kelli wouldn't let it go. 'Just one I came across when I was walking. She was watering her hanging baskets and noticed I was upset, as I approached.' The lie is tripping so easily off my tongue for the second time tonight that it's almost worrying. It's been years since I've lied so blatantly, but it seems that it's coming as naturally now as it did back then.

'You were upset? But you seemed OK when we dropped you off.'

'Well, I wasn't – not really.'

'And she invited you into her home – even though you're a complete stranger?'

I nod. 'Obviously, I don't look like some kind of murderer, do I?' I laugh though the sound is completely hollow. 'Maybe she decided she could use the company.'

'And she's helped you to feel better, has she?'

I nod. 'It's sometimes easier to talk to a stranger, isn't it?'

'Fair enough but please – I'm *always* here for you, Mum.'

Judging by her expression, she has no reason to disbelieve me. And I mustn't feel guilty – after all, she'll know the truth soon enough.

'Right, I'll leave you in peace then,' she continues, 'but we'll talk properly tomorrow, OK? And remember, you're not on your own with all this, you know.'

'Come here you.' She steps towards me and I hold her in my arms, momentarily enjoying her warmth. Kelli is a third of the reason why I stayed so long with Karl. For her and Rylan and Nathaniel. I could never have left my children behind. Though Kelli, the last to leave home, has been gone for several years now. And now Joe's no longer with us either, there's no longer anything to keep me stuck in this situation.

Like I promised Jason, I've got to be brave and gather every shred of my strength together. If Karl *does* carry out his long-standing threat, then so be it. As Jason so rightly pointed out, if this happens, then Karl will be up to his neck in things too. After all, *knowing* about something of the magnitude it was, and turning a blind eye, can be as serious as actually doing what I did in the first place.

'I really love you, Mum, you know.'

'You too, sweetheart. Everything will be OK after a good night's sleep.'

'You've always said that.' She smiles. 'Just make sure you go up soon too. You look done in.'

I sit for a bit, lost in thought as I nurse the glass of wine Rylan poured me earlier. I've never drunk so much as I have during the last three nights while we've been here. I'm still feeling wired so might have another to knock me out a bit more. Then I'll get myself up to bed and hopefully Karl will pass out on the sofa like he often does at home. If he and Martha weren't already in there, that's where I'd be going in the first place.

As I step into the hallway, their drunken voices echo from the lounge. I can't hear the TV so whatever they were watching must have finished. I pause for a moment – I want to know what they're talking about. After all, *things of significance* are more likely to be said by people while they're drunk, and any knowledge I can gain from eavesdropping is definitely power.

'Don't you think you should *force* her to be assessed by someone,' Martha is saying. 'I'm telling you now – I would if it was *Rylan* – if *he* was carrying on like Gill was earlier.'

'*Everyone* in this family's doo-lally,' Karl replies. 'You must have realised that by now. The two of us are the only sane ones.'

She laughs. 'That must be why we get along so well.'

'Like I've told you many times,' he continues, 'you're more like my daughter than my daughter.'

That's exactly what I was thinking to myself earlier. What sort of a father says something like that? I'm just relieved Kelli's already gone up and can't hear him.

'She's too much like her mother, Kelli is.' He still hasn't finished. 'If the truth be known, they both depress the hell out of me.'

'It's probably why Erin gets on so well with them both too. She's cut from the same piece of cloth.'

'I know.'

'It all gets to me sometimes, to be honest.' Martha's voice rises some more. She must think I've gone to bed. Or perhaps she's just too drunk to care. 'You must have noticed how they leave me out all the time?'

'Kind of. Perhaps that's a good thing though. You're obviously out of their league.'

'But they're supposed to be my in-laws. My *family.*' I can imagine her pet lip jutting out as she speaks.

'Does it really bother you so much?'

'I've tried and tried to get on with them all, Karl, but it doesn't change anything.'

'Perhaps I should say something then. I'll have a word with Gill if you like.'

'Would you?'

'Of course – but no matter what happens, you stick with me, Martha. We're two of a kind – you and I.'

Yeah, you can say that again, I think to myself as they clink their glasses together. I wouldn't like to have their livers by the time this week is over. If it ever is over. Each day has felt like a week so far. No – much longer than a week.

'What are you doing, Mum?' I jump as Rylan tugs at my arm. 'Why are you standing here? It's nearly midnight.'

'Shhh.' I put my finger to my lips. 'I'm just listening in.'

'Oh, I see.'

Martha's laughter rings out.

'I was wondering where *she'd* got to.' Rylan shakes his head as he tightens the cord on his dressing gown. 'That's why I've got back up. Are they *still* bloody drinking?'

'Come on, we'll go in here.' I point at the kitchen door. 'Leave them to it. They're the only ones here on the same wavelength. It's been like this since we arrived.'

'She's driving me potty.' Rylan lifts the iron which props the door open and rests it on the breakfast bar. 'Blimey, that's heavy.'

He points at it. 'She's either been drunk or just completely nasty since we got here – you must have noticed it, Mum.'

'Wine or tea?' I point from the fridge to the kettle.

'I'd better have tea,' he replies flicking his fringe from his eyes. 'What no one can drink, however, is whiskey – I think Nate's drunk his own body weight in it today.'

'Really?'

'He's been in bed for hours. I don't know what's got into him lately.'

'What happened with Alice probably shook him up,' I say. 'And he and Erin haven't been getting on so well either.'

'They're not the only ones.' Rylan shuffles himself onto one of the stools and crosses his legs.

'Are you sure you don't want wine?' I pull the cork from the bottle. 'I'm having another one.'

'Oh go on then.' He grins. 'You're a bad influence, Mother.'

'What do you mean, *they're not the only ones*?'

'I'm not going to start loading all my problems onto you, not after the time you've had today.'

'I'm OK now.' I take another glass from the cupboard. 'Really I am. I've let it all out and I'm fine.'

'You sure?' Concern lingers in his eyes, making me feel guilty all over again.

'Honestly.'

'OK, well, I suppose it's nothing major. Just Martha's endless jealousy over Erin which seems to be getting worse.'

'Yes – I've noticed that, but it's nothing new, is it?'

'It's not only that.'

'Yes – I thought there might be something else.'

He sighs. 'You know me too well, Mum. It's the baby thing too.' He lowers his voice and studies his feet. 'Since Dad made a quip about us having one yesterday, I can't get it out of my head.'

'Neither of those things you're talking about sound like *nothing major* to me.'

'What do you mean?'

'For one thing, jealousy would rot *any* relationship.'

'I know.'

'And so will someone's yearning to be a parent when their partner isn't interested.' I could sense something shift when Karl so clumsily started going on about this the other day. 'Have you tried talking to her about it?'

'She's been drunk since we got here.'

'Hmmm. However, you sounded as though you were getting on alright last night.' I laugh. As soon as I've said this, I'm aware that I probably shouldn't have.

'Yeah, right. How embarrassing.' Rylan blushes to the roots of his hair. 'We were both drunk.'

'Sorry, I was only joking.'

'There's more to it all though, Mum.' He glances at the door as though he's making sure that no one's listening. 'I've got all sorts whirring about in my head right now. I keep thinking I've made a mistake. Sure, she's attractive and all that but...' His voice trails off.

'Beauty's only skin deep.' I complete his sentence for him. 'And you *have* got a choice in whether you want to stay married to her, Rylan. You could end your marriage, if you really wanted to.'

'How could I?' He stares down at his hands.

'The last thing I want is for you to make any more of the mistakes I've made. Any of you.'

'But I'd have as much chance of Martha letting me go as you'd have with Dad.' He sighs, suddenly looking ten years older than his thirty-four years. 'Erin was right with what she said when I was fixing Alice's puncture.'

'Why, what did she say? Just hang on.' The low hum of voices and occasional cackle of laughter from the other room appears to have halted. I creep to the door and open it slightly, relieved as Karl's voice starts up again. So long as they stay safely in there until we've gone up, there should be no more trouble this evening. I close the door with a click and return to the wine glasses.

'She said I'd married someone just like my father,' he replies. 'And she's right, isn't she?'

I open my mouth to say what I *really* think is going on here but then think better of it. It can keep. Knowing my son more than anyone else on this earth, I've noticed something in his eyes which spells nothing but trouble.

He still thinks more of Erin than he'd ever dare let on and seeing how she looks at him too, I'd say this is very much reciprocated. Martha's seen it, Nathaniel's seen it and I've definitely seen it. But while things are like they are for this family, I'm not going to coax an admittance out of Rylan. It's not time.

Yet.

'Thanks.' He takes the drink from me.

'Here's to escaping.' I hold my wine aloft.

'What do you mean?'

'One day.' I lower my glass.

'What's going on, Mum?' He narrows his eyes.

'I'm not sure yet.'

DAY FOUR

22

ERIN

'THANKS FOR COMING to pick us up,' I smile at Rylan as he ducks under the doorway. 'Sorry – I haven't got around to folding that back up yet.'

He heads around the side of the lumpy Z-bed I've spent the night on. 'You look shattered,' he says.

'Gee, thanks. Anyway, I didn't expect her to be discharged so early, not that I'm complaining – it's been a lo-ong night.' As he stands in front of me, with his hair still shower-damp, wearing Levi jeans and an expensive-looking jumper, I'm aware of how dishevelled I must look in comparison. I rake my fingers through my hair, still matted from when the wind whipped under it yesterday when we were out on the bikes. Kelli forgot to put a hairbrush in our bag.

'No one else has surfaced yet. Not even Mum.'

'How's Nathaniel been with it all? Dare I ask?' I pull a face. Am I even bothered anymore?

'Let's just say I wouldn't like to have his head this morning.' Rylan lowers himself into the chair beside mine at Alice's bedside and gestures at the crinkled sheets. 'Where's the patient anyway?'

'She's just gone to get a wash. She'll be over the moon to see you. She can't wait to get out of here.'

'I bet.'

'How's your Mum doing? Has she let on where she got to yet? I was texting with Kelli last night and she seems a bit baffled to say the least.'

'Mum's acting really strangely, to be honest.' He shields his eyes from the sunlit glare from the windows facing us. It's even brighter because it's bouncing from the stark, white walls. 'She was at some mystery woman's house last night and when I had a drink with her before I went to bed, she was making weird comments about escaping. It's the first time I've heard her talking like that. Has she ever said anything to you?'

I shake my head. 'Maybe she's finally seen the light.'

As Rylan takes a breath ready to say something, I quickly add, 'I'm sorry – Karl's your dad. I do forget myself sometimes.' My face is burning.

'Don't worry about it.' He laughs. 'You're right. Maybe this week has brought things home to all of us.' For a moment, Rylan has a faraway look in his eyes. Then he looks straight back at me. 'We can't exactly call this a *holiday*, however a break from the usual routine can be quite enlightening, can't it?'

'What do you mean?'

'Oh look, ignore me, I'm warbling on again – it doesn't matter. Oh look, she's here.' Rylan smiles at Alice who's now standing in the doorway, looking comfy in her joggers and hoodie. 'How are you doing sweetie-pie?' He stands from the chair again.

'Uncle Rylan.' Alice rushes over to hug him. 'How come *you're* here?'

'Well I wasn't going to leave you to eat hospital food all day, was I?' He goes to ruffle her hair but must suddenly remember the bang to her head she had yesterday for he stops himself. 'Besides, who else would I have to watch movies on the sofa all day with if I didn't come and pick you up?'

'Yes, that's about all you'll be doing today, Alice,' I say in my most authoritative voice. 'The doctor said you had to rest.'

'Boor-ing.'

'Just for today and then you can get back to normal tomorrow.'

'Does that mean we can go home?' Her voice is filled with hope. 'And get *properly* back to normal?'

'We'll have to see how it goes. But yes, that's probably the plan.'

'Nooo. The two of you can't *leave* the holiday cottage.' A look of horror crosses Rylan's face. 'We've got sooo many exciting things to do.'

Alice looks about as non-plussed as I probably do. 'Such as?'

Rylan appears to be racking his brains. 'I haven't worked them out yet but as soon as I do, I'll let you know.'

'We'll come back to the cottage for *today* only.' I tell Rylan as I collect Alice's painkillers from the nurse's station. 'Mainly because I want to have a proper chat with Gill. After that, well, we'll have to see what happens. Really, I'm dying to get home.'

'Wow! Look at the state of you.' The words are out before I can stop them.

Nathaniel's huddled in the corner in the chair he's been favouring since we arrived. 'Whiskey, I hear.' His hair's more on end than even mine is and he's looking decidedly green around the gills. More importantly, he looks as miserable as sin.

'How come *you* picked them up?' He completely ignores me, but the look he gives Rylan says it all. He's fuming.

'*Someone* had to pick them up, Nate. You're hardly in a fit state, are you? You're probably still over the limit.'

'I'm quite capable of picking my wife and daughter up *myself*, thank you very much. So focus on *your* own wife and leave mine the hell alone.' Nathaniel swigs his water, the pint glass shaking in his hand as he raises it to his lips.

'Go in the lounge, Alice.' Rylan points at the door. 'You pick whatever movie you want and I'll be in shortly with some biscuits.' He watches her go and then bends beside Nathaniel's chair, resting his arm on the edge of it. 'You really are a twat, aren't you? Did you not even think to ask your daughter how she is after her night in the hospital? You're a fucking disgrace, Nate.'

'When I want parenting advice,' Nathaniel begins, his voice weak, yet full of venom. 'You'll be the last person I ask. After all, your missus doesn't even want kids with you. I can't blame her really.'

'What's going on in here?' Then Gill notices me and rushes over. 'Erin!' As we wrap our arms around each other, I notice Rylan rising back to his full height from where he was crouched beside Nathaniel. He'd have been well within his rights to swing at his brother after what he's just said. But he's not like that. Not really. Rylan wouldn't hurt a fly – which is probably why Martha seems to be able to walk all over him like she does.

'How are *you* doing?'

Gill's wearing clothes she'd normally wear for her legs, bums and tums class, instead of the tailored clothes she normally wears, though I suspect they're probably more Karl's preference than hers. She also looks as if she's had about as much sleep as I got last night.

'All the better for seeing you, love.' Her eyes crinkle at the corners as she smiles. 'How's that granddaughter of mine?'

'She's in the lounge – waiting for Rylan and biscuits. They're having a movie morning.'

'Are grandmas allowed to join in?' Gill's smile broadens. 'Though I can't promise not to fall asleep if they're drawing the curtains.'

'I think we could make a space if one were to show up.' Rylan grins at her. It's good to hear his banter with his mother – it reminds me of the old days when I spent every waking moment during the holidays at their house. Karl would be out working and Nathaniel, being older than me and Rylan, was away at University.

He came back just as I left. Before Martha managed to get her claws stuck into Rylan.

'I'll take these into her then.' Gill reaches into the cupboard and pulls out a box of chocolate fingers.

~

'Mum, where's Uncle Rylan?' Alice pokes her head from the lounge as I pass on my way to the stairs.

'I don't know – I thought he was already in there with you.'

'Not yet.'

'I'm sure he'll be along shortly. He said he would be, didn't he?'

'But me and Grandma are waiting to start the film.'

'I'm just off for a shower. Start your film, and you can always start it again if he wants you to.'

'OK.' But she looks disappointed.

As I get undressed, Martha and Rylan's voices echo from the next room. I freeze.

'*Someone* needed to pick them up,' Rylan says.

'But of course that *someone* had to be you, didn't it?'

'Oh give over, Martha. I've had enough of this.'

'Don't think I haven't noticed how the two of you are together. And your brother's noticed it too?' Listening to her raised voice, she clearly thinks no one else is up here. Or maybe she *wants* others to know what she thinks. 'Why do you think he's been constantly pissed since we got here?'

'I don't care what you *think* you've both noticed. No matter what might have happened when we were literally still *kids,* I'm allowed to get along with Erin.'

'Oh, it's more than that.'

'If you can't handle it, then you've got some serious work to do on yourself.'

'And that's all you can say? Are you not even going to *try* to put my mind at rest?'

'Jealousy doesn't suit you, Martha. In fact, you should take a look in that mirror – go on – you'll see how ugly it makes you look.'

'So now you're saying I'm ugly?'

I stifle a giggle. I can just imagine the look on her face right now.

'Maybe I should just clear off and leave you to rekindle things with Erin.'

'Now you're just being daft.'

'I don't think so.'

I flick the shower on in the en suite to drown out their voices and I don't care if they know that I've heard them. Hopefully, she'll hear the water running and feel really stupid.

I feel a million times better after having a shower, and return downstairs for a much-needed coffee. The rumbles of what sounds like a Harry Potter film emit from behind the lounge door as I pass. I get the impression they're all in there, apart from Nathaniel. He's still slumped in exactly the same place as he was when I first got back over an hour ago. Thankfully, he's fallen asleep.

I tiptoe to the other side of the kitchen and silently thank whoever it is who's left a jug of coffee, keeping hot on the stove.

Then I slip on my cardigan and take my coffee out into the autumn sunshine. It might be the only chance I get today for a few moments to myself.

I sink to a chair on the decking, noticing probably for the first time since we arrived, just how beautiful it is around here, no matter what we discovered in the shed on day two. I don't normally notice things like how the sun on a cobweb creates such a kaleidoscope of light, or the motion of the leaves as they flutter from the branches. Yet for some reason, this morning, I do.

Yes, I've got problems, but I'm hugely grateful that Alice is largely unscathed after what happened. I'm also starting to feel more clarity about my own situation. I know now that I want to be free again. I'm well into my thirties and am only too aware that life is passing me by.

I stare at a flock of birds as they set off in formation to warmer climes and wish I could join them. They're as free as I felt when I used to be with Rylan. He allowed me to be who I wanted to be, which couldn't be any more different to how his brother is. He won't be happy until he's turned me into a carbon copy of Gill. Subservient and obedient. One thing this trip has shown me is how much my marriage is choking me and how badly I want to escape from it.

'Hey, you.' I nearly slop my coffee as Rylan appears in front of me. 'How dare you think you could sneak off for a bit of peace?'

'Guilty as charged.' I squint in the sunshine as I look up at him. 'It's stunning round here, don't you think?'

'It's just a shame about the family.' He grins as he follows my gaze to the hills in the distance.

'I'm sorry for causing trouble between you and your wife.' The word *wife* sticks in my throat. There was once, in my teenage fantasies when I thought I'd end up in that role.

'What are you on about?' His grin fades as he threads his thumbs through his belt loops and faces me.

I might as well be honest with him. 'When I went up for a shower before, I heard her going on at you – I didn't mean to listen but well, I couldn't help but overhear.' I stare down into my coffee. What a pair of idiots me and Rylan have been. We could have been happy *together* but instead, he's married Cruella Deville and I'm lumbered with Dick Dastardly.

'*You* haven't caused any trouble.' He steps towards me. 'As I told her before, she's the one with the problem. She'll get over it.'

I let a long breath out. 'I'm just sick of all the drama, Rylan. Life's hard enough without being married to...' My voice trails off. I'd better shut up before I say something I come to regret.

'Hey, are you OK?'

A tear plops down from my chin onto my hand. My emotions are all over the place at the moment. 'I'm really sorry. I'm just tired. And stressed. I want my life to be exactly like this.' I stretch my arm out at the view in front of us. 'Looking at hills and watching birds.'

'I know, Erin. I really do.'

I'm not sure I like the way Rylan's looking at me – it's as though he can see right to my soul. But then, I suppose, he always could. 'I feel like I'm just *existing* with him, in there. The whole thing's having a terrible effect on Alice.'

'She's a grand lass.' He gestures to the house. 'She obviously takes after her mother, doesn't she?'

I can't reply. How can I? I dab my sleeve to my cheek. I can't believe I've allowed myself to get upset. One minute I was feeling at peace, out here on my own, the next, I'm an emotional wreck.

'Come here you.' Rylan holds his arms towards me. 'We can't have you crying when you're supposed to be on holiday.' I allow myself to be pulled to my feet and then to lean into him for a moment. Really, accepting a hug from my brother-in-law is probably one of the stupidest things I can do.

Particularly as my husband is now standing at the window, watching us with an expression on his face which I know only too well.

23

ERIN

THE DOOR SLAMS against the wall as Nathaniel storms towards us. I spring back from Rylan.

'What the fuck do you think you're doing?' Nathaniel grabs him by the scruff of the neck and rams him up against the shed.

'Get your hands off me.'

'Come on then – I'm waiting for an answer.'

'I was comforting her actually.' Rylan reaches for Nathaniel's arms, trying to prise him off, but his brother's rage is holding all the power. 'Which is more than you ever do.'

'Get off him, you bloody idiot,' I shriek. 'We weren't even doing anything.'

'Like hell, you weren't.' He lets go of Rylan then comes at me. 'I just saw you.' He grabs my arm. 'You can get yourself back in here.' He swings his free arm around to point at the house. 'And you can start getting your stuff together. We're going home. *Today.*'

'I'm going nowhere with you.' Fury engulfs me as I shake my arm out of his grip. 'You've been an absolute maniac this week. You're more than welcome to go where the hell you want, but I'm staying right here until my daughter's properly recovered after being in hospital all night.'

'Do you really think I'm going to leave you alone with *him*?'

'How many times? Nothing is going on. I was upset – because of *you*. Rylan was just making sure I was alright.'

'So that's what you're calling it now.' Nathaniel's face twists into a sneer.

'What's all the carrying on out here?' Karl pokes his head from the door. 'Oh, I might have known.' He looks from Rylan to Nathaniel who promptly steps away from me. 'The two of you never fail to disappoint me.'

I sink back to where I started on the decking. I should have known better than to think I could come out here for some time and space on my own. What an utter joke.

'Mum, why won't Dad talk to me?' Alice flounces into the lounge where I'm trying to concentrate on reading a book when really, I'm struggling to keep my eyes open. 'He just said, *see your mum,* when I asked him what we're going to do when I'm better.' She sits beside me. 'He's been ignoring me all day.'

'It's not your fault, love.' I reach out and squeeze her shoulder. 'It's *me* he's upset with. I'm just sorry he's taking it all out on you.'

'I wish Uncle Rylan was my dad.' Alice pouts and luckily, doesn't watch for my reaction as her words strike something into the very core of my being. If she were to look at me more closely, I'm sure my face would give me away.

'Dinner's ready,' Martha calls from the kitchen. I'm still amazed she agreed to cook. Maybe there is a half-decent bone in her body after all. That's assuming that she hasn't laced my portion with arsenic.

'Well, this looks fabulous,' Gill says as she helps herself to a baked potato from the dish in the centre of the table. 'I'm so tired, it's been great not having to cook.'

'Perhaps you shouldn't go clearing off until all hours of the night then, should you?' Karl snaps. 'And I'm still waiting for a proper explanation from you.'

'Not now, eh, Dad,' Kelli says. 'Can't we just have a civilised dinner for once?'

'Civilised, in this family – you must be joking.' Nathaniel fills his plate with salad.

'Give it a rest will you?' It's my turn to snap. 'You've done nothing but ruin this holiday since we got here.' I think I prefer him drunk and insensible this week as opposed to the sarcastic and hungover version that's almost a replica of his father.

'Mum! Stop!'

'*Holiday!*' Nathaniel yells, dropping the serving spoon to his plate with a clatter. 'I'll tell you all something, shall I? My dear wife here,' – he points at me, – 'she didn't even want to be here in the first place, did you, Erin?'

'That makes two of us,' Kelli says. 'And with good reason, judging by the state of things since we've been here.'

'I'll have some of that wine, after all.' Nathaniel grabs the bottle in front of him by the neck and slops some into his glass. 'I might as well just get pissed again, after all, it's not as if I've got a marriage left.'

'That's enough, Nathaniel.' Gill looks close to tears.

'Sorry, Mum, but you know as well as I do that Alice is the only glue holding our marriage together. And it's been this way for years.'

'Oh for goodness sake.' Martha throws her fork onto her plate with a clatter. 'Do we really need all this crap at the dinner table?'

'It makes a change from it being *your* crap, don't you think?' Nathaniel jabs his fork in her direction. 'Anyway, don't play all high and mighty with me – most of the time, Martha, it's *you* that's at the centre of any problems going on in this family.'

'Rylan.' Martha swings around to face him. 'Are you really going to let your brother speak to me like this?'

'Come with me, sweetheart.' Gill grabs hers and Alice's plates and they head for the door. 'You don't need to hear all this. We'll eat together in the kitchen.'

'I'll tell you all something else as well, shall I?' Nathaniel clearly doesn't give a toss about how upset Alice looks as she trudges after her grandma. 'I'm sorry to say this, Martha – you might not want to hear it – but we all know that Erin married the wrong brother, don't we? Maybe it's about time you woke up and smelt the roses.'

Martha, for once, appears to be speechless as Karl gets to his feet.

'I'm going in there as well.' I snatch up my plate before he gets a chance to start on me. 'You need help, you do,' I say to Nathaniel. I feel like picking up the glass of wine and tipping it over his head.

'You can get out as well,' Karl shouts at his son. 'What an absolute disgrace you are. We'll speak about this later.'

'I'm not ten years old anymore, *Dad.* You can't tell me what to do. What will you do if I don't move, eh? Swing a belt at me like you did with Kelli? Put me in hospital to be stitched up? If I'm a disgrace, I learned from the master.'

'Kelli, Ben,' come with me.' I lower my voice as I pause at the door. 'Let's leave them to it.'

As they gather their plates and follow me out, I turn to Kelli and say, 'I think I'm going to get mine and Alice's stuff together. Before someone in this family kills someone.'

24

KELLI

'If you're leaving, I'm going as well.' I follow Erin into the kitchen. Though I have to say that she's handling things pretty well given the state of my brother. He's still ranting and raving with Dad and Rylan. 'But we can't leave my mum with all this.' I set my plate down on the breakfast bar. I'm not even hungry anymore.

'Can't leave me with all *what*? What are you talking about?' Gill looks up from her plate.

'Erin's on about going home, Mum.'

'Now? Today?'

'I want to stay with you, Grandma,' Alice wails. 'I'm not going home with *Dad*.'

'I knew coming here was a mistake – right from the start,' Erin cries. 'What on earth were you hoping for, Gill, getting us all together like this? It's an absolute cesspit.'

'Hey – it's not Mum's fault.'

'Well Joe's certainly getting his wish, isn't he?' Erin closes her eyes for a moment. 'He wanted to bring everything to the surface and shake us all up.'

'It would be almost funny if it wasn't so sad,' says Mum as she rubs at her head.

'Are you alright?'

'It's just a headache. But don't worry about me – I'll be fine.'

I stare back at her. No matter what I've just said to Erin about leaving too, there's no way I'm leaving my mother with this lot to contend with on her own, not without me around to keep an eye on her. The situation is like a volcano.

'This is getting ridiculous.' Karl appears in the doorway. 'Everyone at each other's throat like this. So we'll sit at the table like a proper family and enjoy the food Martha's so kindly prepared for us.'

'*So kindly,*' I mock. 'The woman can do no wrong in your eyes, can she, Dad?'

'Kelli.' Mum frowns at me. 'Look Karl, let's leave things alone until it all calms down – everyone can eat where they feel most comfortable. A civilised family meal is out of the question.'

'You need to watch your mouth.' As Dad's glaring at me, Ben gets up from the stool to stand beside me. I can almost feel the tension crackling from him – he's said all along that he'll step in if my father goes too far. My father doesn't like that I'm seeing him for who he really is. *What* he really is.

'Or else?' I square up to him. 'I'm alright Ben. I can handle this.'

'Kelli, please.' Mum's voice is full of desperation. However, I can do this. I've *got* to do this. I've spent so many years trying to appease and please this man, but finally, I don't care anymore.

'Go on. What are you going to do?' I hold his gaze as he tries to eyeball me.

'Don't push me, Kelli.' Dad's spittle lands in my face and I resist the compulsion to wipe it away. He wants a reaction – *any* reaction.

'Are you planning to clout me over the head again? Because if I need stitches *this time*, I won't be lying to protect you – I'll be pressing charges instead. That's my biggest regret ever – I should have hung you out to dry.'

Alice's jaw is hanging open. Erin's probably going to kill me for carrying on like this in front of her but putting my father in his place is long overdue.

'I'm warning you—'

'Yeah, that's right.' I glance around at my audience. 'This loving father of mine had some issue with my mother when I was eight. I've no idea what it was – it was certainly bugger all to do with me.'

'I mean it—'

'But what I *do* know is that he thought it was perfectly acceptable to take his nasty frustrations out on me–'

'You little—' He raises his hand and I flinch.

'You lay one finger on her and I'll—' Ben jumps between us and amazingly, my father steps back. He'll know that he wouldn't stand a chance against my six-foot-two strapping boyfriend.

'Yeah, Mum knows, don't you, Mum? I had to lie through my teeth at the hospital, then I was kept off school until my injuries healed.'

'I only did what I had to do. We'd have had social workers breathing down our necks. You could have all been taken into care,' Mum sobs.

'You've been a wonderful mother, it's not you I blame for all this – but him…' I jab my trembling finger into my father's face. 'If you think you can carry on threatening me, or my mother, or anyone else for that matter, I've got news for you.'

'You–'

'OK, let's all calm down, shall we?' Rylan comes up behind Dad and looks at me. 'What he did to you back then was despicable, we all know that, but harking on about the past won't solve the present. Come with me, sis.'

'How dare you?' Dad swings around to face Rylan.

'I want to go home too – I've changed my mind. I can't be around that man for a moment longer.' I look at the ever-reddening face of my father as I shake my head.

'Just come with me, will you?' Rylan tugs at my arm. 'Let's have a chat about this.'

Ignoring my father's orders that we apologise to him, I follow my brother towards the hallway, wondering what on earth he could be planning to do or say to me that could change my mind.

He leads me into the lounge and closes the door. 'Right firstly, come here.' He pulls me into a hug and I sob into his shoulder. They're more tears of rage than of sorrow because I've allowed my father to get to me – yet again. 'What an absolute mess this family is – I wouldn't even call it a family, would you?'

'Me, you and Mum are OK, aren't we?' He holds me at arm's length. 'And Alice and Erin?'

'And Ben,' I sniff, gesturing in the direction of the kitchen. 'He could have gone running for those hills with all that's been going on this week. And I could hardly blame him.'

'He's a keeper, Kelli, and you attracted him into your life because you're a decent lass too.' He squeezes my arm. 'Look, I know this is a mess but we've got to see it through. It's only for a couple more days.'

'But it's madness for us to stay – we're just feeding into Dad's need for drama. Why would you not want to leave?'

'I think something's going on with Mum.'

'Like what?'

'Something's going to happen – I don't know what exactly, but trust me on this. And if something *did*, and we weren't here to protect her, we'd never forgive ourselves.'

'What do you mean? Has she said something to you?'

'Kind of – I got back up last night – I was looking for Martha at first.'

'After I'd gone to bed?'

'Yeah, just after. Anyway, I was talking to Mum for a while and sussed out that there's *something* she's not telling us. Not yet, anyway. Something's going to come out – I can just tell.'

'You don't think she's ill or something, do you? She has been a little off lately.' I think back to how adamant on the phone Mum initially was when she contacted me about this holiday. 'Maybe that's the real reason she got us all together like this. To break some news. She might be waiting until the last day.'

'I get the impression that it's something to do with Dad. I've no idea what, but I reckon she's waiting for the right moment. So it's up to us to make sure we give her that chance.'

'OK...'

'So can you hang in here for me Kel – and if we can persuade Erin to do the same? There are only three days left now – we're more than halfway through it.'

'Gosh, whoever says that about a so-called holiday? You're supposed to not want it to end, not to be willing it to pass as quickly as possible.'

'I don't know if Grandad knew exactly what he was doing with ordering us together like this, but I need you to stay.'

'OK.' I sniff. 'But I'm doing it for you and Mum – and no one else.'

25

KELLI

'WHAT'S GOING ON? Where's Ben?'

Martha jumps back from the window and joins Karl as he falls about laughing. Everyone's gone from screaming at one another to – well I don't know what. I really *don't* know what.

'I heard something outside again.' Alice shivers in her nightie. 'Ben went out to look and to make sure no one's there.'

'So where is he then?' I turn around to check the chair in the corner.

There's a banging on the window behind me.

'They've locked both of the doors.' Alice points from one to the other. Then in a softer voice she says, 'They seem to think it's funny to have locked him out.'

'It was her, not me.' Karl points at Martha and fresh laughter erupts from both of them.

I barge between them. 'You're both pathetic.' My voice is a snarl as I twist the key in the lock and open the door. 'Ben,' I call into the darkness before looking back at my father. 'Why would you do such a thing?'

'The lad needs taking down a peg or two.' Dad leans against the breakfast bar and folds his arms as he mutters to Martha. 'I don't know who he thinks he is.'

'It's alright.' Ben steps into the kitchen. 'There's no harm done, is there? Just leave it.' He rests one arm on my shoulder and the other on Alice's as he ushers us out of the room. 'They're not worth it,' he whispers as I turn to head back into the kitchen. 'Don't give them the satisfaction of letting them see how upset you are.'

'Go back to your room and get warm Alice.' I give her a gentle push towards the stairs. 'I'll bring you some hot chocolate in a few minutes.'

'I'll make it,' Ben says. 'You need to keep well away from your father, so stay out of the kitchen for now.'

'Actually, I think we need to stick together. What if he says something untoward when you go back in there?'

'It's like water off a duck's back.' He grins. 'You've heard the stories about my dad, haven't you? Don't worry – I can more than cope with yours after *him*.'

'I'm sorry about what they did to you just then.' I shiver. 'I can't even begin to fathom what they'd get from it.'

'If you could, I don't think we'd even be together.' He laughs. 'Thank God you take after your mum instead.'

'I'm off to find Erin,' I say. 'She seems to be lying low – not that I blame her.'

'Hopefully, she hasn't changed her mind and started packing. The sane ones amongst you need to stick together for these last couple of days.'

'Erin's only staying because I've begged her to, and I'm only staying because Rylan's begged me to,' I tell him. 'And as I mentioned before, it's all for Mum's sake – *only* for Mum's sake. Rylan reckons there's going to be some sort of revelation about something – but Mum seems to be biding her time with whatever it is.'

Ben nods. 'I'm getting that impression as well. So when it happens, we need to be ready for it.'

'It's so quiet around here.' Ben stares up at the ceiling, shadows in the moonlight casting shapes onto his face. 'Especially after all today's aggro.'

'It's reached another level, hasn't it? I warned you this would happen.'

He turns over and traces a line with his finger down the edge of my cheek. 'I didn't say it at the time, but I was proud of you earlier. For standing up for yourself like that.'

'I was quaking inside though.' I shudder at the memory of Dad's face as he eyeballed me.

'It must have taken a lot of guts, but it's the only way not to be brought down by a narcissist.'

'Is that what you really think he is?'

'A hundred per cent.' He leans back onto his pillow. 'And you'll never change him. But you can change yourself, as you are doing.'

'Well, I'm not that defenceless eight-year-old any more, am I? He can't hurt me like he used to.'

'That doesn't mean he won't try. But you've done well staying here – I know you've been feeling like just running away.'

'If it wasn't for Mum...' My words trail off.

'I know.'

We lie in companionable silence for a few minutes, seemingly lost in our own thoughts, until, probably lulled by the sudden peace, and drowsy from the beer he's drunk tonight, Ben's breathing falls into a regular pattern. I envy him for being able to fall asleep so easily, but now he has, I can either lie here with my racing mind or try to distract myself.

I reach for my phone. I'm so wired that I don't know how I'll get any sleep tonight but I'm not getting back up in case anyone's still down there. I've had enough drama for one day and can't face any more confrontations. The amount of alcohol everyone's drinking is pouring even more fuel onto the fire – the later in the day it is, the more volatile things have the potential to become.

I've barely looked at Facebook since I got here, but I've been tagged in a few of the pictures a couple of the others have posted. To an outside eye, we probably look like a normal happy family having a wonderful time together, squirrelled away here in the Yorkshire Dales. Yet that couldn't be further from the reality.

Martha took a picture of us all sitting at the dinner table on our first night. *A very civilised dinner with the in-laws,* says her caption. It was anything but *civilised.*

I flick onto her page. She's also taken a photo of the recycle bin, which with the amount of empties dumped into it, looks shameful. She's written *families drive you to drink.* I untag myself from that one. There's one of her and Dad, captioned *couldn't ask for a better father-in-law,* and I feel like spitting at my phone screen as the words blur before my eyes.

Next, there's a picture of her and Rylan with their arms around each other when we went for our soggy walk on the second day, entitled *my gorgeous hubby.*

Ben's tagged me in a slideshow of pictures he's taken of the hills and fields, saying *beautiful place with my beautiful lady.* I smile at his sleeping form. Several years ago, I couldn't have handled any of this family crap, but now, with him by my side, I can cope with anything and anyone. I love the bones of Mum and Rylan but Ben's my family now and I can only hope I never lose him.

It's after one in the morning. Every time I close my eyes, I see my father's face and the contempt in it when he looked like he was about to hit me earlier. He might have felt guilty for putting me in hospital when I was eight but whatever he might have felt back then seems to have manifested itself as contempt towards me ever since. Ben thinks Dad subconsciously justifies what he did by keeping me at arm's length and treating me as he does.

Half an hour later, and I'm still lying awake. Dad's face has become Martha's and her cackling laugh when she locked Ben out for a 'joke' won't stop echoing in my ears.

Suddenly I wake with a start. I *must* have drifted off for five minutes. But for a moment, I'm unable to separate fact from imagination.

Did I hear Dad's raised voice and my mother crying in the next bedroom? Was I dreaming or was it real?

26

GILL

'I CAN'T STOP THINKING about where you might have been last night.' Karl pokes at my arm. 'What you said earlier just doesn't stack up.'

I don't believe this. He really doesn't give a toss about me – he knows how tired I am after last night. 'I was nearly asleep then.'

'I need to know, Gill.'

My eyes burn with fatigue as I force them open, taking in the shadowy shapes in this unfamiliar room. 'I'm so tired. Just let me sleep please.' I can see myself having to go and sleep on the sofa. That's if he allows me to.

'You're making a complete fool of me.' His voice sharpens. 'I know you are.'

His tone affirms there's no way he's going to leave me alone. And if I don't at least *attempt* to appease him, he'll wake the whole house. We've managed to prevent Erin and Alice and then Kelli and Ben from leaving here by a gnat's hair today, so I need to keep things calm at least until tomorrow. That's when I'm planning to come clean about Jason – I don't think I can put it off any longer.

But tonight I need to shut him off and get back to sleep. I've had enough; *everyone's* had enough for one day and besides, judging from the silence that now surrounds us, the rest of them are sleeping – lucky sods.

Karl leans out of bed and flicks the bedside lamp on. 'Look at me, Gill.'

'Why?' My eyes ache in the sudden glare. He's the last thing I want to look at but if I don't, I'll only make things worse.

'Because I'm your husband and I'm asking you to.'

I turn over to face him, keeping my head on the pillow. He's sitting up now and I study the shadow of his emerging beard in the lamplight. He's still such a good-looking man. The other girls used to be so envious when we first got together. But I'm living proof that looks are not an attribute worth going for. By the time he showed me the ugly side of his personality, it was too late as I was already expecting Nathaniel.

'What is it?'

'You were gone for over *five hours* last night and I still haven't had a straight story out of you.'

'You have – I told you where I went.'

'I want to know exactly who this *woman* was – whose house you claimed to have been in. Then tomorrow, I'll be able to check it out.'

'She's just someone who was kind to me, that's all. Like I've already told you.' His reaction if I were to tell him the truth would be unimaginable. I wouldn't dare to tell him without anyone else present to protect me. I'm not sure how the others will react yet, but at least it won't be with the threats that Karl's capable of.

'She must have asked about *me*. What did you tell her?'

As is always the case, Karl has to make it all about *him*. He's only bothered about what other people might be thinking or saying. But at least he seems to believe that I *was* at some woman's house. Maybe soon, he'll leave me alone and allow me to sleep.

'Nothing much, to be honest.'

'So you *were* talking about me then. This is why I don't trust you, Gill. I'm not having you going around bad-mouthing me behind my back.'

'I haven't bad-mouthed you to anyone. Look, Karl, please. I'm so tired. Just let me go to sleep.'

'You've changed, you have – and not for the better.' Karl's voice has changed too – over the last minute or so, it's become more of a snarl.

'I haven't. But I just want to sleep.' It's not the first time he's prevented me from sleeping. It's one of his control tactics. Sometimes I think it would be easier if he just clocked me around the face to keep me in line, instead of subjecting me to this. Especially since I know exactly what will be coming any time at all.

'What are you really up to Gill? You've been behaving oddly this week. In fact, it's been going on since my dad died.'

What he means is that I'm not bowing down to him as much as I used to. Plus, I've been defending myself a bit more – being around Jason has made me stronger.

'I haven't. It's just, well, things are bound to be different this week when we're around all the family instead of being here on our own, aren't they? And I'm missing your dad as well.' Since *he* mentioned his dad, I might as well bring him in too – it might just distract Karl from his initial line of questioning. What I'm hoping for, is that he doesn't try to extricate the 'woman's' address from me – so he can carry out his threat of checking things out himself.

'Oh, and another thing – that bloody *Ben* should never have been allowed to take part in this holiday.' Karl leans back against his pillows. Perhaps the relaxed stance he's suddenly adopted means he's starting to tire of our conversation and will leave me alone soon. Though I'm probably too agitated now to be able to fall asleep. I can't believe I'm still stuck here, with *him*. I'm sick of living like this and I'll be damned if I'm spending what's left of my days in this way.

'Why?'

'My father specified that this was to be a *family* holiday and Ben is *not* family. But as usual, my wishes were totally disregarded.'

'He and Kelli *live* together.'

'*She's* changed as well.'

'No, she hasn't.'

'You heard how she spoke to me earlier, and I might add, you did absolutely nothing to challenge her about it.'

'I happen to think—'

'Well, if she thinks she's going to get away with it, she can think again.'

'Please Karl. Just let me go to bloody sleep, will you? Can't we just leave this conversation until the morning?'

'I don't know who the hell you think you are, taking that tone with me. What's got into you?' He props himself up on his elbows as he hisses the words into my face.

I turn away. The smell of his wine-laced and sour breath is not something I want in my face. I swallow hard. Now I've decided to do something about how I've been living, I can hardly believe that I've managed to survive as I have for so long. What an utter waste of my life. Why didn't I do something about it sooner?

'Like I said before,' he continues. 'I don't like this change in you and if it continues, well you know exactly what's going to happen.'

Here we go. Yes, I know *exactly* what he's capable of inflicting on me. Which is why it's for the best if I get in there *first* and tell my side of things to my family before he does. Tomorrow. It's going to have to be tomorrow. No way can I put up with another night like this again.

'Do you want to lose everyone, Gill?' Karl's voice has an almost mocking edge. 'And *everything*.'

'Of course I don't.' The tears I've been holding back since he woke me well up in my eyes. Why have I been so weak? How have I let myself end up like this? Cowering from him in a dark bedroom because I'm frightened of disturbing the others. Apart from Martha, everyone else is fed up with all the drama too.

'You *know* what you're risking if you carry on as you are, dear.'

How can he call me *dear* when he's threatening me like this? As time progresses, he's becoming more and more warped.

'I honestly thought we'd got through all this, but clearly, you need a reminder, Gill.'

'You've spent the last twenty-odd years controlling me with it all – I hardly need reminding.' I can't hold the tears back anymore. I lean against my pillow and let them roll from the corners of my eyes, down the sides of my head and into my ears. I'm sick of crying and I'm even more sick of allowing *this* man to be the one who makes me cry.

We fall into silence for a moment as I stifle my sobs and try to cry silently. I've become good at it over the years. If he catches me crying, it either irritates him or further empowers him.

As I swipe at my tears, he turns to face me. 'Eh, don't cry love.' He brushes a tear from the side of my head. He's bloody deranged. Every last one of my blinkers has fallen away and I know I won't go back on what I've decided to do. 'There's no need for things to be *this* unhappy between us. We just need things to go back to how they were, you know, *before*.'

'Before *what*?'

'Before we came here. Before Dad died. Oh, I don't know – I just don't like this new version of you.'

'I don't know what you mean.'

'Yes, you do. You clear off when you feel like it, you argue back, but Gill, to be totally honest – it's the way you look at me these days – it's awful – I don't know what's got into you.'

'Maybe your dad's death has brought it home to me about how short life is.'

'What's that supposed to mean?'

His question hangs between us for a few moments. Really, we both know what it means.

'And while we're on the subject of people changing, you'd better have a word with Kelli in the morning.'

'About what?'

'She can't speak to me like she did earlier. I won't be ridiculed like that. Especially in front of strangers.'

He's back to Ben again. 'Ben's not a stranger – he's Kelli's partner.'

'So you'll do that for me will you, Gill?' His voice is gentle as he completely ignores what I've just said. 'You'll help our daughter to see sense?'

What choice do I have other than to nod?

'Because I'd hate to be *forced* to turn our family against you. I can't imagine what the truth would do to them all, especially little Alice.'

'You couldn't turn them against me.'

'Oh, I think we both know that I could.'

Fresh tears begin to erupt. Maybe he's right – maybe he really could. Nathaniel and Rylan have spent so much energy in previous years trying to court favour with him that they might be easy for Karl to manipulate.

'More importantly—'

Bloody hell – he's still going.

'I'd hate for our revelations to land you in prison. And you would go to prison, Gill – after what you did.'

I turn my head away from him and scrunch my eyes together, letting some more tears squeeze from beneath my eyelids. 'I hear you, Karl. Now please, leave me be and let me sleep.'

DAY FIVE

27

GILL

EVENTUALLY, sleep takes hold of Karl. After the amount of drink he seems to be consuming, it was only a matter of time. But I hardly dare breathe, let alone move, for fear of waking him again. Not until I'm certain that he's fallen into a deep enough sleep. Then I'm out of here.

Every atom of me is screaming to get away from him. He's threatened me relentlessly ever since the children were little – mainly about how my past actions would put me in prison if he were to decide to take us down that road. And he's dangled it like a noose above my head for long enough.

It's got to the point where seeing my days out being locked up in a cell would be preferable to how I've been living all this time, trapped in misery with Karl. And now Joe's passed away, there's even less to imprison me in my marriage – at least Joe used to stick up for me. When he was there, I had someone on my side.

However, there's one other person on my side now and even if the others are unable to forgive what I have to tell them, I know that I've got Jason firmly in my corner.

'Karl would be incriminating *himself* for not speaking the truth back when he had the chance,' he said, more kindly than I could ever have predicted.

'You're the only person other than Karl who now knows my secret from the past.' Despite the gentleness of his words, I was still shaking. I'd built up and built up to telling him and had prepared myself for, and had come to expect the worst.

'It's totally safe with me but I do think you need to bring it out into the open once and for all.' He refilled my glass, clearly sensing that I needed a drop more of something to settle me down. 'If only to break the hold he's had over you for so many years.'

'I know.' My voice was small and every bit of me sagged at his words.

'I can be with you when you tell them if it makes it easier.'

I stared back at him, knowing he really meant it, and would be more than willing to put himself in that position for me. It invited fresh tears to my eyes.

'There's also,' Jason continued, 'the possibility Karl could be charged with blackmail and coercive control.'

'Do you think so?'

'Definitely. It'll be a lot for you to handle but if you can stay strong, I'm sure you could see it through – obviously, I'd be with you every step of the way.'

'I really don't deserve you,' I sniffed.

Karl's breathing has become a rhythmic snore. I turn my head and stare into his face, now silhouetted in the moonlight which filters around the edge of the curtains. To think I once *loved* this man. However, five years his junior, I guess I was more in love with what he represented. He took me out all the time and showered me with expensive perfume and jewellery. He wanted to spend every waking (and sleeping) moment with me, and within less than a month, he was staying at my flat every night.

Within another month, his constant presence was enough to drive my beleaguered flatmate to the point where she left in a fit of temper.

'This was supposed to be *our* flat,' she screamed at me. 'I can't believe you've allowed him to force me out like he's doing.'

'It *is* our flat.' I reached for her arm. 'Come and sit down. Let's talk about this.'

'Either you get rid of him or there's nothing to talk about.'

'Come on – he's my boyfriend. You can't give me an ultimatum like that.'

'He's a controlling lowlife.' She snatched her arm away. 'You need to wake up and smell the shit he's going to shovel your way.'

'You're just jealous.'

'Of *that*?' She gestured towards a framed photo of us that he'd stood on the mantlepiece. 'He's taking you over. Why can't you see what I can see? You're in trouble, girl, you mark my words. You stay with him and you're in deep trouble.'

'Why are you being like this? Why can't you just be happy for me?'

'*Happy?*' Her voice became a screech. 'You should have heard what he said to me earlier.'

'What?'

'Ask *him*,' she said. 'Anyway, there's no way I'm sticking around here. If you're going to choose some arsehole of a man over a ten-year friendship, I'll leave you to get on with it.'

She banged out of our flat and I watched from the window as she slid into her car which was already laden with her bags and boxes.

I rang her over and over but she wouldn't speak to me again. So I never found out what Karl had said to her.

In the coming months, I unwittingly shed my other friends one by one until there was no one left. Even my sisters faded into obscurity.

'You've changed,' one said, shortly after my wedding to Karl. 'And it's not for the better.'

'How do you mean?' I carried on stuffing washing into the machine, keeping my back to her as my face flushed. Really, I knew exactly what she meant.'

'Where's your fire gone, Gill? All your hopes for your career? Your daredevil spirit?'

I glanced towards the photo of the kids stuck on the fridge and shrugged. 'Things have changed, haven't they?'

'But you've become so…' she seemed to be searching for the right word, *mouse-like*. We've both noticed it.'

My other sister didn't mince her words when I visited her a couple of days later.

'Do you do *everything* he tells you?' She shook her head as I threaded my arms into my coat. 'You've only been here for an hour.'

'I said I'd be back for five, that's all.'

'Why? Oh, don't tell me. He'll want his dinner cooking.'

'He likes us to spend our evenings together. We've got his mother moving in next month so he wants to make the most of the time before that.'

'So no doubt we'll see even less of you after that.' She rose to her feet and came towards me. 'You're in the prime of your life.' She rested a hand on my arm. 'Yes, I know you've got responsibilities but that doesn't mean you can't have a *bit* of freedom now and again. He's treating you like his servant,' she went on. 'And it's perfectly obvious that he doesn't like *us* coming round.'

'He does. He's just a bit reserved around other people, that's all.'

'We're not *other people*, Gill. We're family. He's trying to cut you off – you really need to see it for yourself.'

My lovely sisters are both dead now, having eventually given up on me. In the end, we only seemed to get together for births, deaths and marriages and never managed to capture the closeness we'd once known as girls. I can see now that this was Karl's plan all along. He didn't want me to be close to *anyone.*

With his own mother, he was even insecure that she preferred me to him and, to be honest, she probably did.

'Why do you suck up to my parents like you do?'

Instead of being grateful that I was sitting and wrapping Christmas gifts that I'd bought for Joe and Marilyn, he was sneering at me.

'I don't – I just think it's important that the kids have plenty of contact with them.'

'You do it for *you,* not for them.'

'You should be pleased that I get along with them so well, not berating me for it. What the hell's up with you?'

'It's just, that, if I wanted to spend so much time with my parents, I'd have never moved out, would I? And you're just as bad with the children.'

'What's that supposed to mean?'

'Pandering to their every whim. All Kelli has to do is whimper from her pram and you're there in a second.'

'It's called being a parent, Karl.' I stopped myself from adding, *you should try it sometime.*

'The sooner she joins the others and goes to nursery, the better. I might have some semblance of a wife back then.'

'Don't wish their time away – it goes so fast as it is.' I glanced towards Kelli as she kicked in her bouncer. The six months since she'd been born had passed in the blink of an eye.

'It's like you're obsessed with the three of them, that's all. Look.' He waved his arms around wildly. 'Do we really need so many photographs of them cluttering up the place?'

'Yes, we do.' I silently dared him to do anything with my precious pictures.

The sound of his snoring is making me seethe. His mouth has dropped open, making a hellish clicking sound. I can't bear to remain here, at the side of him. The morning feels a long time away.

I edge from the bed, an inch at a time until my feet sink into the deep pile of the carpet. Then I feel around in the darkness for my dressing gown. Wrapping myself in it is like someone giving me a warm hug. And after Karl's words before he went to sleep, I badly need one of those right now.

I grab my phone and get to my feet, my head swooning with the movement. It takes a few moments for the dizziness to subside but when it has, I tiptoe to the door and out of the room, grateful to be free of him, if only for a few hours. As I close the door after myself, I hold my breath as he grunts. Then after a few moments, his snoring falls into a louder and slightly longer rhythm than it was before. It'll be a miracle if no one else hears the sound that's now literally vibrating through the house.

I tiptoe down the stairs. Hopefully, he drank enough earlier to anesthetise him for the remainder of the night. I can't imagine getting much sleep with everything I've got on my mind right now but I have to try. Especially with what I've got coming.

The pan of hot chocolate Ben made earlier is still lukewarm. While I wait for it to reheat, I tug my phone from my dressing gown pocket and try to focus on the words that are blurring in front of my eyes.

I have a new message. Oh my God, it's Jason. Just because I've promised to bring everything out into the open shouldn't have given him the green light to text me. Not when our agreement is for me to *always* text him first. Karl could have so easily picked my phone up and seen this. I let a long breath out and open it up.

I haven't heard from you since I dropped you off last night. I'm really hoping everything's OK and that you haven't changed your mind. Please let me know what's going on as I can't think about anything else. Not only that, but I'm worried about you. xx

The message was sent two hours ago, so it's too late to reply to it now. I hit delete, slide the volume button to silent in case he thinks to text me again, and drop the phone back into my pocket.

The hot liquid sizzles as I pour it into a mug and then fill the empty pan with cold water. Curling my fingers around the warmth of the mug, I lean back against the kitchen counter and sweep my gaze over the room. There are shoes, jumpers, glasses, books and magazines *everywhere.* All signs of habitation by a family. My family. I wonder what it was like before – when Joyce and Bruce lived here. I sigh again. Life is just so short. I'm terrified about what's coming but there's no other way. Tonight is probably the last night where everything is still as it was.

Tomorrow, everything is going to change.

28

ERIN

RYLAN'S an absolute natural with Alice. They're probably not aware of how closely I'm watching them over the top of the book I'm feigning interest in.

'Oh no,' he yells as she overtakes him on the racetrack. 'You're far too good at this for me.' He shuffles forward to the edge of his seat.

She laughs as she tosses her hair back behind her shoulder. 'Told you I'd whoop your arse.'

'Alice Hawthorne. You're *not* allowed to say that word.'

'Why?' She glances sideways at him. '*You* said it when we first arrived.'

'I did no such thing.' He doesn't take his eyes off the screen.

'You did! When you wanted to play Monopoly.'

'Oh gosh – Don't remind me about that.' He pulls a face. 'Oh look, now what have you gone and made me do – I've crashed.'

'It's not my fault you're rubbish, Uncle Rylan. You keep crashing into all the trees.' Her brows knit in concentration as she narrows her eyes at the TV screen, letting out a whoop as she crosses the finish line.

'High five.' Rylan rests his controller on the coffee table and raises his palm towards her.

She reciprocates, laughing. 'Rematch?' Her eyes are shining for the first time since we arrived here. I might not always approve of the PlayStation but today, I'll give it the benefit of the doubt. Though really, the uplift in her mood is all down to Rylan.

If only things could have turned out differently.

'I don't know about that. You're far too good for me. Anyway...' He pats his belly. 'How about we have some breakfast before I have another go at beating you? Are *you* ready for some, Erin?' He turns to look at me.

It's heartwarming, yet also painful to see them together like this – to observe how she lights up when she's in Rylan's company. It's the polar opposite of what she's like when she's with Nathaniel. Around him, she wilts like a dying flower. Even more so, lately.

'Uncle Rylan's right.' I get to my feet. 'It's time you had a break from that and had some breakfast. Let's go and see what there is. I'm thinking... pancakes.'

'Yeah!' She jumps up. 'Can we? I'll make them – Uncle Rylan, you can help me.'

'Oh I can, can I?' He laughs. 'I can definitely see a mini-Erin in the making here and it's not just the red hair that's the convincer.'

Alice races from the lounge and as we follow her out, we're just in time to see her disappear across the hallway into the kitchen.

'It's hard to believe this is the same girl who was laid up in the hospital with a concussion just over twenty-four hours ago.' Rylan laughs.

'The whole thing's completely shaken me up though. If that car had been going any faster, who knows what could have happened to her?'

'I know.' He rests his hand on my shoulder. 'But it didn't, did it?'

'And all because your stupid brother's head,' – I'm on a roll now, – 'was so far up his own arse that he wasn't watching her properly, even when she was right beside him.'

'If it's any consolation, he's really beating himself up about it.'

'Where's your mum?' I pause in the doorway of the lounge and glance up the stairs. 'I haven't seen her yet this morning.'

'She's gone back to bed for a bit,' he replies, stopping in the doorway of the lounge. 'She said she hardly got any sleep last night and that she's got a splitting headache.'

'I could hear someone snoring if that's what it was,' I reply. 'I'm so glad I brought my earplugs, that's all I can say.'

'Kelli thinks she might have heard them arguing in the night,' he continues, ushering me back into the lounge. He waits for the door to fall closed behind us before he continues. 'And Mum *crying*. I found her on the sofa when I was going out for my run this morning.'

'*Crying*? You're joking.'

'This is why I need you and Kelli to stay. Mum needs all the support she can get.' Then his look of concern becomes a grin as he winks at me. 'Well, that's *one* of the reasons.'

There's a light in his eyes that I remember only too well but I can't allow myself to linger there. No way. I don't know why he seems to be flirting with me all of a sudden. He's rejected me twice in the past so I'm not going to let him have a third opportunity. Therefore, I need to keep the topic of our conversation on Gill.

'But she's still got to go home with your dad when this week's over and done with.'

'Which is why I'm going to talk to her as soon as I get a chance,' he replies as he pulls the door open and pokes his head into the hallway. 'Sorry, I'm just making sure no one's hanging around and listening in.' He pulls a face as he closes it again before lowering his voice some more. 'Kelli's been on about Mum potentially staying with her and Ben.'

Something lifts within me. With *two* of her kids on her side, Gill may be more willing to do something about her situation at long last. And if *she* can do it... 'God, I know I shouldn't wish a marriage split on anyone but that would be a really good step forward. I can't believe what I've seen from your dad this week. There comes a point where enough has to be enough.'

'Tell me about it.'

As I follow Rylan into the kitchen, I allow myself to admit that I'm not only referring to Gill and Karl's marriage with that statement.

'Where have *you* just come from?' Nathaniel glances up from his phone and eyes us with suspicion. Shit. I should probably have allowed a few minutes after Rylan before coming in here instead of entering the kitchen at the same time.

'I've just been in the lounge watching Alice on her game.'

'But she's in *here*.' He points at her as she opens and closes all the cupboard doors.

'I went to the loo,' I fib. 'Do you require any further information, Nathaniel?'

Rylan locks eyes with me for a moment and I feel a twist within my chest. This is another reason why I didn't want to be here this week – I knew all my old feelings would come flooding back. I've buried them as deep as I can for so many years but am not sure I can do it anymore. And from the way Rylan looks at me, I'm almost certain he feels the same.

'Mum, what do you want on your pancake?'

'Oh, er, you're making *me* one? Maple syrup for me please.'

'Of course.' She smiles at me.

I hover around the breakfast bar, unsure whether to hang around under my husband's scrutinising gaze, or go in search of Kelli and Ben whose voices I can hear elsewhere in the house. I'd quite like to know more about how they're planning to convince Gill to stay with them.

Martha's sitting in the armchair nearest the fire, filing her nails, in what has been Nathaniel's usual perch up to now. It's the one place in the room where getting warm is possible. It's chilly everywhere else. She might pretend to be engrossed in what she's doing, but she'll be listening closely to all that's going on around her.

Sinking to a stool at the opposite end of the breakfast bar from my husband, I watch Alice and Rylan enjoying themselves as they prepare the pancake batter.

'There's more flour on you than in that bowl,' I laugh, pointing at my daughter. 'And your grandma will have a fit when she sees the floor.'

I glance up to notice Martha scowling at me. There's a surprise. Perhaps I'd better keep quiet.

And just watch.

Without planning or wanting it to, my mind drifts back to the last place I usually allow it to go. Back to twelve years ago, when the path of my life altered beyond all recognition.

'I've had a *massive* row with Martha.' There was a scratch down the side of Rylan's face, a crust of blood beneath his nose and his shirt was torn. 'She's thrown me out of the house.'

A flicker of hope danced within me as I opened the door wider. They'd rowed before but this one looked like she'd turned violent. *Surely he wouldn't put up with that*?

'Sorry to hijack your evening, Nate,' Rylan called as he slipped his trainers off on the doormat. 'I hope you've got some beers in the fridge.'

'He's away on a course tonight.' I gestured at the lounge door. 'Go through. I'll get you a beer – you look like you could use one.'

'Oh, I don't know if me hanging around if Nate's not here is such a good idea,' he replied. 'You know what—'

'Don't be daft. Besides, where else are you going to go? Gill would have a fit if you turned up at her house in that state.' I leaned against the wall as I looked at him. Closer inspection showed scratches on his arms as well. 'It must have been *some* row. You look like you've been in a boxing ring with an alley-cat.'

'I feel like I have.' He pauses. 'I guess I could go to one of my mates, but then Martha would be more likely to look for me there.'

'Don't you think she'll look *here*?'

'After all that's gone on, she's less likely to. She doesn't even know that Nathaniel and me are back on speaking terms.'

'What's the problem then? Go and sit down, then you can tell me all about it.'

'So what happened?'

'Martha got into my work phone and went through my messages.' He swigged from his bottle.

'And?' I raised mine to my lips as well.

'I'm friendly with one – a female colleague called Becky.'

'Friendly?

'Yeah – we have to work together quite a lot and she's been going through a bit of shit at home so we've messaged outside work two or three times. She's my mate and I care about her. Anyway, she puts an x on the end of some of her messages – but she does that with everyone,' he adds quickly.

'You're definitely just friends?' I leaned forward in my seat.

'Absolutely. But you don't need me to tell you how Martha doesn't like me anywhere *near* other women.'

'So then what happened?'

'Well. Martha rang Becky and was bloody awful to her – God knows how I'm going to explain it away at work. And then, when I tried to grab my phone back, Martha hit me in the face with it. Things went from there really – slapping, punching, you know – the usual.'

'Please don't tell me what she's done is usual.'

He nodded and closed his eyes. 'She's fine, most of the time, really she is. It's just these jealous and violent rages she gets into. Oh, I'm sorry – I shouldn't be landing all my problems on you.'

'You absolutely should. You can't be going through this on your own. You need support, plus, as I'm sure you don't need me to say, you need to leave her.'

'It doesn't happen that often, really, in fact—'

'You mean if you fall into the line she wants you to walk and do as you're told? Come on, Rylan, if one of your mates was going through this, what would you tell them to do?'

'Right now, the only thing I want to say is, have you got any more of these?' He held his beer bottle aloft.

'Blimey, you've soon downed that!'

As the drink flowed and the evening flew by in each other's company, beer became brandy, and counselling became reminiscing. It was the first time we'd been alone since Rylan had ditched me for Martha when we were eighteen. Eight years had elapsed but what hadn't, it seemed, was the attraction between us.

'Oh my God,' he said as we lay in each other's arms on the sofa. 'That should never have happened.'

I closed my eyes as he stroked my hair. It felt so right to be back with him – it was like I'd finally come home. 'You have to leave her.' It was more of a question than a statement. When he didn't respond, I added, 'and I'd leave Nathaniel.'

I opened my eyes but what I didn't see in his eyes was reciprocity, instead, it was fear.

'Nathaniel and me have only just got things back on track.' He sat up and covered himself over with a cushion, moving slightly away from me. 'And I know things can be rocky, but I *do* love Martha.'

'Men who love their wives don't sleep with their former girlfriends.' I suddenly felt cold, not just at the loss of his warmth but at the rejection I sensed was coming my way.

'I forgot myself, Erin. I was enjoying being in your company again. But I made my decision back then and I also made my wedding vows. *Shit!*' He reached for his boxers. 'I can't believe I allowed this to happen. She might have accused me of it, but I've never been unfaithful to her before. Ever.'

'And I've never been unfaithful to Nathaniel either.' I reached for the dress I'd been wearing and held it against myself, feeling suddenly vulnerable for being naked in front of Rylan. 'But it's not as if we're strangers to each other, is it?'

'It can't ever happen again.' Rylan stepped into his jeans and tugged them up. 'Ever.'

'You wanted it as much as I did, so you can't put all the blame onto me.' I held the dress tighter against myself.

'I'm not trying to but, God, I feel terrible.' He shrugged himself back into his ripped shirt. 'I've cheated on my wife. I've slept with my *brother's* wife. Oh Erin, what have we done?'

Tears were running down my face by then. 'You're making me feel so *used*. I let you hurt me once before and now—'

'Sssh.' He leapt back to my side on the sofa and enveloped me in his arms. 'The last thing I'd ever want to do is to hurt you.'

'But you have. Twice now.'

'Listen to me, Erin – in another life, in another time—'

'It should have been in *this* life and in *this* time.' The tears flowed faster. 'I've always loved you, Rylan.'

'So why did you marry my brother? That's what I don't understand.'

'He was there. It was easy and I was stupid. Need I say more?'

'He can't ever find out about this, Erin.' Rylan held me away from him and we locked eyes. 'I couldn't do it to him. Or Martha. Plus, can you imagine how my parents would react?'

'Why does it have to be about everyone else?' I wailed. 'And why are you still talking like it's all my fault? You're the one that came here – you let it happen as much as I did.'

'I'm sorry – really I am. This wasn't supposed to happen. But I'm going to have to go home – back to my wife.'

Then he gasped and sat back beside me as though he'd suddenly been winded. 'Shit – I can't believe we've been so irresponsible. I obviously wasn't planning to— so I didn't bring any— What if?'

'It's OK. I'm on the pill.' I tugged my dress back over my head and raked my fingers through my hair which felt like a bird's nest after our previous activity. An image of Martha's sleek, shiny hair and perfectly made-up face flashed into my mind. I would never be able to live up to her standards. No wonder he was going back.

'Thank the Lord for that. Look, Erin.' He reached for my hand. 'Can we just draw a line under this and pretend it never happened? It would blow the whole family apart if it ever got out.'

'I'm hardly going to say anything, am I?'

'I'm really sorry. Truly I am. But I'm going to go now. I need to try and sort things out with Martha.'

'I'd suggest you take a shower first.' I pointed towards the door.

'Good point. I'll just tell her I've been to the gym.'

While the water ran in the en suite above me, I hugged a cushion to my chest and wept. Rylan had made a very valid point when he'd asked why I'd married Nathaniel.

At the time, I was fond of him – maybe I even thought I loved him or could *grow* to love him. But I certainly wasn't *in love* with him. Staying in the lives of Gill and Kelli was possibly a factor too. And because my mother had recently died, perhaps marrying Nathaniel offered safety and security in some strange way. Thinking back, he was just in the right place at the right time. Or in the wrong place at the wrong time, as hindsight has shown me.

And then, exactly six weeks later, I discovered I was pregnant.

29

ERIN

'WHEY, HEY!' Rylan watches as Alice throws her pancake almost as high as the ceiling before catching it in her pan again. 'You've been practicing that.'

'Me and Mum make them at home – don't we, Mum?'

'She does have an unfair advantage, I'll give her that. Anyway, the proof will be in what they taste like, won't it?'

'We should give your mum the first one, Alice, don't you think?'

'Keep it down, will you?' Nathaniel's scowl deepens.

'Sorry.' Alice puts the pan back on the stove and Rylan tugs at one of her plaits as he pulls a face at Nathaniel's expense. She giggles and as I'm the only one who notices the exchange between them, I smile too. They have so much fun together that it's almost criminal that Martha denied him the chance of fatherhood. She should have told him right from the start that she wasn't interested in having children. But by the time she did, she already had him hook, line and sinker.

Rylan folds a tea towel over his arm and slides a plate with the first pancake on it in front of me, as he puts on a funny chef voice.

'This circular delicacy you can see on this platter consists of the finest ingredients in its composition.'

Alice giggles again and I resist the temptation to draw the comparison to the creation of my lovely daughter twelve years ago. As I cut into my pancake, Rylan stands behind Alice and drapes his arms over her shoulders as they await my verdict.

'Perfect,' I declare.

Nathaniel slams his phone onto the breakfast bar. 'I want a word with you, Erin,' he snarls. 'Outside. Now.'

'But Mum's eating her pancake.'

'You finish it, love.' Keen to avoid yet another scene in front of Alice, I push my plate away. 'You can make me another one when I come back in.' The best thing to do is to take whatever Nathaniel's about to rage about well away from everyone else. 'Come on then.' I glare at my husband who twists on his heels and marches to the door in front of me.

'Is everything OK?' Rylan mouths as I turn to look at him.

'Mind your own bloody business,' Martha snaps from the corner.

I follow Nathaniel to the same spot I was sitting in yesterday when Rylan found me. 'So what's your problem then?' I turn to face him and fold my arms, unconsciously creating a barrier between us.

'You are.' His teeth look as yellow as a rat's out here in the autumn sunshine. He hasn't shaved all week and doesn't appear to have brushed his teeth either. 'I've been watching you.'

'Evidently,' I retort. 'And what have you concluded this time?' I allow my eyes to meet his and see nothing in them other than hatred. It's sometimes hard to imagine that I was ever in love with him – perhaps I never really was.

'What's going on with you and Rylan?' He jerks his head in the direction of the house. 'Because *something* is. And I'm not the only one who's noticed.'

'Nothing's *going on* as you put it. Just because he happens to be a damn sight better company than you've been this week doesn't mean—'

'I've noticed that he's all over Alice as well. I want to bloody know what's going on.'

'He's probably trying to make up for *you* not spending any time with her. How you've behaved this week is disgraceful, Nathaniel.' I almost sound as though I'm chastising Alice here. 'What the hell's the matter with you?'

'Don't you *dare* try to shift this onto me.' He leans closer. 'I'm the one asking the questions here.' He points his finger towards his chest.

'Ask away then.' I lock eyes with him. Not that I'm going to tell him this yet but we are so over. The moment we get home, I'm off straight to see a solicitor.

'I need to ask you something.' His voice softens slightly but I don't relax. 'It's been eating away at me for a while.'

'God – what now?' My stomach clenches in anticipation of what could be coming.

'And I want the truth for once in your life.' There's a slight shake in his finger as he points at me. It's either anxiety or drink withdrawal. Or perhaps a combination.

'*What is it?*'

'Is—' He pauses and swallows. 'Right, I'm just going to come out and ask this.' He swallows again as he continues to lock eyes with me. 'Is Alice even *my* daughter?'

I step back from him and something in how I look away from him and direct my gaze to the ground must betray me. I quickly avert my eyes to reconnect with his but before I've had the chance to reply, he gets in there first.

'She's *his,* isn't she?' His face is pinched and white, his hands curled into fists as they hang at his side. How I handle this from now on will determine whether one of those fists will end up being swung into my face. 'My *brother's* kid.' He spits the word *brother* out like a piece of fatty meat.

'What on earth makes you think that?' I keep my arms folded and rub at the tops of them as though trying to comfort myself, all the time looking back into his eyes as though that, in itself, will portray my innocence.

'I can't believe I've been so stupid – not when the truth's been staring at me all along.' He gestures towards the kitchen window. If I were to tear my gaze from his, I'd probably see everyone standing there, watching us.

'What truth? What are you talking about?'

'Don't lie to me! Don't you dare lie!'

'Of course she isn't—'

'She even looks like him.' His voice cracks as he steps closer to me and I move back again. 'The spitting image, in fact.'

'He's your brother for God's sake,' I reply, my voice almost a squeak. 'That's hardly a surprise. Her hair's a totally different—'

'You've been fucking him, haven't you?' He's bellowing now. 'What an absolute *idiot* I've been. All these years I've been bringing up my *brother's* kid!'

We both turn to the movement in the porch. There, hanging onto every word, is Martha.

'Is this true?' She storms over to me, grabbing me by the scruff of my jumper and ramming me against the pergola before I have the chance to defend myself.

'Of course it isn't,' I squeak as her grip tightens on my neck. 'It's just some half-baked theory my husband's concocted. So get your hands off me.' I thrash my arms out in an attempt to free myself.

'He's bloody right, isn't he? It's only now, that I can see it for myself.' She tightens her grip on me. 'I always knew there was something between the two of you. You're an absolute snake, Erin.' She tugs me towards her and then rams me back so hard and fast that my head smacks against the wood behind me. I wrestle again to get away but I'm no match for her. She's at the gym nearly every day from what I've heard.

'Martha. Stop it!' Rylan's voice echoes from the doorway.

'You fucking bitch.' She bangs my head against the pergola for a second time and my head swoons. Is someone going to help me or are they just going to watch until she knocks me unconscious? I can only pray someone's taken Alice into another room where she can't see what's going on.

'You walk around as though you're some kind of fucking saint when all the time you've been fucking my husband.'

'Once.' Rylan comes up behind us.

'So it's true then? You—'

'It happened *once*. We were drunk and—'

'And that's supposed to make me feel better, is it? You're nothing but a lying, cheating bastard.' Letting me go, she swings around and lunges at him. But at least she's given me the chance to get away from her. 'After what you've done—'

'What the hell's going on out here?' Karl appears in the porch.

'Let me past.' I push past him. 'I need to get to my daughter.'

30

KELLI

'AREN'T you glad we decided to stay up here out of the way this morning?' I reach for Ben's hand as we lay side by side on the bed, each with our noses stuck in a book. 'It sounds like it could be all kicking off down there again.'

'I'm still looking forward to the horse riding.' He rests his book face down on his chest. 'It'll be the highlight of the week.' He winks at me.

'Well we're not joining the others until the *last* minute,' I say. 'At least up here, we can just *be*, instead of having to navigate the endless angst and family politics swirling around down there.'

'I agree but we're going to have to show our faces soon,' he replies. 'If only to check that Alice is OK.'

'Auntie Kelli, they're all fighting out there and I don't know what to do.'

'Speak of the devil.' I sit bolt upright at the sound of my niece's voice at our bedroom door.

'Can I come in?' She sounds really upset.

'Of course you can.' Ben drops his book onto the bedside table and swings his legs over the side of the bed. 'Come in.'

I do the same as Alice rushes into the room, her face streaked with tears.

'What on earth's going on?'

'Auntie Martha had her hands around Mum's neck and she hit her head. And everyone's yelling at each other in the garden.'

'That's what all that noise was.' Ben jerks his thumb in the direction of the other side of the house from where we are. 'At first, we thought it was the TV.'

'Come here you.' I pat the bed by my side and Alice sits in the space I've created. 'Do you know what they've fallen out about?'

She shakes her head. 'One minute, Mum was eating a pancake which me and Uncle Rylan had made for her, and then the next, Dad was dragging her off outside and they were arguing and—'

'Hang on,' Ben says. 'What do you mean, *dragged her*?'

'Well, he told her to *get outside now* but then Martha went out too, and that's when she grabbed Mum and,' – she takes a jagged breath in, – 'I'm scared she might have hurt her. I wanted to stop it all but I didn't dare to go out.'

'Oh, you poor love.' I wrap my arms around her. 'They shouldn't be carrying on like this in front of you. None of them should.'

'I heard someone saying my name as well.' Alice's voice wobbles. 'And I didn't know if I'd done something wrong. And then Grandad went out there and he was shouting too.' She buries her face into my shoulder. 'What if he comes up here and starts shouting at me next? He doesn't even like me – I know he doesn't.'

'I'd better find out what's going on?' Ben says but just as he stands from the bed, Mum comes rushing in, looking breathless and red-faced.

'Have you heard all that down there?' She stops in her tracks as she notices Alice. 'Oh my poor sweetheart, are you alright?'

'No,' she sobs. 'I'm really scared.'

'How much have you heard, Alice?'

'I don't know.' She looks down at her hands.

'None of us know what's going on. Do you?'

'Ben, would you do me an enormous favour?' Mum says as she steps more into the room. 'Just take Alice somewhere out of the way while I speak to Kelli for a few minutes.'

'Why can't I stay?' Alice wails. 'I want to stay with you, Auntie Kelli.'

'I tell you what, let's get her *completely* out of here.' I stand from the bed and scan the room for my trainers. 'Ben, take Alice down to the car and I'll be along in a minute when I've had a quick word with Mum. Is that alright with you, Alice?'

She nods and wipes at her tears with the back of her hand. 'Can we go out the front way though? I don't want to walk past everyone. I don't want anyone to shout at me.'

'The poor love.' I sink back to the bed as the door falls closed behind them. 'What the hell's going on down there, Mum? Did you hear much of it?'

'Every single word, unfortunately.' She stands facing me as she lets out a long sigh. 'My room's only just above the kitchen, isn't it? And my window was ajar.'

'And?' I look at her.

'Nathaniel was accusing Erin of keeping something pretty big from him. *Really* big.'

'Like *what*?' Perhaps this might explain why he's been more miserable than usual this week. Normally, I'd have bet every penny I had that he'd be responsible for any problems the two of them might be having. But by the tone of Mum's voice, the responsibility may lie with Erin.

'Like the fact... are you ready for this?' Mum's voice is shaking. It's always like this when she's imparting big news.

'Just tell me.'

'Like the fact that *Rylan* might be Alice's dad, *not* Nathaniel.' She sits beside me.

I turn and stare at Mum. 'No – that's totally ridiculous. They split up well before Alice was ever even heard of.'

'That's what I thought at first.' Mum shakes her head. 'But I've been listening to them all for a few minutes. Nathaniel was raving on about how he's always had a feeling something didn't add up and the way Erin reacted to him, well—'

'What do you mean?'

'Well – let's just say, her denial didn't sound very plausible at all. And Rylan even admitted that something had once happened between them. He said it was *only* once.'

'So it's true then? But what about Martha? Presumably, from her going for Erin, she knows?'

'You could say that. From what I could hear from up here, she just exploded when Rylan admitted things. So I'm staying out of the way until things have calmed down.'

'Why don't you come with us?'

'No – I'm going to stay here.'

'But why?' I stare at my mother wondering why on earth she'd want to stay amongst this lot with what's going on.

'When Erin's ready to talk, she'll need someone to be here for her. I don't care what she might or might not have done in the past – I can't leave her at the mercy of *that* lot.'

'What's going to happen now?'

Mum's shoulders slump. 'Oh, I don't know. I've got to the point where little would surprise me with this family anymore.'

'I'd better get down there – to Alice.' I slide my phone from the bedside table. 'Listen, we won't go far and we'll be back straight away if you need us to be.' I tap my phone. 'Call if you need me, and if it really gets out of hand, call the bloody police on them.'

'Don't worry.' She sniffs. 'I've already considered that and I don't give a monkey's what your dad thinks.'

I tuck my knees up into my chest, shielding my eyes from the sun as Ben teaches Alice how to skim stones across the water.

As I sit beside the tranquil tarn which reflects the hills and valleys around it, I feel calmer already. The sound of birds which have not yet migrated and distant sheep has lowered my stress levels and it's good to feel the warmth of the autumn sun combined with the gentle breeze on my face. I'm free of the lot of them. For now, anyway.

I keep telling myself that no matter what fresh hell has broken out today, we've made it to day five. Only two more days to go and then we're out of here. However, I still need to work on Mum to persuade her that staying with Ben and I is a far better option for her than continuing as she is with Dad.

'Yes,' Alice cries out. 'I did it.' She twists herself around. 'Did you see that, Auntie Kelli – I skimmed one!'

'Of course,' I call back. 'I was watching the whole time.'

Ben turns around and grins. 'She's a natural. She's better than me already.'

I can't help but recall how good *Rylan's* always been at skimming stones and as Alice turns again to invite me to join in, for the first time, I see Rylan's dimples, the slant of his eyes and the angle of his forehead.

Why the truth has suddenly come out after all these years, I have no idea.

'I just need to check something on my phone, hon,' I call back to Alice. 'You keep practising and I'll be with you shortly.'

> Just checking you're OK, Erin. Mum's probably told you that we've taken Alice out of the way of it all. If you need us, we're only ten minutes away. xx

I don't really expect a response but immediately the dots appear on the screen, signalling that she's replying.

Thanks. I really appreciate it. And yeah, I've got away from it all. I'm currently locked in the bathroom - lol! xx

It's the best place for you by the sounds of things. We'll give it a bit longer for things to calm down – Mum said she'd text when it's safe to come back. We can talk then, if you like. xx

No prizes for guessing what you'll want to talk about... xx

As Ben flops beside me, I show him Erin's text. 'It's all true then.' He looks up from the screen. 'It's a bloody mess, I'll give you that.'

'She does look like him, you know.' I nod towards Alice. 'Rylan, I mean. I can't believe I've only just seen it.'

'Are you coming, Auntie Kelli?'

'Just give me a couple more minutes while I have a quick word with Ben. I say we then go and find somewhere that sells ice cream.'

'Yessss. I'm hungry now.' Her face falls. 'Since I didn't get my pancakes.'

I turn back to Ben and lower my voice. 'Did you hear what she said about my dad before?' I tip pebbles from one hand into the other as I speak. 'It breaks my heart.'

'What does?'

'How Alice thinks it's all her fault and she's frightened that her grandad's going to shout at her. I can't bear to think she's suffering so much – especially with the same fear I was forced to grow up with.' I watch as she continues skimming stones, her hair billowing out behind her in the breeze. It's good to see her playing like a child instead of being caught up in all the grown-up crap.

'I know – it's awful.' Ben's voice takes on a darker tone. 'I know he's your dad but he really needs cutting down to size. For him to make his own granddaughter feel like she does is shameful.'

I glance at Ben, taken aback by the uncharacteristic venom in his voice and the hard line of his jaw. He's a gentle giant usually, but I've gathered from a few people in his past that he's got a sting within him. It takes a lot to push him over the line but once he's gone over it...

'Look, Uncle Ben. I just did one three times better than before.'

'She called me *Uncle* Ben.' He nudges me as his face relaxes into a smile. If only my father's anger dissolved so easily.

'Can we go and find some ice cream now?' Alice brushes her hands down her jeans.

'Of course we can.' I smile, then to Ben, I say, 'Then we'll probably have to go back and face the music.'

31

KELLI

NATE'S OUTSIDE on the decking as we pull up on the gravel beside him. It's an unseasonably warm late October day but I'm not grumbling – far from it. I might have one of the most dysfunctional families on the planet, but there can be no denying that we're staying in the most beautiful of places with this unexpected gift of sunshine. One thing having such a difficult relationship with my father has taught me is to count my blessings wherever I can.

'You two go inside,' I say, giving Alice a gentle nudge in the direction of the door. 'I'll just have a quick word with your dad.'

Who isn't your dad by the sounds of it.

'Come on Uncle Ben,' she says as he ducks under the door. 'I'll teach you how to play Kart Rider.'

'You OK?' I say to my brother as I sit beside him and tug my jumper off.

'What do you think?' He swigs from a beer bottle, his words already slurred. I don't think I've ever seen him looking so unkempt. Usually, he hasn't got a hair out of place and he wouldn't be seen dead scruffing around in the holey joggers he's wearing.

Whatever's been going on between Rylan and Erin, they've done a good number on him.

'You won't find your answers in the bottom of a bottle.'

'No, but I can try.' He looks at me with watery eyes. 'I take it you've heard then?'

'Mum's told me bits and pieces. Thankfully, I was out of the way when it all kicked off before. So, have you managed to sort anything out yet?'

'Like what?'

'I don't know, but everyone shouting and being violent isn't going to achieve anything? Where is everyone?'

'*She's* gone upstairs with Mum.' His voice hardens.

'Who? *Erin*?'

'Yeah, she's the one in the wrong, yet she always manages to get all the sympathy, doesn't she? It's *me* Mum should be talking to and supporting, not *her*.'

It's like he can't even bear to say Erin's name. 'Where's everyone else?'

He shrugs. 'Don't know – don't care. But with a bit of luck, Rylan's getting the shit kicked out of him by either Dad or Martha.'

I strain to listen for any commotion but thankfully, all I can hear is birdsong and the flutter of leaves. Rylan's car isn't here, whatever that means. I wouldn't blame him if he's cleared off – not one bit.

'I always suspected I wasn't Alice's dad.' Nathaniel stares straight ahead, his voice flat.

'Give over. No, you didn't.'

'I did – deep down. I just wouldn't admit it to myself.' He drains his beer and then reaches under his seat for another one.'

'Have you got one for me?'

'I suppose so.' He takes the lid off the one in his hand, passes it to me and reaches for another.

I enjoy the feel of the first swig sliding down my throat as I wait for Nathaniel to continue.

'We were barely having sex back then,' he says. 'In fact, it pretty much stopped apart from the rare time when we were drunk – it was like that from the moment we got married.'

'Whoa!' I hold my hand up to him. 'TMI.'

It really is too much information. I'd prefer *not* to know what my brothers get up to, or in this case, *don't* get up to.

'Then suddenly she was up for it all the time,' he goes on, ignoring what I've just said. 'I always thought the dates were completely off when she told me she was pregnant, but whenever I brought it up, she insisted Alice had just been born early.'

'I remember you saying something about it at the time.'

'Two months early.' He takes another swig from his beer. 'I mentioned the baby's so-called prematurity to the midwife when Erin was in labour but she didn't seem to know what I was on about. I should have sensed something was wrong there and then. Perhaps I did – I just chose to bury it.'

'You've *never* mentioned any of that to me. Look Nathaniel – since you seem more *together* than I was expecting you to be, perhaps you need to talk to Erin? Get things out in the open between you, once and for all.'

'That's what I was trying to do before, but all hell broke loose when I asked her for the truth, didn't it?'

'*Talking* to her. Not *shouting* at her.'

'What's the bloody point? Look, I've brought that girl up as my own, and now I find out...' His voice trails off and his head bows. I turn to look at him, shocked to see tears in his eyes. My brother *never* cries. Rylan's told me that he cried when our grandma died but I was too young to remember that. She'd been a fixture within our home for several years from what I've been told, always there to spend time with when Nathaniel and Rylan got home from school, and then suddenly, after several months confined to her bed, she was gone. I have little memory of her, or this time but apparently, it hit Nathaniel really hard.

'It sounds like you don't even know for certain yet. She could still be yours.'

'I do know, Kelli – I really do. I should never have just ignored it like I did,' he says. 'Instead, I've let it gnaw away at me like a disease, this suspicion that she might not be mine. I tried, I really did, just to bury it.'

'Just talk to your wife, Nate.'

'I might not be the best father in the world but I happen to love that girl.' His eyes bulge with tears now.

'I know you do.' I reach for his hand.

His tears spill over. I'm probably the only person today who's shown him any kindness. 'I just can't believe this is happening, Kelli – that Erin could do this to me. I mean, what sort of a woman *knowingly* lets a man bring a child up that isn't even his?'

I stare down at the floor. I haven't got an answer for that.

'Look, the person who's the most important in all this is *Alice*. Whatever happens now, you have to remember that. And until you know for sure—'

'I'm not saying she isn't, but what about *me*? What am *I* supposed to do now? We can hardly all go on living together.'

'Well, if you won't talk to Erin, then I will. We're all jumping to conclusions yet we don't know her side of the story yet.'

'OK.' He rubs at his eyes. 'Look, I know I've been a dick this week but I've had my reasons. Things haven't been good for a while and I haven't known how to handle it.'

'Come here.'

I lean in for a hug and miraculously, my brother reciprocates. It's the first time he's hugged me since I came out of hospital at eight years old.

I poke my head into the lounge as I pass. Ben and Alice are absorbed with the PlayStation game.

'Who's winning?' I ask.

'Alice, of course.'

She giggles as I let the door fall closed and tiptoe over to Ben. 'Thank you,' I whisper into his ear. 'You're a love. I've spoken to Nathaniel and now I'm off to find Erin. Can you keep this one entertained for a bit longer?'

'Of course I can.' He smiles without averting his eyes from the screen. I squeeze his shoulder. He doesn't look like he minds too much.

'Can I come in?' Mum and Erin are sitting together on Erin's bed as I push the door into her room. 'It's only me.'

'Thanks for taking Alice.' Erin sniffs. She looks as dreadful as my brother does. Whatever she might have done, she certainly seems to be paying the price for it.

'It was no trouble at all. We just went skimming stones and had an ice cream.'

'She'll have liked that.' Mum looks grateful for my intrusion. If I know her correctly, she'll be struggling with her role in this situation – she hates to be stuck in the middle of conflict.

'Ben's well chuffed because she called him Uncle Ben for the first time.'

'Aww, that's nice,' says Mum. 'Where is she now?'

'She and Ben are on the PlayStation,' I reply. 'She's OK. She knows something's going on, but hasn't got a clue what it is yet.'

'I'm going to have to talk to her.' Erin lowers her gaze. 'What's going on needs to come from me. I can only hope that somehow, she'll be able to forgive me.'

'So it's true then?'

Her silence says it all.

Mum nods.

'It only ever happened once.' Erin wrings her hands in her lap as she speaks. 'Rylan turned up one night when Nathaniel was away on a course and we both had too much to drink.' She stares down at the carpet as she talks. 'We regretted it bitterly afterwards and vowed it was a one-off and no one would ever have to know.'

'But then you were pregnant?'

She bows her head even more. 'At the time, I thought there was still a *chance* it could have been Nathaniel's.'

'Oh, Erin.' I sink onto the bed beside her as fresh tears roll down her face. Part of me wants to be angry with her but I've known her for the best part of twenty years and love her like a sister. Instead, I take her hand and say, 'So what happens now?'

'I don't know.' Her voice is a whisper. 'Where's Rylan? How's he handling all this?'

'He's gone off somewhere,' Mum replies. 'Probably to get his head around it all. It's not every day you suddenly become the father of an eleven-year-old, no matter how wonderful she is.'

'What about Martha?'

'She's gone with Karl, looking for him.' Her expression darkens. 'I can only hope they don't manage to find him.'

32

GILL

THE COTTAGE IS EERILY quiet as I venture back downstairs. I've left Kelli with Erin in her room while I go to check on Alice. I poke my head into the lounge, but instead of finding her and Ben in there, I find Nathaniel passed out on the sofa. I stare at him for a moment – I can't imagine the agony he must be in, having learned not only that he isn't Alice's father, but also that his wife and brother were unfaithful to him. It might have been some years ago but that won't stop it from hurting like hell.

As I allow the lounge door to close behind me, I walk closer to the sofa. He's a little too still for my liking and I can't see his chest moving up and down. 'Nathaniel.' I shake him. It's reminiscent of the days when as my firstborn, I'd sit beside his cot for hours, obsessed with the rise and fall of his chest.

'What?' He turns over to face away from me and promptly falls straight back to sleep. As I step away, a familiar thud of pain lands behind my left eye. This, along with the sudden dizziness, sends me sprawling into the chair behind me. I sit for a few moments, as I allow the pain, along with the wooziness to subside. As I've been warned, mornings are the time when I most need to take it easy.

And this morning, I did anything but. And I can't imagine that the stress and lack of sleep are helping me.

'Where's Alice?' I ask Ben, who's preparing some food in the kitchen. I still feel a little spaced out but after a snooze in the armchair, the pain seems to have shifted.

'It's very kind of you to be sorting that,' – I gesture at the dish, – 'but I can't imagine there'll be much of an appetite for food at the moment.' I for one, couldn't eat a thing.

'Well, it'll be here if anyone wants it when it's ready. As for Alice, I'm not sure.' His smile fades and he takes on a troubled expression. 'Martha said something to her when she came back with Karl, and I haven't seen her since.'

'Martha did? What did she say? Did you hear?'

'I didn't catch it, to be honest. But Alice didn't hang around after that.'

'So where's Martha now?'

'In the other room, with Karl.' He gestures in the direction of the dining room.

'Just them?'

'As far as I know.' Then he lowers his voice to say, 'I don't think anyone will be flocking in there to join them.' He smiles again. It's easy to see what my daughter sees in Ben – he has such a twinkle about him. He peers more closely at me. 'Are you OK, Gill? You're looking a bit peaky.'

'I'm fine, thanks. I've just had one of my headaches again.'

'It's no wonder with all that's been going on.'

I open the kitchen door, noticing the gap where Rylan's car usually is. 'I take it Rylan hasn't turned up yet then?'

Ben shakes his head. 'I can't say I blame him.'

'It's an utter mess, isn't it? To be honest, you've done well to hang around this week.'

'I can't say it's been easy but as you know, I love Kelli,' he replies as he sprinkles cheese over the dish he's assembled. 'I came to support her and I want to support *you* as well.'

The familiar heat of tears stabs at the back of my eyes. 'I know. She's told me you're on board if I were to decide to come and stay with you.'

'And we *really* think you should.' His eyes are warm and sincere. 'We'll look after you, you know.'

At his kind words, the tears threaten to spill over and I do my best to blink them away. 'Let's just see what happens, shall we?' What I can't tell him is that he might just change his tune when he hears what I've still got to reveal to them all. With everything that's gone on today, I haven't been given the chance to come out with it yet and I keep wondering if this is fate's way of forcing me to keep quiet. However, I can't imagine how Jason would react if I were to go back on my commitment to tell the truth at long last. No – I wouldn't do that to him. I don't think he'd let me anyway.

'Was Alice OK when you were both playing the game before?' I jerk my head in the direction of the lounge.

'She seemed to be – it definitely distracted her from it all.'

'I'd better go and look for her. She needs to hear about it all from Erin – and no one else.'

'So it's definitely true then?'

I nod. 'I'm afraid so – subject to confirmation from a DNA test. What an absolute mess.' I lean into the hallway. 'Alice.' My voice rings into the void. 'Come in here for a minute, will you?'

As I wait for her footsteps to reverberate on the stairs, I head back into the kitchen and slide a mug from the cupboard. Really, I want wine but I'd better keep a clear head for now. There's far too much going on within our pressure cooker of a family. Who knows what's going to come next?

'You could be forgiven for pouring something stronger than coffee.' Ben laughs as though he's read my mind. 'Especially after the day we've all had so far.'

What I don't say is how, when I've said what I've got to say, it's going to get a whole lot worse.

I'm both excited and terrified in equal measure.

~

'Has a car just pulled up?' Ben closes the oven door and folds the tea towel into quarters as he glances at where headlights permeate the edges of the kitchen blind.

'I think so.' I pull the curtain to one side. Even in the semi-darkness, there is no escaping the outline of my youngest son. 'It's Rylan – thank goodness for that.'

Rylan looks uncertain as he pokes his head around the kitchen door. 'Where are they?'

'Who?' The way things are right now, he could mean anyone.

'Dad and Martha, for starters.'

'It's alright. They're in the other room. But never mind them – are *you* OK? I was worried when you took off like that. And then you haven't been answering your phone.'

He steps into the kitchen and shivers. 'Just struggling to take it all in, you know.'

'I bet you are.' I don't add that I am as well. All this has come as a hell of a shock and I can't imagine how it's going to affect poor Nathaniel. At some point, when he sobers up, he's going to need all the support I can give him. And I have no idea how he and Erin will get through this as a couple. Things between them seem to have been hanging by a thread already.

He looks around the room before saying, 'Has Alice got any idea about what's going on yet?'

'Not exactly. Not as far as I know anyway. However...' – Ben's words suddenly come back to me, – 'now you come to mention it, there's every chance Martha could have let something slip to her.' Something twists in my gut and I stop myself from saying what I *really* want to say about Martha.

'There's no way this kind of news should come from anyone other than Erin,' Rylan says, with pain sparking from his eyes.

'You're right – I've tried calling her down and—'

'She's probably keeping well out of the way.'

'I'll check outside, shall I?' He jerks his head back towards the door through which he's recently emerged. 'While you check upstairs.'

I rush from the kitchen, first looking into the lounge even though I've already checked in there. Nathaniel's still sleeping, oblivious to it all, so I head up the stairs, calling Alice's name as I look into her room and then open and close all the doors of all the others.

'What's up?' Erin and Kelli appear in the doorways of their rooms.

'We're looking for Alice. Has she been back up here since I left you?'

They shake their heads in unison, firstly looking puzzled, then panicked.

'I thought she was downstairs.'

'Don't worry,' I try to keep my voice calm. 'I'm sure she won't have gone far.' I return to Alice's room, stepping over a mound of clothes to look inside her wardrobe. Then I drop to the carpet to check under her bed. Really, I wouldn't expect to find her in either place – perhaps when she was small, this cottage would have been perfect for her to have instigated a game of hide and seek, but not now.

'I thought she was in the lounge with Ben.' Kelli's suddenly behind me, in Alice's doorway, tugging her cardigan on.

'She was, but then I think Martha's said something to her, and—'

'She'd better bloody not have done.' As I meet Kelli back on the landing, Erin's darting to the top of the stairs.

'Oh God.' Kelli's hand flies to her mouth. 'What's she gone and said to her?'

'I don't know yet.' We pursue Erin down the stairs. 'But knowing her as we do, it probably isn't anything nice.'

Rylan's in the hallway as we reach the bottom. 'She's not outside,' he says, seeming to avoid Erin's eyes. It sounds like they're going to have a lot of talking to do as well.

'She's not in here either.' I can't keep the panic out of my voice as I gesture back to the hallway. She's eleven years old, it's nearly dark outside and it looks as though Martha's gone and enlightened her in the worst possible way about the situation she's unwittingly at the centre of. Martha's got every right to be upset but to inflict her venom on an innocent eleven-year-old is unforgivable.

'What's going on?' Speak of the devil. Karl and Martha appear in the dining room doorway, one behind the other.

'We can't find Alice, that's what.' Not that I expect any help from either of *them*.

'What did you say to her?' Erin marches towards Martha, stopping with her face an inch away.

'Don't be bloody blaming me for your shortcomings as a parent, Erin.' Her voice drips with bitterness. 'If *you* don't know where your daughter is, how the hell do you expect *me* to?'

'Just tell me what you said to her?'

'That's between the two of us.' A ghost of a smirk is playing on her lips.

I stare at Martha. I've tried, I've really tried over the years to get along with my daughter-in-law, if only for Rylan's sake. However, right at this moment, I want to slap that smirk clean off her face. 'Please, Martha – it's important – what did you say to her?'

Martha looks thoughtful but also looks to be relishing her moment of power.

'Just bloody tell me – we don't know where she's gone,' Erin snaps. 'Regardless of what you might think of *me*, she's still a kid.'

Karl twists his neck to look at her, which seems to be what she needs to force her into speaking.

'I reckoned that she had the right to know what sort of people her parents are. Her *real* parents, that is.'

'You're a nasty bitch.' Erin flies at her. Instinctively, Kelli and I go after her to prevent a fight breaking out between them but Karl's already in the middle of them.

'People who are unfaithful in their marriages haven't got the right to judge others.' He might have Erin's wrist tightly in his grip but he's looking straight at me.

'Get your hands off me.' She writhes in his grasp. 'I need to find my daughter.'

'You've got no right to raise your voice to anyone after what *you've* done.' Karl lets go of her wrist but pushes her back by her shoulder as she attempts to surge forward again. 'You're nothing but a whore. And as for *you.*' His gaze moves from Erin to Rylan. 'I'm ashamed to call you my son.'

He lets Erin go and she immediately lunges towards the door. 'I'm going to find my daughter.'

As Karl steps towards Rylan, I hold my breath. Yes, Rylan's behaved terribly towards his brother but if Karl lays one hand on him I won't be responsible for my actions.

'I'm not scared of you, Dad.' He stands firm and squares his shoulders. 'Not anymore. Nor do I give a shit about what you think of me. In fact, the only person's opinion that matters to me is my mother's. She's *always* been there for me, no matter what. While *you...*'

'I reckon it's time you all knew the truth about your *mother*.' He spits the word out like it's something that's been stuck between his teeth. 'How she's not the saint you all seem to think she is. What do you say, Gill? Do you want to tell them or shall I?'

A prickling sensation is crawling up my back. Even if Karl doesn't say what I'm certain he's about to right at this moment, he's certainly opened the floodgates for me to be questioned by everyone later.

I swallow hard. This could be it now. I need to stop him, though really, maybe everything *should* come out into the open. Not only about what I'd already planned to tell them about Jason but *everything* else as well. *The whole lot.*

However, my granddaughter is still goodness knows where and finding her comes first. 'The most important thing before anything else is that we get out there and find Alice,' I say. As if I'm having to convince Karl of this. He's supposed to be her grandad.

'No. Go on, Karl. I want to hear what you've got to say first.' While still glaring at Erin, Martha steps forward and stands at Karl's side. I dread to think what she's said to poor Alice that's caused her to run off.

'Go on then, Karl.' The strangled voice coming from within doesn't even sound like me. This is the moment I've dreaded for nearly two decades but I can't let him have his power over me any longer. 'Do your worst – I don't care anymore. One thing this *holiday* has shown me is that I can't go on with you anymore. So, when we get home I'm going to stay with Ben and Kelli. And then, I want a divorce.'

'Oh, you think so, do you?'

'No – I know so. No matter where I end up after this, I'm going to be *free* of you.'

My gaze darts from Karl to Kelli who looks smug as she stares at her father.

'You don't have to stay with him,' she's been saying this over and over for months now. 'You'd be far happier without him, Mum, I know it would be hard to start with, but eventually, you'd be able to properly *live* again.'

If only.

Since Joe died, Kelli's reminders of how I can *live rather than just exist* have increased in intensity.

'I worry now Grandad's not around to keep an eye on things,' she's told me more than once. 'Please Mum, you've spent your life looking after us lot – let us look after you for a change.'

She thinks there's nothing to stop me.

Only she's wrong.

Still, at what I've just said, Karl's turning a rather interesting shade of crimson. But any moment now, he's going to explode – thank God the kids are here. Hopefully, he'll just storm off somewhere rather than taking his anger out on me.

'There's only one place you're going, *lady*, and we both know exactly where that is.'

'Tell me what he's going on about, Mum?' Kelli looks from him to me. 'And don't worry. There's nothing he could say that—'

'You need to face facts,' Karl roars. 'The lot of you. Gill here, pure as the driven snow Gill – well she isn't the person you all thought she was. Far from it, in fact.'

How Nathaniel is still asleep through there is anyone's guess.

'So who is she then?' Rylan laughs. 'Go on *Dad*, enlighten us, why don't you, instead of playing your warped mind games. I for one, am sick of listening to them.'

'I'll tell you exactly who she is, shall I?' Karl's face hardens. 'What she is.'

'Get on with it then.'

'Your mother is *nothing* but a murderer.' He spits each word out one at a time, enunciating each one.

For a moment, silence cloaks the room and a hand of fear squeezes at my stomach. My head's pounding behind my eyes again. I knew this week wouldn't be pretty but I had no idea just how ugly it could possibly get.

'How on earth have you worked that one out?' Rylan laughs, breaking the quiet.

'*She,*' he points at me. 'Killed your grandmother.'

A second hush sweeps over us that's so palpable, I could almost reach out and touch it. I can't look at anyone – how can I after what he's just told them? They'll know from my face and my silence that he's telling the truth.

'Yeah, that's right.' He looks from one face to another. 'She *murdered* my mother.'

Kelli spins around to face me, her expression difficult to read. 'Is this what he's had over you all these years, Mum?' Her voice is far calmer than I would have expected. 'All his veiled threats and barbed comments?'

I nod – I don't trust myself to speak. What can I say anyway? Karl's telling his version of the truth and I always knew this would come out one day. But now it has, I'm scared – really scared. Of going to prison, naturally, but I'm even more scared that my children will turn against me – they'd have every right to.

'Didn't you all hear what I just said?' Karl bellows. He's obviously not quite received the reaction he was counting on.

'Yeah, we heard you, Dad.' Rylan's as still as a rock as I wait for him to fully react. He adored his grandmother and the way I'm standing here, just rooted to the spot, will be confirmation enough of what he's just been told. But what nobody's been told yet is *my* version of the truth.

Karl laughs. It's a manic sound, matching the look in his eyes. The fact that Rylan and Kelli don't seem to be responding in the way he probably thinks they should, probably means all hell is about to break loose. 'You're both looking at me like *I've* done something wrong – not *her*.'

Thank God Nathaniel's stayed asleep. At least one of them is in blissful ignorance from all this. For now, anyway.

'Tell us what happened, Mum?' Rylan's voice is surprisingly even. He's probably in shock.

'She forced a pillow over a poor defenceless old woman's face while she suffocated to death, that's what happened.' Karl jabs his finger in my direction. '*Your* grandmother's face. I've kept her nasty secret for all these years so you lot didn't have to grow up without a mother, when really, I should have let her rot in prison.'

'It's what she wanted me to do.' My voice is so small, it's barely perceptible. 'She begged me to help her.'

For a moment, nobody moves, not even Martha. The faces of

my children and Ben display shock and possibly, though I can't quite read it – horror.

'So it's like what happened with the couple who lived here before?' Kelli eventually asks.

'And you've known about this for all this time, Dad?' Nathaniel emerges from the lounge with lines from the sofa down one side of his face. He must have been listening.

'Who rattled *your* cage?' Martha glances at him. 'Decided to sober up now, have you?'

'You'd better all get saying your goodbyes to her.' Karl lowers his voice as he pulls his phone from his pocket. 'For I've kept quiet about what she did for long enough. It's time for your mother to be where I should have had her sent in the first place.'

'No – Dad – just wait!'

I feel sick. And I feel like I can't breathe. I need to get away from them all. I need to get out of here.

Now.

33

GILL

I GRAPPLE for my bag which is still hanging on the back of one of the breakfast bar chairs as I dash through the kitchen.

'Stop right there,' Karl yells, but I'm out of the back door before he can come after me. Hopefully, even in their shocked state, one of my kids will manage to hold him back for a few minutes to let me get away. I hurtle towards the car but as I fumble to get the keys in the ignition, he's already out of the door and closing in on me.

I grapple around, managing to lock the doors with a second to spare before he yanks at the handle.

'Oh my God – oh my God.' The car doesn't start straight away. 'Come on.'

I can hear the muffled shouts of my husband as he thumps against the window. If I don't get away soon, he's going to smash his fist right through the glass.

'Come on – come on.' I twist the key again.

The others burst from the doorway as the engine suddenly roars into life. 'Thank God.'

As I ram the gearstick into first gear, Karl lurches to stand right in front of the car. I rev the engine, once, twice, three times. What will I do if he doesn't move? He knows I won't drive the car at him in front of our children.

Or maybe I will.

With the fourth rev, I let the handbrake off. Karl dodges to the side just in time. I glance in my mirror to see him shaking his fists after me. Perhaps I *should* have run him over. If I could get away with it, I'd love to permanently be free of this bully, the man who's made my life a misery for as long as I can remember.

But now that I've managed to get away from him, all that matters is finding my granddaughter.

Tears roll down my cheeks as I comb the country roads, shining full-beam headlights into each nook and cranny. It's been well over an hour since anyone saw her and according to the car's thermometer, it's only three degrees out there. She's at risk of being run over, being picked up by some maniac, or being out all night and freezing to death.

If I don't come across her in the next twenty minutes or so, I'll have to find a phone and call the police. Though Erin's probably called them by now – I haven't even got my phone with me to liaise with her.

'Please God, let her be alright,' I mutter into the silence of the car. She's all that matters right now. Everything else can come later. I'd serve a thousand prison sentences as long as she's safe. Then it dawns on me.

I've got an idea where she might have gone. It's a slim chance but I can't think of anywhere else.

I park the car around the back of the row of terraced cottages and open the gate into Jason's backyard while muttering yet another silent prayer for my grandaughter's safety.

Jason wouldn't have been able to call me as my phone's back at the cottage so at least Karl can't track me. Luckily, it's all locked up and if Karl tries to get into it, he'll find out that I've changed the password.

Jason opens the door before I even reach it. 'I had a feeling it'd be you.' He smiles and holds his arms out. 'And you look like you could do with a hug.'

'How did you know it was me?' Briefly, I step into his arms before springing back again. I'm far too wired to accept a hug from *anyone* right now.

'I must've tried calling you umpteen times. To let you know that Alice turned up here.'

She appears behind him and a wave of relief crashes over me. I've never been so happy to see her little face.

'Oh, thank goodness. I've been so worried about you, sweetheart.'

'I'm sorry, Grandma. But I didn't know where else to go and I was wandering around for a while but when I got to this row of cottages, I remembered it was the same ones we'd been to before–'

'She knocked on three other doors before she got to mine.' Jason smiles.

'It's OK.' I draw her towards me and breathe the scent of her strawberry shampoo as I bury my face into her hair. 'Everything's going to be OK.'

But is it?

'Before we get into anything, I'd better send a message to let them all know we're safe – can I borrow your phone, Jason?'

He gestures to where it's resting on the arm of the sofa. 'Have a sit down with Alice and I'll fix us a drink. Do you want your usual or are you planning to drive?'

'My usual would be good, thanks.' I don't answer his question about going back. If I have anything to do with it, there's no way that me *or* Alice are going back to the cottage tonight. I need time to think and to work out how we'll go forward from this. But I can't just leave my kids hanging. I'll have to let them know that me and Alice are safe.

Kelli - it's me. I just wanted to let you know that I'm safe and Alice is safe too – can you let Erin know I've got her?

OMG! I've been in a right panic. Where are you? Whose phone is this?

Never mind that – I've borrowed it from someone. We're going to come back tomorrow and I'll explain everything then.

TOMORROW? No, Mum. Dad's going mental. He's on about getting a taxi to look for you. Me and Erin have told him we're over the limit and can't drive. But when the drink he's had comes out of his system, I don't think we'll be able to stop him taking one of our cars.

Honestly, I really can't come back tonight. I just need to think – and breathe. I'm sorry love. I promise I'll tell you everything tomorrow.

But where are you?

I've found us a bed and breakfast. Don't worry. We're safe.

I hate lying yet again. But if Karl were to find out where we are, he'd tear Jason limb from limb.

Is Alice OK?

She will be. I'm going to talk to her now.

And are you?

I'll be fine. Tough as old boots, me.

I love you, Mum – no matter what might have happened in the past. And nothing Dad can do or say could ever change that.

You too, love – I'll have to hand this phone back now but I'll see you in the morning, I promise.

Jason returns to the room jangling drinks on a tray.

'Do you mind turning your phone off?' I look at him. 'Just in case Karl can find a way to trace it?'

He nods and does as I ask. 'Where is he?'

'He's still at the cottage. Luckily, he's had too much to drink to come after me.'

'Is your phone off as well, Alice?'

'Aww, Grandma, I don't have to turn it off, do I?'

'If you don't turn it off, Grandad might be able to find us.'

Pulling a face, she pushes the slider on the side of her phone. 'Can I watch TV instead then?'

Thankfully, I don't need to offer any information as to who Jason *really* is. Alice seems to have accepted my explanation that he's a tradesman about to start work on our porch. Because of this, I can just deal with one thing at a time. The rest will certainly have to come tomorrow.

'What did Martha say to you before you left the house?' I stare at Alice's face, as the flames of the fire in front of them reflect onto it. It's so much cosier here than it is back at the cottage. I usually only ever refer to Martha as *Auntie* Martha but it seems those days are over. Nothing's ever going to be the same as it was.

Alice's face crumples. 'It was something nasty, Grandma.'

'Just tell me, sweetheart.'

'But it's a bad word.'

I exchange glances with Jason. 'Has she told *you* any of this yet?'

He shakes his head. 'Not a thing. She was just crying and cold when she got here. It's a miracle she was able to find her way, especially as it was starting to get dark.'

'You did well to say you've only been here once before, love. I'm just so relieved you're alright.' I move closer to her and drape my arm around her skinny shoulders. Somehow, in the midst of everything else, she seems thinner and more vulnerable. 'Now tell me what she said – bad word and all. I need to know.'

'I'll whisper it to you then.'

I bend so my ear's nearer to her face.

'She said, '*Hasn't anyone told you that your dad isn't really your dad?* Then she said…' Her voice fades as she pulls away from me.

'Just say it, love.'

She swallows and comes back in to me again. 'She said, '*you're Rylan's little bastard*.'

I shudder at such a word being uttered by my innocent granddaughter. What a way to speak to an eleven-year-old girl. If Martha thinks I'll want anything to do with her after this, she's very much mistaken.

'What does she mean, Grandma?'

I swallow. I'm going to have to explain and the truth is the only way forward here. This would be best coming from Erin but in the circumstances, it's going to have to come from me.

'Do you remember how you learned at school about where babies come from,' I begin, my face burning and not just because of the fire.

She nods.

'Do you want me to leave the two of you alone?' Jason points at the door to his kitchen. Typical male – though I can't blame him for wanting to make himself scarce.

'No, you stay. You're part of it all now – whether you like it or not.'

Something lifts in his face. That was clearly the right thing to say.

DAY SIX

34

ERIN

With Karl and Martha's voices still ringing in my ears, I exit the kitchen and head towards the lounge. With a bit of luck, no one else will come in here for a while.

The heavy curtains are still pulled across as I walk in. But I suppose they would be – Gill's been the one responsible for opening curtains and lighting fires each morning. I head for the window to draw them back, nearly slopping my coffee in surprise at the sudden voice behind me.

'What do you have to go and do that for?'

I turn on my heel to see Rylan hauling himself into a seated position on the sofa while hitching the blanket over his bare chest. I resist the urge to tell him that it's nothing I haven't seen before.

'I–I didn't realise anyone was in here.'

'Well, I could hardly sleep in mine and Martha's room, could I? And I'd had too many sherberts to drive anywhere. I'm going to leave today though – I've had enough.'

'Me too – as soon as I get Alice back. At least I had her room to sleep in last night, or else you and me would have been fighting over the sofa.'

Rylan opens his mouth to say something, but must then think better of it.

'You OK?' I ask. 'We haven't had the chance to speak since—'

'I just don't understand why the truth about Alice had to come out like this,' he cuts in. 'Why now? Why haven't you ever said anything to me before? Don't you think I had the right to know?'

I consider telling him that I never knew for sure that he's Alice's real father. But that would be another lie. I might feel wretched but I also feel a slight relief that at least the truth's finally out in the open. 'How could I?' I reply. 'All you cared about was Martha – you made that perfectly clear at the time.'

'But you've lied to everyone for all these years, Erin. As if there wasn't a ten-foot wall between me and my brother already. It's going to take a wrecking ball to break it down now.'

'I'm not proud of what I did.' Tears stab at my eyes as I perch on the edge of the sofa next to him. 'But I did what I had to do. If I could have that time over again, I–' I pause at the sudden voices I hear in the kitchen. 'Hang on – I think Kelli and Ben have come back.'

'Why, where have they been?'

'They were out first thing, looking for your mum and Alice.' I start towards the door. 'Kelli said she had a couple of ideas of places to try.'

As I get to the door, Rylan's already thrown his blankets off and is pointing his feet into his jeans. Not wanting to be caught here in this room, while he's still in his boxers, I make a quick exit and head back to the kitchen.

'So did you knock at *all* the doors?' Karl's leaning against the counter as Kelli fills a glass from the tap.

'Of course we did,' Ben replies. 'We found two rows of terraces and knocked at every single one.'

'I was speaking to my daughter, not to *you*.'

'And we've driven all around, and also checked at a couple of pubs and farms,' Ben continues, seemingly undeterred by Karl's ever-growing hostility. 'But there's no sign of them.'

'Erin!' Kelli's eyes rest on where I'm leaning in the doorway. 'Are you alright? I can't imagine you got much sleep last night.'

'She doesn't deserve to.' Martha's voice echoes from where she's sitting in front of the unlit fireplace. 'Not when she goes around sleeping with other people's husbands. You're lucky I'm not gouging your eyes out, you bloody slapper.'

'Oh, give it a rest, Martha.' Rylan squeezes past me and heads into the kitchen. 'I've already tried telling you that it was a drunken moment of madness and it all happened a long time ago.'

'*A drunken moment of madness*,' I echo. Well bloody charming. 'That's not what you were saying at the time.'

'Erin – watch it.' Rylan jerks his head to one side, seemingly to let me know that someone's right behind me.

'Get out of my way.' Nathaniel barges past me. 'As if things aren't bad enough already, Erin, you have to make them even worse, don't you? Martha's right – you're nothing but a slapper.'

'Well if you…' My voice fades out as I notice movement at the door. 'Oh my God, Alice! Come here.' I charge towards my daughter and throw my arms around her, trying not to allow the fact that she's as stiff as a plank of wood to dampen my joy at seeing her. 'Gill, are you OK?'

'Yes, I'm only here to explain myself after yesterday. Then I'm going again.'

Alice steps out of my embrace and returns to stand at Gill's side. This show of solidarity towards her grandmother is both heart-warming and worrying at the same time. *How much does she know?*

Gill must read the question in my eyes. 'She knows *everything*, Erin. She's old enough to understand and dare I say it, a damn sight more mature than most of the adults around here.'

'Including what her grandad said?'

'*Everything*. Which is what I'm back here to explain and I

should have taken you all to one side and told you the truth years ago.' She lets her gaze roam from Nathaniel to Rylan to Kelli.

Karl makes a sudden show of reaching towards where his phone's plugged in next to the microwave. It would seem he's wanting us all to know that he's on the verge of having her arrested.

'Just wait, Dad,' Rylan says. 'I, for one, want to hear what Mum's got to say.'

'Me too,' says Nathaniel, his voice much calmer than before.

'What *can* she say?' Karl's voice intensifies. 'She held a pillow over an elderly woman's face until she could no longer breathe. She's nothing but a murderer.'

'Your grandmother was riddled with cancer.' Gill clasps the hand which Alice offers her as she looks around at everyone again. 'And she'd *begged* me to help her end her suffering.'

'Cut the crap, woman.' Karl's voice echoes around the room. 'You murdered her in cold blood. And I should never have let you get away with it for all these years.'

'So why did you then?' Rylan's voice has an accusatory edge and I can't see one flicker of sympathy in his face towards his father.

'I did it for *you*.' Karl waves his finger around. 'Nathaniel, Rylan and Kelli. Like I said yesterday, if it hadn't been for me keeping quiet, you'd have all grown up without a mother.'

'Your grandma had suffered enough.' Gill continues talking with tears now leaking from her eyes. 'And I'd do it all over again if I had to. Joe knew all about it and despite the awfulness of it all, he was grateful that I ended her suffering.'

'Grandad knew?' Nathaniel's voice rises.

'She's lying.' Karl's voice is a snarl. 'It's easy for her to say that when he's no longer here to speak up for himself.'

'You can say what you want about me, Karl, but your parents loved me. They'd have washed their hands of you years before if it wasn't for me.'

Go on, Gill, I say silently. I couldn't be any more proud of my mother-in-law than I am at this moment. Karl's never deserved her. And it appears as though she's finally seen the light.

'You can save all that for the police after they've carted you off.' He does pick his phone up this time.

'Do you know how ashamed your mother was of her misogynist, pigheaded and narcissistic son?' Gill says, her voice surprisingly even.

Karl slams the phone down and steps out from behind the breakfast bar towards Gill. I hold my breath. If he goes for her, I'm more than ready to step in.

'Dad – no.' Rylan dodges into the gap between his parents.

'Get out of my way.' Karl grabs him by the shoulders but Rylan stands firm.

'There's *nothing* you can do to hurt me anymore,' Gill says, her arm still around Alice. 'In fact, if *you* don't tell the police about what I did to help your mother, I'll bloody well tell them myself. You're not hanging it over my head anymore.'

'But Mum, you *will* probably go to prison,' Nathaniel says.

'I don't think she will.'

'And then I'm going to divorce you, Karl.' Gill juts her chin out as though daring him to challenge her. 'Whether I'm in prison, or not.'

I don't know what's got into her but I like this version of my mother-in-law. The subservient people-pleaser has been replaced with someone who's finally found her kick-ass side. Which she's going to need if Karl carries out his threats. And judging by the rising colour in his face and the way his fingers have curled into fists at his sides, he's going to blow any minute.

'I can hardly believe I've wasted so many years of my life being stuck with *you*,' she continues.

'Right, that's it.' Karl shoves Rylan out of the way. 'You don't get to humiliate me like this. Not now, not *ever*.'

'Get off my grandma,' Alice shrieks as Karl squares up to Gill.

'Jason, come quickly.' She twists herself around the side of the back door.

But who the hell is *Jason?*

35

ERIN

ALICE STEPS OUT of the way to reveal a man who looks barely out of his teens. He rushes to Gill's side.

'Get away from her.' He flicks his finger towards Karl. 'You don't get to threaten her any more.'

'And who the hell are you?' demands Rylan.

Maybe Gill's been having an affair. That might explain where her new-found bravado has come from. I stare at Jason more closely. No, surely not. He looks even younger than Ben. Gill's not the sort of person who'd get involved with someone who's so much younger than her. At least I don't think she is. I'd never have thought my mother-in-law was capable of being able to end her *own* mother-in-law's life. Never in a million years. With this in mind, who knows what else she could have been up to?

'This is my family.' Gill seems to be making the most of her brief reprieve from Karl as she gestures from Jason and then to the rest of us. 'Well – they're *your* family too.'

'Eh?' Martha pushes forward from where she's been watching from behind everyone else. 'What on earth are you on about?'

'Yeah, what *are* you on about, Mum?'

'This had *better* not be who I think it is.' Karl's knuckles whiten as he cracks one of them into the other. His lips are thin with fury. 'God help you if it is.'

I lunge towards Alice and nudge her in the direction of the hallway. 'Go to your room – now!' Enough is enough. Whoever this man is and whatever's going on here, my daughter does not need to witness any more of it. She's been through quite enough already this week. This is the final time I'll ever put her in a position like this and as soon as we're out of here, everything is going to change.

'But Mum, I already know—'

'Just do as I say. Plug your earphones in and don't come out of your room until I say you can – promise me, love.'

'I promise.' The tone of my voice must portray that I really mean business for she darts to the door without looking back, her red hair flowing out behind her. Thank goodness she's listened to me. There can be little doubt that this is going to get ugly. Whoever this man is, Alice seems to have already met him. I'll have to speak to Gill – she shouldn't have been telling my daughter *anything* or subjecting her to any situations without my *prior* approval.

'It bloody well is, isn't it?' Karl's top lip curls – it's an expression I know well – one I've seen often enough from Nathaniel, especially lately. 'What the hell is *he* doing here? You said you weren't in touch with him anymore. I can't bloody believe this.'

'Who is he, Mum?' Nathaniel's voice echoes from behind me.

Nobody moves. It's as if everyone is holding their breath and it's no wonder. I'll be gobsmacked if he does turn out to be some sort of boyfriend.

'Answer me, woman!' I jump as Karl's voice slices through the silence of the kitchen. 'I want to know what's going on here?'

Gill moves towards Jason and tucks her arm around him. The way he leans into her provides little doubt that a closeness exists between them. 'Nathaniel, Rylan, Kelli – this is Jason – he's your brother.'

There's an audible gasp as all eyes turn to him. *Their brother*? Blimey. Of all the possibilities, I wasn't expecting that.

'*Brother*?' Kelli's face is white and her eyes widen with shock as she stares at Jason. 'But how? I mean, surely—'

'So I take it you had an affair then?' Nathaniel narrows his eyes at his mother. Trust him to show that as his first reaction. He's more interested in what his mother's been up to than the man who looks like he doesn't know where to put himself who is standing in front of him.

Now I know for sure he's related to them, I can see the resemblance between Jason and Rylan. The angle of their jaws, the broad chests and shoulders. They even stand in a similar way. But if no one knew about him until now, Nathaniel must be right.

'Of course she had an affair,' Karl snaps as he gives Gill the nastiest look I've ever seen. 'So not only was I forced to spend many years concealing what *she,'* – he jabs his finger at her – 'did to my mother, but there's also the fact that she started carrying on with my workmate when I was working away – resulting in this little bastard.' He jerks his thumb in Jason's direction.

'Dad—' Kelli gasps.

'What do you even want from us?' Nathaniel says, his lip curling as he continues to stare at Jason.

'I want him out of here,' Karl continues. 'Or else, I won't—'

'Dad – just stop.' Rylan edges forward, seemingly poised to prevent anyone going for each other. 'It's not *his* bloody fault, is it?'

'One thing I do know...' Jason steps clear of Gill's hold on him, and squares up to Karl. 'There's only one *bastard* around here and I'm—'

'Easy mate.' Rylan forces himself in between them. 'There's enough shit going on here without the two of you coming to blows as well.'

'You lot might allow him to speak to *you* like that, but I'm not—'

'You can't just turn up here like this, throwing your weight around like you are – who the hell do you think you are?'

Your brother, I want to tell Nathaniel but I keep quiet. They've all got enough to take in with what they've heard about their grandmother and now – *this.* It's no wonder they're all in shock.

'But how come we've only just heard about you?' Rylan looks to have aged ten years in the last ten minutes. He looks from Jason to Gill. 'Did you not think we had the right to know we had another brother? I can't believe you've kept something like this from us.'

'I agree with Rylan.' Kelli's voice trembles and it sounds full of shock as she faces her mother. 'We had a right to know. Is there anything else you've kept us in the dark about?'

Gill lowers her eyes. 'I'm so sorry.' Her voice trembles and I want to rush over and comfort her. But this is really *nothing* to do with me, so I stay where I am. Poor Gill. I only hope they all find it in themselves to show her some understanding. 'I should have told you all about Jason years ago.'

'Yes, you bloody well should have done.' Nathaniel's voice is as hard as his face, his lips as thin as Karl's. 'So why didn't you?'

I glance at Martha, relieved that she's keeping quiet for once in her life, but no one could fail to notice the almost-gleeful expression as she observes the unfolding drama. It will certainly give her something juicy to gossip about.

'Your father gave me a choice at the time – an impossible choice.' Gill glances at the young man still standing at her side. 'I could give Jason up for adoption or I could lose *everything*, meaning all of *you*.' She dabs at her eyes with her sleeve. 'Karl was going to throw me out, cut me off and stop me seeing you all for good.'

'He couldn't have done that,' Nathaniel says. 'You could have seen a solicitor.'

I want to tell him to give over. How could she have even paid for one? Karl, as always, it seems, had all the control over her.

'He was also threatening me again with the other thing I'd done – with your grandmother, I mean.' Gill's more focused on Kelli than anyone else as she speaks, as though she's the person she's trying to convince the most. I guess that if Gill has Kelli on her side, she's more likely to be able to pull her brothers around to be more forgiving. 'Looking back now, I should have fought against him harder. But I was pregnant, vulnerable and had no fight left in me.'

'That's no excuse.'

I glare at Nathaniel. Can't he give his mother just a crumb of understanding?

'I know love. I was selfish and stupid and I can barely forgive myself. And if I can't forgive *myself*, how can I expect the rest of you to?'

I glance from Gill's tearful face to Karl's sneer. I can fully believe he'd give her an ultimatum like she's saying he did. But it will have been white noise. After all, without her, he'd have been lost with no servant to childcare, cook, clean and do all his donkey work.

'I do remember you being pregnant, Mum, now you come to mention it...' Kelli begins. 'But—'

'So do I,' says Rylan. 'But there was no baby at the end of it. You were just crying all the time.'

'I'm just so, so sorry.' Gill grips Jason's arm. 'To you mostly,' she looks at him, then again at Nathaniel, Rylan and Kelli. 'I thought, at the time, that I'd done what was best in a situation where I didn't know what else to do.'

'There were lots of other things you—'

'For God's sake, Nathaniel,' I cut in, unable to help myself. 'What's done is done.'

'You can butt out.' He rounds on me. 'You've got absolutely no right getting involved. Especially after what *you've* done. I might have known you'd side with the person having the affair.'

'It's just that for all these years you didn't tell us, Mum,' Kelli begins. 'This is my biggest problem with it. Not with the fact that you had an affair but that we had absolutely no idea about our *brother*.'

'And what about him?' Rylan gestures towards Jason, something in his face evidently softening. 'He's had to grow up without his mum, and without us – he was just abandoned because Dad couldn't handle it. The whole thing is mental if you ask me.'

'I obviously got it all hopelessly wrong, love. And I know it doesn't make anything any better but I didn't just *abandon* him.'

'What do you mean?'

'From the moment I was forced to give him up, I kept in touch with how he was doing and I always knew he was being well looked after by his adoptive parents.'

'No, it doesn't make *anything* any better, Mum.' Nathaniel's voice is still as hard as nails. 'And if you could have abandoned *him* like that, I dare say you could have done the same with *any* of us.'

'Of course she could,' Karl says. 'Just look at her. The woman doesn't care about anyone but *herself.* And she never has.'

'That's just not true.' Rylan stares at his father. 'The only parent we've got who fits that description is *you*.'

'He wants to be glad he didn't grow up as part of this family anyway,' Nathaniel snaps, his face souring some more as he looks around at us all. 'Look what a shambles it is.'

Ben and I exchange glances. Apart from me trying to get through to Nathaniel a moment ago, we're just standing here like spare parts absorbing the toxicity and drama of it all. We can't get properly involved, but no doubt we'll be well and truly caught up in the aftermath.

'So what now?' Rylan says.

'He leaves, that's what now. He had no business turning up like this in the first place.'

'He had every right actually, Dad.' Kelli glares at him then something relaxes in her face as she turns her attention to her newly found brother. 'Surely, we should be making up for lost time now? Surely we shouldn't be letting the past ruin the future?'

'So you think this is some kind of happy family reunion, do you?' Karl's sudden bellowing makes me jump again as he turns toward Jason. 'You – get out of here – right now.' He jerks his finger at him. 'Enough's enough.'

'I'm not going anywhere,' he says. 'And *you* can't make me either.'

'Oh, you think so, do—'

'Actually, I own this place.' Jason stands firm as he waves his arms around the room. 'I grew up here.' He juts his chin out defiantly and it gives me great pleasure to see the expression on Karl's face fall so fast.

'What? So you mean – those-those urns – the ones in the shed,' I manage to stammer.

'My adopted parents,' he explains. 'It didn't feel right to scatter them somewhere else. They loved it *here.* And they'd have wanted to stay together.'

I shiver as the vision of the urns swims into my mind. Particularly the circumstances in which they died. I force my attention back to Jason – the poor bloke. He's only in his twenties and he's really been through it by all accounts.

'I don't care what you say you *own.*' Karl steps forward and Rylan, once again, tries to elbow his way in front of him. 'I want you out of here. And as for *you*—' he reaches around Rylan quicker than he can stop him and manages to take a swipe at Gill. However, she realises what's going on fast enough to dodge out of his reach.

As she lurches towards the hallway, he darts after her. 'You're going to get what's fucking coming to you.'

'Stop it – just leave her alone.'

'Mum,' Kelli squeals. 'Go and lock yourself in the bathroom. Quickly! We'll sort him out.'

But he's pursuing her faster than she can get away and a second or two passes before the rest of us get ourselves into gear and go after them both.

She shrieks as Karl grabs her from behind, grabbing a fistful of her hair as he rams her up against the bannister with a sickening crunch.

'No – Dad, stop!'

'Get your hands off me!' It's the first time I've heard such pain and anguish in my mother-in-law's voice. I rush forwards to help her but I'm not fast enough.

As I try to pull him backwards by the shoulders, he's oblivious to my efforts as he tugs her head back sharply by her hair. As I cajole and shout at him to stop some more, he slams her head back into the wood for a second time. The sound of her skull crashing into the wood causes the bile to rise in my throat. If he can do this to Gill in front of us all, what on earth could he have been doing to her behind closed doors for all these years? He's evil and I'll be only too happy to be part of making sure that he gets everything he deserves after this.

'Get off her!' Kelli shrieks from behind me. 'Get off my mum!'

Blood spurts from Gill's face as she tries to free herself from Karl's grip. But she's in a daze. With a couple more blows to the head like that, he's going to knock her out. Or worse.

'Dad. Please! Let her go.' Kelli forces her way past me. 'Out of my way, Erin.'

'You can say goodbye to them all, you conniving bitch.' He pulls her head back by her hair for a third time and I brace myself for the inevitable.

'You *bastard*.'

The dull thud of iron connecting with bone is a sound I'll never forget for as long as I live.

Then, with a spray of blood into the air, there's a collective gasp as Karl suddenly releases his grip on my mother-in-law and crashes to the floor.

36

KELLI

I SWALLOW the vomit that rises in the back of my throat. He's down on his knees – right in front of me. But he's still trying to get back up. If I don't stop him, he'll go for me – or for Mum again. With blood dripping down the sides of his head, he reaches for the bannister to haul himself up as he twists around to face me. His face is contorted with what could be either rage or pain. Or both.

'You,' he hisses from between bared teeth as he stumbles at me, reaching for the iron in my hands.

I raise it above my head once more. 'You're never going to hurt my mother, or any of us, ever again.'

'No – Kelli - Stop!' My brother's voice echoes all around as I bring the iron crashing onto my father's head for the second time. This time, the blood from his head gushes over me and Martha who's rushed across the hallway to help him. Dad staggers back against the bannister before collapsing to the ground.

'Oh my God. Oh my God.'

Martha crouches at Karl's side. 'Karl, Karl, wake up.' Her fingers fumble for his wrist. She spins around and points at Rylan. 'Call an ambulance, will you? And the police. Quickly.' Panic is etched across her face. 'Karl, can you hear me?'

He doesn't move.

'Someone, call them.' Her anguished eyes sweep over us all. '*Now*!'

But everyone seems to be frozen to the spot. Especially me.

'*Now*!' She shrieks.

Ben drops into a crouch at the other side of Dad. 'Karl, can you hear me?' He feels around on his other wrist, holding his forefinger and middle finger onto it for a few moments before finally shaking his head. 'I think he's dead.'

'No – no – no.'

'You've killed him.' Martha screeches as she falls back away from my father. 'Oh my God – you've really gone and killed him.'

I avert my gaze from what I've done and turn the iron over in my hands. Its unscathed leaden surface offers little clue of the act it's just performed. Once a mere tool for pressing clothes, it now bears the weight of a deadly purpose. My father's death. Covered in layers of dust and grease from years of being used as a kitchen door prop, it has now evolved into something far more sinister – a weapon of murder. Meanwhile, I'm completely numb. I can't even speak. It's as though I've disconnected from my own body and I can't get myself back to it.

Did I mean to kill him? If I'm to be really honest - yes, I did. Can I deal with the inevitable repercussions? The weight of what I've inflicted staining my conscience until the end of my days? No, I don't think I can. But what choice have I got? What's done is well and truly done. Unless Ben's got it wrong and he isn't really dead. I can't shake the feeling that it would take more than two mere blows to the head to silence my father forever.

I bend to place the iron at my feet, as though trying to disassociate from that too. I silently pray for Ben to turn and look at me – I need to see something in his eyes that suggests he doesn't think I'm a raging psychopath, but he's still busy tending to my father, no matter how fruitless he must realise it is by now. Even though I half expect my father to suddenly leap to his feet and begin raging again, I can tell, from his absolute stillness and the seep of blood from his head that he's well and truly gone. And it's all my fault.

'What the hell have you done?' Martha's voice is heavy with accusation as she rises to her feet, her face twisted with hatred as she looks at me. 'You evil bitch.'

The sound of retching emits from one corner – as Nathaniel loses his breakfast into a plant pot. What will they all think of me now? My brothers, my mother, my sister-in-law. What will I do? Their watching faces merge into one, united in shock, each expression impossibly unreadable. Martha's question was fair – I must admit. What *have* I done? What will my young niece think of me for *killing* her grandad? *What the hell have I done*?

Several eyes flit between me and the body of my father, slumped in a pool of blood between us all. I open my mouth to speak but still, no sound comes out. I close my eyes – willing the horror before me to disappear when I open them again. Not to see my father, the man who once carried me on his shoulders and tickled me until I begged for mercy, lying in his own blood. That *I've* caused.

But he was also the father whose moods could be darker than a midwinter day, the father who once injured me badly enough to warrant hospitalisation, while threatening and terrorising me, my mum and my brothers on an almost daily basis. And now, as I've found, the threats and terror he inflicted on my mother were far worse than I could have ever imagined.

But inevitably, as I open my eyes again, the horror is still there – in all its gory technicolour. As is the unspeakable horror that's emerging on each face as I continue to look around. One thing is certain – my fate is no longer in my own hands – it's now in the hands of my family.

There is nothing I can do to undo what I've done. And there is nothing I can do to change whatever may lie ahead for me.

'Are you sure he's dead, are you really, *really* sure?' Rylan's words are a gabble as he creeps towards our father. He looks as frightened as he used to do when he was a little boy.

'Of course he's dead,' Nathaniel replies, seemingly unable to tear his eyes away from the corpse of our father. 'Just look at his eyes.'

'Shit, shit, shit, shit, shit.'

'What are we going to do?'

'What do you mean, *we*? I want no part in this – any of it.'

'Oh my God, this is a total nightmare.'

'We've got to stop Alice from coming down here – she'd be scarred for life.'

I allow my gaze to roam to Dad's glassy stare wishing I had the guts to manually close his eyes so I'd feel less like he's still watching me. He probably is – in fact, he'll probably haunt me forever and I'll deserve it. I've never seen a dead body before, not even that of my grandad. But here is my father and it's *me* who ended his life so brutally. I wait for someone to say something, *anything* to me but no one seems to want to even look at me, let alone *speak* to me.

The adrenaline's starting to leave my body and is being replaced by an unrelenting shaking, a force so fierce it's making my teeth chatter. I never knew I was capable of such violence. And judging by his avoidance of returning my gaze, neither did Ben. He's probably going to leave me after what I've done. That would make Dad happy, anyway.

'Mu-um.' I reach out to my mother as I allow myself to slide into a crouch against the wall. I can't trust my legs to hold me up a moment longer. Then, as I hit the bottom, the tears begin to flow. Just a few at first, then a torrent of them. 'Mum?'

They'll all hate me now, after what I've done and I don't blame them. If only someone would hug me, tell me that what I did was warranted – and that I won't go to prison for it. That I won't lose my partner, my friends, my family, my teaching career, that they'll all stand by me. But no one will look at me, not even Mum. 'Mum please – I was only trying to stop him from hurting you.'

'Just a minute.' She's clutching her head. 'I don't feel so good. I've gone a bit...' She leans into the wall next to me.

'Someone help her,' I shout.

'Mum, what's the matter?'

Oh my God – she's going to die as well. Those blows to the head—

'I'm OK.' Helped by Rylan and Jason, she slumps down beside me.

'Mum, are sure you're alright?'

'Of course she's not,' Nathaniel snaps. But at least *someone* has acknowledged me. 'Didn't you see how hard he rammed her head into the bannister?'

'Of course I did. Why do you think I intervened like I did?'

'I'll be fine,' Mum says, appearing to take deep breaths in between her words. 'I'm just a bit woozy. It's nothing I haven't suffered with before.'

'Maybe you should get checked over,' Jason says.

'Just butt out,' Nathaniel glares at him. '*We'll* look after her.'

'Please.' Mum's voice is weak. 'Enough.'

'Jason's right,' Erin says. 'You need checking over.'

'I'll see how I go – just wait a few minutes.' Mum's still taking deep breaths. 'Is Alice still in her room?' She finally allows me to hold her hand as she looks at me with her watery eyes. I can't read what's in them.

'Yes,' Erin replies. 'I'll go up in a moment – when I know you're OK.'

'Go now.' Mum grips my arm tighter. 'She can't come down here and see what's happened.' She scrunches her eyes together to avoid looking at her dead husband. Will she ever truly be able to forgive me for what I've done?

She's clearly in pain, physically and mentally and yet the thoughts for her granddaughter always come first. However, we could end up being side by side in prison. Mum, for what she did to Grandma – me, for what I did to Dad. Our whole world has changed beyond recognition while we've been at this damned place.

Jason crouches in front of us and rests his arm on Mum's arm. 'It's OK, Mum.' His voice is calm and not dissimilar to Rylan's. 'Everything's going to be OK.'

Even in the haze and shock of what I've just done, to hear this *stranger* calling her *Mum* is the weirdest thing I've ever heard.

'*Mum,*' Nathaniel echoes. 'No – this isn't right, and I'm afraid that I just can't get to grips with it all.'

'No one would expect you—' Jason begins.

'Don't you think *you* being here,' – Nathaniel points at him as he cuts him off mid-sentence, – 'has caused *enough* damage without you continuing to hang around us? I think you should leave us to it.'

'It's his house, remember,' Rylan says. 'And he's part of our family whether you like it or not.'

Jason's hold on Mum's arm doesn't waver. And neither does his voice. 'I've missed out on more than enough years as it is, without allowing *you* to drive me back out. I'm here now and I'm not going *anywhere.*'

'It's not Jason's fault, Nathaniel – Rylan.' Mum's voice is trembling so much it hardly even sounds like her as she looks from one of them to the other. 'If all this is anyone's fault, it's mine.'

Martha rises from beside Dad. 'Are you all mental or what? He's lying here dead, and you're all discussing your fucking family tree.'

'We're making sure Mum's alright, actually.' Rylan's nostrils flare as he replies to his wife and there's nothing in his eyes apart from disdain towards her. Their marriage isn't going to come back from all this – not in a million years.

'Your father is fucking *dead*,' she shrieks.

'Shut your mouth.' Erin turns to look at her, her eyes flashing with anger. 'My daughter is up those stairs.'

'Well, she's going to know sooner or later what you're all capable of, isn't she? Especially you.' She points a heavily manicured yet blood-smeared finger in my direction.

I look back at her, trying to filter my father's body out of my vision. I can't look at it. He's probably still here in this hallway, somewhere, hovering in a corner between earth and hell, watching my every move. I'd do *anything* to turn the clock back and undo what I've done. It all happened so fast that I did what I did without stopping for a moment to consider the consequences.

Pass me my phone,' Martha orders Erin with a flick of her finger. I swallow. The phone call she's about to make will see me thrown into the back of a police van and then into a cell. Who knows when I'll see daylight again after what I've done? I've taken a life – the life of my father and I've probably lost my entire family too. The man ruined my childhood and now, I've gone and let him ruin my future as well. I might as well have died with him.

'Go and make sure Alice is alright,' Mum says again. 'Please – someone.'

But Erin remains where she is, as still as a rock. 'Just wait a second first, Gill. Don't we need to work out exactly what we're going to say to the police before we do *anything*?'

'Erin's right,' Rylan says. 'We need to protect Kelli from what might happen from here, no matter what.'

Everybody averts their gazes from Dad's body to me. There's no malice in anyone's eyes apart from Martha's. If the rest of them don't hate me, that's something at least.

'Like hell we do.' Martha stamps past us all and makes towards the kitchen. '*She's* a murderer and she needs locking up. So if you won't get on the phone to the police right now after what she's done, then I bloody will.'

'Someone stop her.' Mum's voice suddenly takes on an extra strength as she points at Martha's retreating form. 'Don't let her phone *anyone* just yet.'

'Thanks, Mum.' My own voice is barely audible as I haul myself back to my feet. As long as I've got my mother in my corner, I can handle the rest of it. Perhaps I've still got the others in my corner as well.

Ben jumps up and runs after Martha. 'Just wait, will you? We need to consider what to do for the best here.' He grabs her arm as she reaches the door. 'And we all need to stick together.'

'Like hell we do – so you can get your hands off me.' She squirms around to break his hold but he appears to tighten his grip.

'Rylan,' Ben says. 'Find her phone – in fact, *any* phone lying around in there and put them somewhere where she can't get at them.'

Martha points at Gill. 'Your husband's lying dead after having his head stoved in and all you care about is what happens to *her*? What's wrong with you?'

'She's my daughter. But I wouldn't expect *you* to understand that kind of loyalty.'

Martha's face twists. 'He was your *husband*.' She points at him. 'You make me bloody sick, the lot of you.'

Right on cue, Nathaniel retches into the plant pot again. 'I can't believe this,' he sobs as he comes up for air. 'I can't believe any of it. He's dead – he's really dead.'

'I told you we should *never* have come to this damn place,' Erin snaps. 'I knew something dreadful would happen as soon as you mentioned it.'

'Don't you even talk to me. Not after what you've done – have you got that?'

'I'm going to make sure you *all* go down for this.' As cupboard doors bang from the kitchen, Martha, points around at us all with the arm that's not in Ben's grip. 'Every last one of you – is there really only me here who cared about him?'

'Right – stop it. Everybody.' Rylan moves amongst us, holding his hands in the air. 'I don't know about the rest of you but I can't stand in here, looking at–' He glances at Dad and swallows. 'I say we go in there, pour a stiff drink each and work out what the hell we're going to do next. How are you feeling, Mum? Do you think you can move?'

'I'll be OK,' she replies. 'I think it's just about passed.' She stretches her hands out. 'Can you help me?'

'He was your father,' Martha cries as Jason helps her back to her feet. 'And all you can think about is pouring a *drink*. This is absolutely *mental*.'

'If he'd been *your* father,' Rylan replies. 'You'd understand how we feel.'

37

KELLI

As Rylan slops brandy into tumblers and passes them around, Martha appears to be still looking for a phone. But hopefully, they've all been found and stashed somewhere. I'm busy scrubbing at my hands in the sink, trying to get rid of the blood. Perhaps Martha should be doing the same thing, instead of bleating her head off about getting *help* or *justice* for the last man on this earth who should ever receive either.

'We need to get someone here for him,' she cries. 'And *she* needs to be held accountable for what she's done.' She pulls a face in my direction. 'Right, if you won't give me my phone, I'm off to find some help.' She yanks some car keys from the counter and makes towards the door.

'I don't think so.' Ben goes after her and blocks her exit. 'Just wait, will you?'

As I wipe my hands onto my clothes, Jason comes up beside me and squirts the sink with bleach spray. 'Just in case,' he says. 'We're going to need to have a thorough clean of the place.'

'I'm so glad you're here,' I sniff. 'It's a huge shock, obviously, but—'

'We just need to focus on *now,* now.' He wipes the sink around and rinses the cloth. 'We'll focus on the rest later.' It's the kind of thing Mum might say.

Other than Martha, the rest of them seem to be rallying around to cover this up. Maybe this isn't the end of my life after all.

'It hasn't sunk in yet, just what I've done.' I lean against the counter. 'I can try to say it was a moment of madness, and perhaps it was, but if I saw him smashing my mother's head into a bannister ever again, I'd do exactly the same thing.'

'You just got there first,' Jason said. 'He needed stopping.'

'But not like I stopped him. Are you OK, Mum?' I sidle up to her as she sits onto one of the breakfast bar schools, still looking ill and paler than I've ever seen her.

She dabs at her bloodied face with some tissue. 'I'm feeling much better, thanks. But I don't know how I'll explain this away to the police when we eventually have to face them.'

'Will we really have to? Face them, I mean?'

'Short of digging our own hole for him.' She stares down at her hands. 'We'll have to let them know *something* soon. It's just a good job we're in the middle of nowhere and have got time to decide how we're going to handle all this.'

'Now you've wiped your head, Mum' – Rylan peers at her – 'It doesn't look as bad as it did. You could even say you were bending down and someone accidentally opened the car door on it.'

'Do you think they'll believe me?'

'They'll have to, if we're all telling them the same thing. Are you sure you're OK? You had quite a turn back there.'

'I'm just in shock, I think.' She dabs at her eyes. 'I can't believe he's dead.' She gestures towards the hallway. 'I'm expecting him to suddenly jump up and rush at me again, if I'm honest.'

'Me too.' And I wish he *would* suddenly jump up. At least if he did, I wouldn't be facing a murder charge and my life wouldn't be over. Why did I do it? Why the *hell* did I do it?

'I'm sorry, Mum.'

'From where I was standing,' Erin says. 'You did what you had to do.'

'Have you heard yourself?' Martha's voice is a shriek. '*You did what you had to do.*' She steps towards me and for a moment I think she's going to go for me. 'You've killed your father. You're a murderer – just like he said *you* are.' She points at Mum as she says the word *you*. 'Like mother, like daughter. Well if you think I'm going to stand by and—'

'Right, shut up everybody.' Rylan shouts over us all. 'Here's what we're going to do.'

Jason stands beside Mum, hopping from foot to foot. In the last twenty minutes, I've gained a half-brother and killed my father. I feel sicker than I've ever felt but I still take a glass of brandy from the counter. It might numb the pain for a while after I'm thrown into a cell, which if Martha has her way, won't be too far away.

Everyone looks at Rylan who seems to have taken charge. I'm relieved *someone* has. God knows what he's got up his sleeve but I'm all ears. If anyone can dig me out of all this, my brother can. I can hardly even drink from the glass, I'm shaking so much.

Ben comes up to the other side of me and draws me to him. I'm so grateful for his close proximity at last that I want to collapse into him. I want to weep into his chest but I'm too numb to even think straight.

'Right – we're all going to go for a walk,' Rylan begins, jerking his thumb in the direction of the door. '*All* of us.' He glares at Martha as though daring his wife to disagree.

'Are you off your head?' She cries. 'A *walk*? Oh my God, let's brutally kill someone and then what shall we do? Oh yes, we'll go for *a walk*. Wake up, Rylan.' She throws her hands in the air. 'You need to call the police *now* and let *them* handle this.'

'We'll take Dad's phone and wallet with us.' He turns his back on Martha. 'We'll get rid of them, and then we'll come back here after an hour or so – only *then* will we ring the police and report his death.'

'Wow,' Martha exclaims. 'You really are surpassing yourself this time.'

'And tell the police *what* exactly?' Erin asks.

'We'll tell them this is how we found him when we came back from our walk. That he must have been attacked by intruders.'

Ever so slightly, my shoulders relax. If everyone joins in, this really could work. I certainly haven't got any better ideas.

'Don't be so ridiculous,' Martha cackles, her face breaking into a sarcastic smile. 'They'll be looking at the forensics – and at CCTV. You're talking absolute crap if you think they'll believe someone broke in.'

'We've all been in and out of this cottage all week,' Rylan replies. 'That'll explain any of our DNA. We'll clean up the iron, and–'

'I never want to look at it again.' I choke back a sob as I scrunch my eyes together. I should have let the others hold Dad back and keep him pinned down. *They* could have stopped what he was doing to Mum – I didn't need to do what I did. Even in death, he will have managed to ruin the rest of my life. Even if we *can* pull off Rylan's plan, I've still got to live with the guilt.

'And there's no CCTV around here,' Jason says. 'None whatsoever.'

'How can you be so certain?' Everyone turns to look at him, this new and uninvited family member. There'll be time for more questions about the situation with him later, but for now, it seems like Rylan's plan could be the only way forward.

'I've lived around here all my life,' he replies.

'We *are* in the middle of nowhere,' adds Erin.

'I suggest we do what Rylan says.' Nathaniel's voice is suddenly softer than it was a few minutes ago. 'What other choice do we have? We've got to protect Kelli.'

I shoot my brother a grateful look. He's the last person who'd usually speak up for me but these aren't usual circumstances.

'I agree.'

Nathaniel glares at Jason. He might have just agreed with him but it's going to take a lot more than that to help Nathaniel come to terms with his new-found brother.

'It's the only way out of this mess as far as I can see,' Rylan replies. 'I honestly can't think of any other way of doing things.'

'You tell the truth, you moron.' Martha slams her fist onto the counter. 'That's the *only* way of doing things.'

'We find our way over this initial mountain,' Rylan continues, ignoring his wife. 'We get the police off our backs and then we can sort the rest of it out later.'

'We're still a family, no matter what's happened here today,' Mum agrees. 'Things can't get much worse than they are, can they? So if we can just all pull together–'

'What if I don't want to *pull together*?' Martha looks around again, presumably in another attempt to find a phone. 'She,' – she points at me. – 'Needs to get what's coming to her. And *he,*' she jerks her head in the direction of the hallway, 'deserves justice.'

38

GILL

'WHERE HAVE you put my bloody phone, Rylan?' Martha hisses into Rylan's ear. They're standing close to the hallway where Karl's feet are still in plain sight. I'm longing to kick the door shut so I don't have to look at him but Alice is still up there and we need to listen out in case she comes out of her room. 'Give me it and I'll just go. I won't say anything but I don't want to be part of this.'

'You can't go *anywhere,*' I tell her. 'Look, I know you disagree but we've got to stick together. Please, Martha – please do this for *me.*'

I'm probably the only person in this room who has a chance of reasoning with her. She's usually so eager to please me and so eager to sideline the others that perhaps I've still got a chance of getting through to her. Though she'll probably know that she's fallen right out my favour after what she did with Alice. Telling her the truth about Rylan and Nathaniel like she did.

Somehow we need to get Alice out of here without her seeing her grandad in the state he's in. We'll have to cover him over while we get her down the stairs, as Rylan suggested. But like Jason said, that risks presenting forensic evidence that might complicate our story. *Why did you cover him over?* Will be the first thing they'll ask.

Personally, I think it's a risk worth taking. We can say that it was to protect Alice from having to see him.

Martha picks things up and throws them down as she slams her way around the kitchen. 'You can't do this to him. He deserves justice.'

'*Justice,*' Rylan scoffs. 'Since when did he know *anything* about justice? He deserves nothing.'

This is going to take some getting over. The face of the man I once fell for emerges in my mind and I blink it away. I've felt like killing him myself many a time but never dreamed that one of our own children would end up doing it.

'Do you really think the police will believe someone got in here and did it to him?' Kelli's face is still etched with terror. She doesn't know this yet but there's no way I'll allow her to go to prison. If it starts to look as though things could go that way, I'll take the blame for what happened myself and say I did it. After all, I'll spend a damn sight less time in prison than she'd end up spending.

'We'll make it look that way, won't we? Look, if we stick to the story and do this properly–'

'We need to stay away from here for a couple of hours, I reckon.' Nathaniel stares down at his feet. 'Put some footprints down in the woods and carefully get rid of stuff like his wallet and phone.'

'God I can't believe what's happening here.' Erin lets a long breath out.

'What's happening here is that we're going to let the police know *now.*' Martha squares up to Rylan. 'Because if you're not going to tell the truth to them, like I said, I *am.*' Suddenly, she reaches behind him and plucks his phone from his back pocket. Before he has the chance to stop her, she rushes into the hallway with it.

I'm the first one after her as she trips over Karl's legs and sprawls onto the hallway floor beside him. The phone bounces from her grip and lands beside the front door.

'I'm calling the police,' she snarls as she slips in the blood going after the phone and falls down again. 'I'm going to do the right thing – someone has to.'

'*You* wouldn't know the *right thing* if it slapped you around the face,' Erin edges around the hallway towards the phone and tosses it over Martha's head back to Rylan. 'I'm going to see to Alice,' she continues. 'I'll stay up there with her until we're ready to leave.' She stares at Karl and swallows. 'I agree with what was suggested before – we should cover him over.'

'We'll get it sorted,' Rylan replies. 'When we have, we'll open the front door, ready for you to get Alice straight out of it.'

'She's going to ask what's going on – she's bound to. I actually can't believe she's done as she was told and stayed up there.'

Rylan looks at Karl and also swallows. 'As long as she doesn't look over the top of the bannister,' – he nods towards it, – 'just make sure she goes straight out of *that* door...'

'We'll shout up to you both when we're ready,' Nathaniel says. 'Don't let her out of the bedroom before then.'

I watch my son. Even after what he's been told, he still cares just as much about Alice as he did before he found out. Yet another issue to be dealt with once we get through *this*. If we do.

'But what shall I tell her in the meantime?'

'Nothing yet. We'll tackle it all together when we get out of here.'

'Give me that phone back – I mean it, Rylan.' Martha gets to her feet, slipping once again in the blood as she lurches towards him.

'As if.' He backs into the kitchen.

'I'll be able to tell them the truth sooner or later.' She juts her chin out in defiance as she steadies herself. 'And *none* of you will be able to stop me.'

'With all of *us* saying the same thing,' Rylan looks back over his shoulder as he walks away. 'We'll just make you look like an idiot.'

'First, I find out you were carrying on with *her*.' Martha stabs her finger in the direction of the staircase after Erin. 'And then–'

'Give *me* the phone.' I stretch my hand out to my son. 'We'll sort this out once and for all.'

'What do you mean, Mum?' Kelli rushes at me as I return to the kitchen.

'You haven't done anything the rest of us wouldn't have done, has she?' I sweep my gaze over the others, hoping they're all going to stay on the same page as me.

There's a collective shaking of heads. Thank goodness, because this really could go either way.

'I'm just not prepared to go along with your lies – and you can't expect me to.' Martha points her finger around at us all as she speaks, her eyes fizzing with anger.

'Not if I tell them it was *you* who hit him with that iron.' I hold my palm towards Rylan, more forcibly this time. 'Rylan – give me the phone.'

'What do you mean? What are you going to do, Mum?'

'After her slip just now, Kelli's not the only one covered in his blood now, is she, Martha?' I let my gaze travel from Nathaniel to Jason to Rylan and then Ben. 'Are you all with me here?'

One by one they look at the blood-soaked Martha and slowly nod back.

'You wouldn't – you *couldn't*.' Martha flies at me but is held back by Ben and Jason.

As she squirms like a fly caught in a spider's web, Rylan unlocks his phone and passes it to me. 'Thank you.'

'You're supposed to be my *husband*.' She spits the word *husband* out like a lump of gristle as she snarls the words in Rylan's direction. 'You can't possibly be willing to go along with this? You'd *really* send me to prison for something your *sister* did?'

'Do your worst, Martha,' Rylan replies and my heart swells with pride. It's the first time I've ever heard him truly stand up to her. She normally has him wrapped around her perfectly manicured little finger. I've heard all sorts of rumours about her being violent towards my son over the years so to be seeing her comeuppance is long overdue.

'No one will believe you,' she retorts. 'When I tell them the truth – plus there'll be plenty of forensic evidence to back me up – you won't be able to get rid of *all* of it.' She feels in her pocket, presumably for the keys she picked up a few minutes ago. 'I respected Karl, even if I'm the only person here who did.'

'Have you seen yourself Martha?' Rylan gestures at her bloodied hands as she holds them in front of herself. 'And don't forget, *everyone* knows what a temper you've got now. I'm sure our neighbours back home will vouch for me as well. They've heard you go for me more times than I've had hot dinners.'

Her angry eyes narrow in my direction. 'You're bluffing, Gill. Besides, you'll never get away with it.'

'It'll be the word of six against one,' Nathaniel retorts.

'Our word against yours,' Rylan adds.

'You wouldn't dare.' Martha reaches for the phone as I raise it to my ear. 'Gill, for God's sake, what are you doing? Give me the phone!'

I dodge out of her way as she tries to pluck the handset from my grip.

'I said, give me the phone!' Her voice is more insistent and a flash of fear sparks from her eyes.

Not taking my eyes away from Martha, I speak into the phone as though I'm merely ordering a taxi.

'Yes, I'd like the police please,' I say, then as Martha once again tries to lunge at me, I add, 'I need to report a murder.'

Then as she comes at me for the final time, 'I add, 'of my husband – and I know who did it.'

39

MARTHA

I FEEL as though I'm in some kind of trance as I listen to my mother-in-law on the phone.

I need to report a murder. And she's pinning it on *me.*

I can't get the phone out of her hand – I can't even get to her. I've tried three times and been pushed back by the others. If I stick around here, I'll get arrested for sure and if they all stick together, I've no doubt they *really* could blame what Kelli's done on me and it would be my word against all of theirs.

'Just let her go,' Nathaniel shouts as I reach the door. Evidently, someone must have set off to try and stop me.

I turn before I open it. 'I'll never forgive you for what you've done,' I mouth the words to Rylan.

And I won't. He's standing by while his mother makes that call as well as what he's already done behind my back with Erin. I always knew I couldn't trust either of them.

'Just do one.' He comes after me. 'It's not as if anyone will stop you.'

'How could you do this?'

'I could ask you the same question,' he says. 'All the times you've tried to control me and lost your temper.'

'You're pathetic, Rylan. And you'll never be half the man your father was.' I glance back to the open door of the hallway and fresh tears fill my eyes at the sight of Karl's feet. He had my back, my father-in-law. I can't believe what they've done to him and it's inconceivable to think that I could end up being the one arrested for it.

'You might be beautiful on the outside, but on the inside, you're the ugliest person I've ever known.'

'Unlike *Erin*, you mean?' I stare into Rylan's face, a face I thought I could trust forever.

'The police are on their way,' Gill calls out. She has a manic, almost threatening edge to her voice. She isn't the person I thought she was, far from it.

'Don't think you've heard the last of me.' I hiss into my husband's face. 'And if you think you can bring me down, I'll fight you every step of the way. I'll get the best solicitor money can buy.'

'Good luck with that one.' He smirks – quite possibly having the same thought as me.

I shouldn't have mentioned money. As soon as I get away from the house and get a phone signal, I need to transfer everything we've got into my account before he sorts it for himself. I reckon he'll be too preoccupied with Karl's body to deal with our bank accounts yet.

Karl's body. I still can't believe it.

'The lot of you need to be watching over your shoulders. Especially Alice. I'll probably start with her.'

'You come anywhere near her and I'll—'

'You'll *what*? I'm out of here, Rylan – I'll leave you all to play happy families.' I laugh. 'What an absolute joke you all are.'

With the breeze whooshing in my ears as I rush to the car, I don't hear what he shouts after me. But with the police possibly en route here already, I need to get home, get clean of this blood and work out what the hell I'm going to do next.

40

GILL - 30 MINUTES LATER

'Come on everyone,' Rylan says. 'Let's do this.'

'I still don't see how we're going to pull it off.' Nathaniel threads his arms into his jacket. 'Not in a million years. Perhaps we just need to tell the police what *really* happened. After all it *was* self defence.'

'But she smacked him twice with that iron,' Rylan replies. 'Which probably makes it *murder*. I'm not prepared to take that chance. Besides, you know Kelli as well as I do – she'd go to pieces if someone were to lock her in a cell. No – pretending an intruder's attacked him is a much better way forward.'

At least Nathaniel and Rylan are sort of speaking again. It's just a pity it's taken such a dreadful event for them to put the situation with Alice aside – for now, anyway. It's also taken the heat out of the situation with Jason. My head is swooning with the stress of it all and I lean against the wall to steady myself. This is no time for one of my turns.

'It's now or never,' Rylan adds as if he needs to convince us.

Erin taps on the kitchen window. She's got Alice at her side. 'Hurry up,' she mouths.

'Two minutes,' I call from the door. 'We're just getting sorted.'

'Pass our coats out, will you, Gill?'

'Why are we having to wait out here?' Alice says to her mum as I close the door. I sigh out a long breath. Erin's somehow managed to get her out without her peering over the bannister and seeing Karl. If she had, it would have been a disaster.

Kelli shuffles into the kitchen with damp hair and fresh clothes.

'Are you feeling any better, sis?' Rylan looks up from tying his boots.

'Not really,' she replies. 'Nothing can truly wash what I've done away, can it?' Her eyes are red from crying.

'We've all got your back, you know.' Rylan rises to his feet and squeezes her arm. 'No matter what, we'll get you through this.'

'Have you cleaned the shower after yourself? They're bound to search the cottage, aren't they?' I button my coat up. I've probably watched far too many crime shows where villains try to get rid of their evidence. Never in a million years did I imagine that I'd end up at the centre of our own.

She nods. And my clothes are all in here.' She raises a bag into the air, holding it away from herself as though it's diseased. 'I never want to see them again.'

'We'll get rid of them,' Nathaniel says, pointing at it. 'They can go in the bag with Dad's things. We need to make it look like a robbery.'

If anyone were to try to stop our current course of action, I would have expected it to be Nathaniel. After so many years of trying to win his father's attention and praise, I'm shocked that he's joining forces with the rest of us. At least protecting his sister has won out in the end.

'It needs to be switched off.' Rylan takes it from him. 'We can't have it picking up a signal once we're away from *here*.' He takes it from his brother and inspects it. 'Yeah – it's off.'

'And these.' I slide my rings from my wedding finger. Rings that have felt like a ball and chain for as long as I can remember. Removing them is liberating. 'If we can say some jewellery that I left by the sink has been taken as well, it looks like a more plausible robbery.'

'I've cleaned the bannister down – and the iron.' Ben turns the tap off. 'The cloths are all rinsed and soaking in bleach.'

'I've done the floor,' Jason says. He's another person where I'm shocked that he's going along with things. They must be aware that they could *all* go down for this. It's *perverting the course of justice.* But none of them know of my Plan B – to take the blame *myself* for Karl's death if it comes to it.

'I can't imagine what we've done will get rid of *every* single trace though, will it?' Kelli passes her bag of clothes to Nathaniel. 'He grabbed Mum, didn't he? He was close to her. Before I…' Her voice trails off. 'Mum's DNA and the fibres from her clothes will be all over him.'

'They were married,' Jason replies as if I could ever need reminding of that. Everyone turns to look at him as if they're still not really understanding who he is or what he's doing here. 'So that's easily explained.'

It's surreal having Jason around the others. The entire thing is surreal. I keep wondering if I'm just having one of my funny turns and any minute at all, I'm going to come around from it.

'How can you all be so calm?' Kelli's voice is etched with pain. 'He's lying *dead* through there. And I killed him.'

'You were looking after Mum,' Rylan says. 'If you hadn't reacted first, maybe it would have been me, or Nathaniel that went for him.'

'Or maybe Mum would be lying where *he* is now.' Nathaniel says and I feel the weight of his hand on my shoulder. 'Which doesn't bear thinking about.'

'But I didn't hit him just once, did I?' She wails. 'He got back up again. I finished him off.'

'Rylan and Nathaniel are right.' Jason's voice is quiet. 'You got there before anyone else. What you did is to be applauded, not punished. He can't hurt anyone anymore.'

'Applauded?' Kelli looks at him with wide eyes. 'How can you say that?'

'What are you doing?' Nathaniel nudges Rylan. 'We need to be getting out of here.'

'I'm just checking something. Ah yes,' – he waves his phone in the air – 'as I suspected, she's emptied our joint account already.'

'She's taken *everything*?'

'I don't care. It's only money, but the fact that she's moved it *already*,' – Rylan glances up from his phone, – 'tells me she's running scared. She knows full well we could pin Dad's death on *her* if we all stick together.'

Dad's death. It still hasn't sunk in. Karl's been my shadow and controlling my every move for most of my adult life. I'll *never* take the freedom that's coming my way for granted – for as long as it lasts.

But first, we've got a hell of a lot to get through, starting with having to convince the police of an *intruder*. With luck on our side, they won't even *suspect* any of us could be behind Karl's death.

'It was a pretty good performance – phoning the police back then, Mum.' Jason squeezes my arm and Nathaniel gives him a funny look, which for a moment, reminds me of the expression he used to have after Rylan was born and he realised he'd have to share me with him.

'It got rid of her though.'

'How are we going to dispose of this stuff then - his phone and his wallet?' Nathaniel tears his jealous gaze away from Jason and averts it to Rylan. Everyone seems to be naturally looking to him as he seems to have had most of the answers so far. I'm just relieved *someone*'s taken charge. I seem to have turned to mush at the moment. And I can't shake this weird feeling in my head, it's like de-ja-vu or like I'm not really here.

'I say we put it all in a bag and let it go in the tarn.' Ben's voice pierces the quiet after a few moments.

'What tarn?' Everyone looks at him.

'We were skimming stones in it the other day – when we took Alice out of the way.'

'How deep is it?' Nathaniel drops the rings I was wearing into his pocket and reaches for Karl's wallet from the shelf above the breakfast bar. He really is taking all this surprisingly in his stride. They all are. No doubt we'll all fall apart later.

'If we head for the jetty, I reckon it'll be deep enough there,' Jason says. 'I know it well around that area.'

'As soon as we've got rid of it all, I'll make that call to the police for real,' I say.

'Let's just hope they're aren't too many people out walking at the tarn,' says Nathaniel.

Jason raises an eyebrow. 'There shouldn't be. This place isn't exactly renowned for visitors.'

'There wasn't a soul around when we took Alice there the other day,' Ben says.

'But what about Martha?' Kelli's much calmer than she was before she went upstairs, but her face is still as white as a ghost. 'Surely she won't just leave this – she'll want her pound of flesh.'

'You leave Martha to me,' Rylan replies. 'Besides, her thinking that Mum was ringing through to the police could have done the trick. Now she's taken that money, I reckon she'll end up hiding out somewhere.' He shrugs into his coat.

'But she and Dad...' Kelli's voice trails off.

'All Martha cares about,' Nathaniel replies. 'Is *Martha*. As long as she saves her own skin, that's all that will matter to her.'

'Come on, we've kept Erin and Alice waiting for long enough out there.'

We leave the door ajar. It doesn't need to look like a forced entry – as Jason's already said, the handful of people who live in this area only ever lock their doors when no one will be at home for a prolonged length of time. And Karl, as far as the police will be aware, is at home. Or *was*.

As we get to the end of the drive, I squint in the afternoon sunshine as I glance back at the cottage. 'How could such a dreadful thing have happened on such a beautiful day?'

And how many more of these beautiful days will I see anyway?

'All I know,' Nathaniel says. 'Is that when we return, all hell's going to break loose.'

'I can't help but worry that Martha's going to go to the police before we even get back,' I reply.

'Look, Mum.' Rylan thrusts his phone in front of me as we crunch through the leaves. We fall still as the others continue to stride on. 'This should set your mind at rest.'

'What is it?' Nathaniel also stops and cranes his head to look over my shoulder.

'It's my door-cam footage from five minutes ago.'

Martha's closing the door with something between her teeth. She then heads to her car, laden with a case in each hand and two rucksacks.

'She didn't waste any time getting back there.' Nathaniel steps away again.

'I said she'd be running scared, didn't I?' Rylan continues staring at his screen.

'Is her hair wet?' I peer closer.

'She'll have had a shower,' Rylan replies. 'Remember, she had as much of Dad's blood on her as Kelli had. However, I bet she hasn't thought to clean the car as well.'

'What are you getting at?'

'If she *did* decide to push things with the police, we'd just send them looking for wherever she ends up leaving the car – there's bound to be microscopic particles of Dad's blood inside.'

The sickness I've been feeling all day intensifies. And I'm chilled to the bone. I pull my jacket tighter around myself. Yes, this holiday was supposed to shake things up amongst us and I knew all along that things would be blown apart one way or another, but I never dreamt someone would be killed. Especially at the hands of another family member.

'What's she got in her mouth?' Jason leans over my other shoulder.

'Her passport by the looks of it.' Rylan presses the screen and then peers at it more closely. 'Yep, it's her passport alright.'

I hardly dare believe that my fake phone call to the police has got rid of her so spectacularly, but it's certainly looking promising. If I've managed to get her out of my son's life once and for all, I'll be a very happy mother.

'What are we going to tell Alice about it all?' Rylan gestures towards where she's walking ahead with Erin, Ben and Kelli.

'I'll worry about my daughter, thank you very much.' Nathaniel stiffens. Evidently, he's gone into denial mode about the whole thing. The situation will have to be dealt with when we get home but for now, as a family, we've got more pressing concerns.

'Since Erin managed to get her out without her seeing her grandad,' Jason begins, 'perhaps the story Alice needs to believe should be the same as the story we give to the police?'

I nod. 'You're probably right.'

'She needs distracting while we dispose of this bag.' Nathaniel holds it up.

Rylan opens his mouth to say something but I give him a slight shake of my head as if to say, *leave it.* Until DNA tests give us some definite answers, Nathaniel's right. Rylan needs to stand back. If he had any ideas about being the person who goes to distract Alice, he should think again.

'Ben said they were here, skimming stones with her the other day,' I suggest. 'So finding flat stones might be the best way of distracting her for a minute or two.'

The weighed-down bag containing our evidence barely creates a ripple as Nathaniel lets it go beneath the surface of the lake.

'Let's get back to the others,' he says, his jaw tight and resolute. 'And get the next part over with.'

The afternoon sun filters through the branches, streaking the ground with patches of light and dark as the leaves crumple beneath our feet. As we head deeper into the forest leading back to the cottage, our group splinters into pairs; Kelli falls back and into step with me, Alice and Ben are out in front, Erin walks with Jason and Rylan and Nathaniel are behind, albeit, they're not speaking to each other as they walk, but at least they've settled on being civil. Until they know for sure who Alice's father is, it's going to be a tricky road to navigate. And after that, who knows?

This could just be a normal family afternoon walk. Not one where we're on our way back to my dead husband. Plus, we've sent another family member out on the run. It's all utter madness. I stare into the sky, the brightness sending tremors of pain behind my left eye again. I don't know how much longer I can go on like this.

'Will the police make us leave the cottage when they get there?' Kelli clutches my arm.

'They'll have to,' replies Rylan. 'They'll have searches to carry out.'

Kelli, who's been slightly calmer since we left the place pales beneath her freckles. 'They're bound to find something – and what if we haven't cleaned enough?'

'We have,' Nathaniel replies. 'With that Dettol spray as well.'

'We've all been staying there for nearly a week, love.' I bring her arm tighter into me and pat her gloved hand with mine. 'Our prints and DNA will be all over the place anyway.'

'But won't they be able to tell that things have been cleaned?'

'People clean – end of,' replies Rylan. 'It'll be OK.'

'They'll want statements from us too – what if someone says the wrong thing? Or something that doesn't tally with everyone else?' I've never seen so much panic in her eyes. I can't help but feel guilty that she did what she did because she was protecting me. I should never have allowed things to escalate as far as they did and should have never put my kids in the position I did.

But I thought things would be safer around them. Now our sons are grown-up men and more than capable of overpowering Karl, he was no longer violent to me in front of them. Until today when he lost all control.

'It's fine, love.' I throw my arm around her shoulders. 'We all know exactly what we've got to say, don't we?

'Yeah,' Rylan agrees. 'We've been over it once and I'll go over it with everyone individually now as we're walking back.'

'Do you really think we can get away with this?' Her voice is almost a whisper as she pauses again. It's as though she doesn't want to reach the cottage – ever, and I don't blame her. But I'll get her through this if it's the last thing I do. 'Oh Mum, I couldn't cope if I was sent to prison.'

I stop in my tracks and spin her around to face me before ensuring that no one else is listening in to what I'm about to say. 'If they don't believe our story about intruders, I'll tell them it was *me* who killed him, alright?'

'Don't be so ridiculous.'

'Obviously, it'll be as a last resort.' I tilt her chin so we're looking into one another's eyes. Hers fill with fresh tears. 'You were protecting me from him and I'll *never* forget that. Who knows what might have happened if he'd carried on slamming my head into the bannister like he was.'

'But you don't even seem upset that he's gone, Mum. Nobody does.'

'I think we're still in shock. But no, I'm not upset – I'll *never* be upset that he's gone.'

'Not at all?' Her voice rises.

'Well maybe I am in a sense – but only because of all those lost years which I've wasted with him – however, where he's gone, it's as Rylan says, isn't it? He can't hurt anybody anymore. *You've* set everyone free.'

EPILOGUE

GILL - SIX WEEKS LATER

ALL EYES ARE on Nathaniel when we realise who he's talking to. Thankfully, he's been staying with me since he and Erin separated, though she and the rest of them call in most days to touch base.

Our 'holiday,' if it can be called that, has certainly had the effect of bringing us closer together.

'It's all over.' Nathaniel replaces the receiver. 'They're releasing his body this afternoon.'

Everyone's eyes stay fixed on my eldest son. I for one, can hardly dare believe what I'm hearing. 'What does that mean then?'

'Like I said,' a ghost of a smile plays on Nathaniel's mouth. 'It's over.'

'So that's it?' Kelli's eyes widen. 'I can stop panicking at last?'

'The police have done everything they needed to do,' he replies. 'All the appeals for witnesses have come to nothing and there's obviously no CCTV up there either.'

'Well, that's bloody amazing.' Rylan darts across the kitchen and wraps Kelli in a hug. 'See, I told you everything would be alright.' He pushes her back to arm's length and tilts her face so they're looking straight at each other. 'You just need to forgive *your-*

self now.' He looks back around at Nathaniel. 'Are they actually closing the case – did they say?'

'Unfortunately not,' he replies. 'Not completely, anyway. The DI said it'll stay open in case any new evidence comes in, but because they've drawn a total blank with any DNA, they're not doing any more *active* investigating.'

'I hardly dared hope for this,' Kelli whispers. 'They've believed our story – they've bloody believed it.'

I think back to that fateful afternoon when somehow we all held our nerve and stuck to the same version of events. We managed to shield Alice from seeing the greying corpse of her grandfather as we reported the 'robbery' we'd suffered. Then several of us took Alice to Jason's house while the others stayed to deal with the police.

'The DI was even *apologetic*,' Nathaniel continues. 'He said they'd done all they could but since *Dad's assailants*,' – he draws air quotes around the two words, – 'could have been wearing gloves and there were *no witnesses* to what happened,' – he draws air quotes again, – 'they've little hope of ever catching anyone.'

We all look around at one another, clearly too stunned for a moment to say anything.

'So we've got a funeral to plan, have we?' I eventually cut into the silence. Since Karl's gone, I've begun feeling almost like the person I used to be before we met. *Almost.* But as soon as I relax into it, my reality catches up with me. There's no denying that the headaches and dizziness have ramped themselves up in intensity since Karl died. I should see a doctor really, but they'll only tell me what I already know. That my time is running out.

Amongst everything else, the relentlessness of having to act like a wife in mourning for the sake of appearances has taken its toll. When I can't cry, people conclude that I'm numb. There have been cards, flowers, messages and so much high praise for a man who kept his true self hidden so successfully from anyone who wasn't his family. I can hardly wait until the final curtains draw around his coffin and I can return to a semblance of normality for as long as is possible for me.

'Well, I won't be going to his funeral.' Kelli's eyes fill with tears. '*How can I*? It was me who put him where he is in the first place.'

'We *all* need to be there,' Nathaniel says. 'How bad will it look if one of us isn't?'

'So I've got to play the role of his grieving daughter?' She sniffs. 'I really don't know if I can.'

'We've come this far, haven't we? This is the very last push now.'

If only Nathaniel knew the irony of his words.

'Well, I for one,' says Rylan, looking around at the others, 'am off to the pub. Who's coming?' I'm heartened to see that his gaze rests on Jason before anyone else. Out of the three of them, it's with Rylan who Jason has hit it off the most. And he's finally been able to bring himself to scatter the ashes of his adoptive parents next to the tarn, and is also planning to put the cottage back on the market at a lower price for a quick sale. Though who'd want to buy a home that's been the setting for so many recent deaths remains to be seen.

'I'm in.' Jason gets to his feet from his seat at the kitchen table and my chest swells with pride. I'm so pleased I've been able to stick around for long enough to see him become a proper part of my family.

'Me too.' Kelli blows her nose and brightens somewhat. 'I'll tell Ben to get his coat on.'

'That's the nearest you've come to smiling since it all happened,' I tell her. 'Keep it up.'

'It's good to see,' Erin adds, not moving from the table as she cradles her mug.

'We were right to hold our nerve.' Rylan plucks his jacket from the back of the chair as Kelli disappears from the room. 'Things could have been very different if we hadn't managed to overpower Martha like we did.'

I nod and smile. It turns out Martha needed a little more over-powering than my son knows but he doesn't need to find out about that *just* yet.

'Are you going with them, Erin?' She's making no move to join the others. It's been a sad situation, seeing her and Nathaniel separate, but for Alice's sake, they've been civil about it. Though who knows if it will stay that way once the dust settles and divorce comes into the mix.

'I don't think so – I'll just stay here with you and Alice if that's alright?'

'Go on, get your coat on – it'll do you good.'

She looks sideways at Nathaniel. They're amicable, yes, but since the DNA results ruled that Rylan *is* Alice's father, they still need to work out a way forward. Thankfully, Erin and Rylan's drunken encounter is so far in the past, that Nathaniel's agreed to draw a line under it, as far as their relationship as brothers is concerned. However, if we hadn't had what Kelli did to Karl to contend with, it could have been a very different scenario.

'It's fine with me.' He sniffs. 'If she *wants* to come, that is.' But he doesn't look back at her.

'I'll sit with Alice while you're gone.' I nudge Erin. 'I'll see if I can prise her off that PlayStation.'

'Kelli's still got to get Ben off it as well.' She smiles. 'I think he and Alice are well and truly addicted to that game.'

'Don't you want to come with us, Mum? Alice will be OK on her own for an hour. Or she could even come with us?'

'As long as we're very careful about what we mention,' says Nathaniel.

'No – Alice and I will be fine *here*. I'd like to be quiet for a bit anyway. Gather my thoughts.'

'Are you OK?' Jason peers at me. He's such a lovely lad. Thankfully, his adoptive parents gave him a wonderful start in life and he bears no malice about how I was forced to give him up. He's finding his way in with the others and in time, I'm sure they'll all get there. Eventually, it will be as though they never grew up without each other, even if it's my own death that cements them.

'Yes – I'm fine. Really, you go.' I nearly add *and enjoy yourselves* before reminding myself of the reason they're going. A drink to mark our exoneration of murder might be cause for relief – but hardly enjoyment.

'We should raise a glass to Martha while we're there.' Rylan reaches for his phone. 'After all, without her disappearing like she did, it might have been a very different story.'

'Have you still not heard from her?' Nathaniel looks up from tying his shoes.

'Not a word.' He shrugs. 'And I can't say I'm too bothered.'

'Will you divorce her?' I ask.

'I guess so. Though I'll have to find her first.'

As I watch them all head down the drive, I ponder about when and how I'll let Rylan know the *truth* of Martha's whereabouts. In time, he'll need to know we've been in touch.

'If you really want me to keep quiet, Gill, it's going to cost you.' Her voice was acidic and something I'd hoped I'd never have to hear again.

'What do you mean, *cost* me? Rylan's told me you've already emptied the bank accounts.'

'What else was I supposed to do? I had to get away from there, didn't I?'

'So where are you?'

'Like I'm really going to tell *you.' Then suddenly, she seemed to change tack and her voice filled with pain.* 'I honestly thought I could trust you, Gill – and that we had some kind of friendship. I can't believe how it's all turned out. And Rylan won't even take a call from me.'

'Things are probably best left alone for now.'

'So he's with Erin now, is he? Is that what you're saying?'

'I don't want to get into all that. I just want to know what it's going to *cost me*, as you've put it, for things to stay as they are.'

'The whole time we were at that cottage, I knew something was bubbling between them. Why do you think I did what I did?'

'What do you mean?'

'The glass in her drink – none of you should ever underestimate me, Gill.'

'As if we ever would. So it was *you*? I suppose you'll be the one responsible for slashing her tyres that day as well?'

'I hate her and if I ever see her ag—'

'El próximo tren que saldrá del andén uno es el servicio de las 19:17 a Sevilla.'

'So you're in Spain, then.' And waiting for a train by the sounds of it.

'I want to know what you told the police about me?' Her voice was quieter then. Less antagonistic, though she didn't answer my question about being in Spain. 'Are they still looking for me? I haven't seen anything in the news.'

'Let's just say you're a person of interest,' I lied. 'So you're definitely better off staying where you are for now.'

'I need money for that,' she replied. 'If I can't come home and if Rylan won't speak to me, there's no one else I can ask.'

'How much?'

'If you want me to stay away, it's going to cost you fifty thousand.'

'*Pounds*?' I shrieked. 'You've got to be joking.' But I was already doing a mental reckoning of what I could shave from where. I'd made a generous provision for the kids and what they didn't know wouldn't hurt them.

'You should be quids in with the insurance from Karl's death, not to mention his pension. Maybe I should make it a hundred.'

'We'll say fifty,' I agreed quickly. 'But how do I know that'll be *it* from you.'

'You don't,' she replied. 'And perhaps when that's run out, I'll be back for more.'

I smiled, knowing that I wouldn't be here to have to deal with that. And by that time, Karl's funeral would also be over and done with. 'I'll need your details then. I also need an address to forward things on to you.'

'Oh yeah – as if I'm going to trust you with that.'

'We've got an agreement, haven't we, Martha? Fifty thousand pounds and you stay away. This is between the two of us now – no one else.'

I've left her contact details in my letter of wishes – after all, one of my plans when I initially set this holiday up was to drive a wedge between her and Rylan to set him *permanently* free from her. Which ultimately means a divorce.

As the strains of Kart Rider echo from the lounge, I wander around the kitchen collecting mugs and glasses before dumping them in the sink.

As I head to the fridge to fix Alice a drink, my gaze falls on a family photo from ten or so years ago pinned to the door. Rylan clutches onto Martha as though his life depends on it – as he did back then. Thankfully, as time's progressed, he's realised that she wasn't the best choice of life partner for him, and gradually, a distance has emerged between them. But she was always able to reel him back in on a whim.

At least now, those days are over.

As the picture blurs before my eyes, so does the image of Karl as he presides over us all in the photograph. The whole thing's been an utter nightmare, but the long and short of it is that I'll be able to rest in peace, knowing my children are free of the bullying influence that's dominated them for so long.

I pour two glasses of orange juice, arrange some biscuits on a plate and head into the lounge. If I was able to stay around, I'd probably sell this place but as things stand...

'Grandma, are you OK?' Alice drops her controller and rushes towards where I'm leaning against the door. 'Here, give me that.' She takes the tray from me, sets it down on the coffee table and rushes back over to me, taking my arm. 'Come and sit down.'

'Sorry love. I just came over a bit woozy, that's all.'

It's happening more and more. When I was first diagnosed with my tumour, I could almost pretend it wasn't happening. But my last scan, only a week before the holiday, showed its progression, and the area where it's pressing more and more onto my brain.

As the dizziness eases, I draw Alice towards me, enjoying her warmth as my gaze rests on the wedding photo of me and Karl on the mantelpiece.

When the funeral's finally over, I can take it down. My eyes move to the photo of my in-laws, Marilyn and Joe. At the time, I thought my guilt for how I'd released her from her suffering would never end, but as the years elapsed, it gradually faded. I might hardly have thought about it if it wasn't for Karl either using it as a stick to beat me with or a threat to keep me in line.

Joe regretted telling him the truth *immediately*. I'll never know how he thought Karl could ever show compassion and understanding. He and I sat together, talking about the situation many nights after Marilyn had gone. He missed her beyond words but was also grateful that I'd ended her suffering.

So much so, that when I asked him for some help several months ago, after his own terminal diagnosis, he readily agreed.

'I need you to put it in writing,' I said. 'It has to look like *your* dying wish.' Instead of *mine.* But I didn't say this. I've still not told a soul about my prognosis. But the time is coming when I'll have to.

'And you've even found a cottage already.' He laughed as he glanced at the photo on my computer screen. 'You know I'll do *anything* to help you out, Gill.' He wrapped his arm around my shoulders and drew me towards him.

'So you think it's a good idea then?'

'Anything that could shake our family up and bring it back together has got to be a step in the right direction.' He studied the photo on the screen more closely. 'Nice place. I wish I was coming with you.'

'Me too.' Tears filled my eyes at the prospect of him no longer being around. Or maybe the tears were more for the fact that I'd be joining him soon after.

'Do you really think they'll all need so much persuasion?' He looked from the screen to me.

'Oh yes. It'll take something *monumental* to throw that lot together for a week,' I replied.

'Perhaps it being my *dying wish* won't hold enough sway.' He looked thoughtful. 'But if we throw the threat and promise of *inheritance money* into the equation...'

As I began to plan the holiday, I even managed to convince *myself* that it had all been Joe's idea rather than my own. Jason's offer of his adopted parents' empty cottage had felt like an omen. Everything was falling into place. I'd use the safety of everyone being there at once to tell them about *him* and also to confess to what had really happened with Marilyn.

Even if they hated me for what I'd done, at least they'd see Karl even more for who he really was and would be able to make an informed decision about their relationships with him in the future.

He smiles at me from our wedding photo, as if he's still taunting me. Perhaps, wherever he is, he's waiting for me – I guess I'll find out soon enough.

I've often blamed myself for his death, but really, it was his own fault. If he hadn't attacked me so violently, what ensued would never have happened.

I'm devastated that Kelli has such guilt and pain to process but I'm convinced that with the support of Erin and her three brothers, that guilt she's so tormented by will fade in time.

Time is something that's in short supply for me now, however it's still plentiful for the rest of my family. They'll get through this – I know they will.

I'm sad to soon be leaving them but will go on to wherever it is I'm headed, far more at peace than if I was leaving them at the mercy of Karl and Martha.

Before you Go...

Thanks for reading The Holiday Cottage - I really hope you enjoyed it!

If you want more, check out The Ex-Wife on Amazon, my next novel, where you'll meet Carla, who's been invited to gatecrash the Christmas festivities of her ex-husband's family. You'll also meet Natalie, who's spending Christmas for the first time with her in-laws and certainly hasn't factored Carla into her plans. As their forced hours together tick by, tensions rise and it becomes apparent that one of them may not live to see in the new year...

And for a FREE novella, please Join my 'keep in touch' list where I can also keep you posted of special offers and new releases. You can join by visiting my website www.mariafrankland.co.uk.

BOOK CLUB DISCUSSION QUESTIONS

1. When you began reading the story, did you have any thoughts on who the victim would end up being?

2. What were your reasons for this? Were your predictions correct?

3. Similarly, what were your thoughts on who the killer might be?

4. Discuss the intentions behind the initial wish for the family to take this holiday.

5. Back when Kelli was eight, the services involved didn't act on her hospital admission after her father attacked her. Discuss whether and how times have changed since then.

6. What were Erin's reasons for living her lie? Did this revelation change your opinion of her or Rylan?

7. Gill also lived a lie for many years, on two counts. What were her reasons for this and where do your sympathies lie?

8. Should Karl have been also held responsible for covering up the circumstances around his mother's death as he did, and then using them to blackmail his wife?

9. How might the police have acted if this truth had ever come to light?

10. What were your thoughts on Nathaniel? By the end of the story, did you feel any sympathy towards him?

11. And what about Alice? How should she now be helped and supported to get through the next phase of her life as unscathed as possible?

12. What might become of the other characters now the 'holiday' is over? How will they cope without Gill?

13. If a sequel were to be told of this story, in whose viewpoint should it be told from?

HIS EX WIFE - PROLOGUE

Fear catches in my throat. There's no pain, just blood. More blood than I've ever seen in my life.

Instinctively, I reach for my arm with my other hand. But within a split second, it's flooding in between my fingers.

The expressions of those gathered around me tell me all I need to know. It's nasty – seriously nasty.

'Help me.' The words somehow form themselves as I stagger back against the counter, looking for something, anything to press against the flow of the blood.

They continue to stare, still as rocks, doing nothing, their eyes full of horror. How could one simple action, from the pierce from a blade produce so much blood?

They'll know that there's nothing any of them can do to help me. An arterial vein has probably been sliced. There's nothing I can do either.

Other than to allow myself to slide to the floor and hope that death comes easily and without the pain that life has been bringing me.

Find out more about His Ex Wife on Amazon.

INTERVIEW WITH THE AUTHOR

Q: Where do your ideas come from?

A: I'm no stranger to turbulent times, and these provide lots of raw material. People, places, situations, experiences – they're all great novel fodder!

Q: Why do you write domestic thrillers?

A: I'm intrigued why people can be most at risk from someone who should love them. Novels are a safe place to explore the worst of toxic relationships.

Q: Does that mean you're a dark person?

A: We thriller writers pour our darkness into stories, so we're the nicest people you could meet – it's those romance writers you should watch...

Q: What do readers say?

A: That I write gripping stories with unexpected twists, about people you could know and situations that could happen to anyone. So beware...

Q: What's the best thing about being a writer?

A: You lovely readers. I read all my reviews, and answer all emails and social media comments. Hearing from readers absolutely makes my day, whether it's via email or through social media.

Q: Who are you and where are you from?

A: A born 'n' bred Yorkshire lass, with two grown up sons and a Sproodle called Molly. (Springer/Poodle!) The last decade has been the best ever: I've done an MA in Creative Writing, made writing my full time job, and found the happy-ever-after that doesn't exist in my writing - after marrying for the second time just before the pandemic.

Q: Do you have a newsletter I could join?

A: I certainly do. Go to https:www.mariafrankland.co.uk or click here through your eBook to join my awesome community of readers. I'll send you a free novella – 'The Brother in Law.'

ACKNOWLEDGMENTS

Thank you, as always, to my amazing husband, Michael. He's my first reader, and is vital with my editing process for each of my novels. His belief in me means more than I can say.

A special acknowledgement goes to my wonderful advance reader team, who took the time and trouble to read an advance copy of The Holiday Cottage and offer feedback. They are a vital part of my author business and I don't know what I would do without them. I would especially like to acknowledge Gill Puttock, Kelli Sanders and Martha Dreeling who had characters named after them in the story.

Thanks also to my talented cover designer, David Grogan, who as always, has produced a great cover for me.

I will always be grateful to Leeds Trinity University and my MA in Creative Writing Tutors there, Amina, Martyn and Oz. My Masters degree in 2015 was the springboard into being able to write as a profession.

And thanks especially, to you, the reader. Thank you for taking the time to read this story. I really hope you enjoyed it.

Printed in Great Britain
by Amazon

48041914R00179